MW00639829

THE OVERLOOK MURDER

THE OVERLOOK MURDER

A WINTERGREEN MYSTERY

PATRICK KELLY

CHAPARRAL PRESS LLC

The Overlook Murder. Copyright © 2022 by Chaparral Press LLC

All rights reserved. No part of this book may be used or reproduced in any manner whatsoever without written permission except in the case of brief quotations embodied in critical articles and reviews. For information contact Chaparral Press LLC, 2402 Sutherland St., Austin, TX 78746.

Published in print and ebook by Chaparral Press LLC.

Cover design by Sleepy Fox Studio.

This is a work of fiction. Some of the locations, restaurants, and other places referenced in the novel are real; however, the names, characters, and incidents either are products of the author's imagination or are used fictitiously. Any resemblance to actual events or events at a particular locale or to persons, living or dead, is entirely coincidental.

ISBN 978-1-7342392-4-9 (Print)

ONE

Near sunset, a soft breeze rustled maple leaves on a suburban street in Charlottesville. The homes were brick, some painted white and others a natural red. Idle chimneys extended above the shingled roofs. A large two-story home was decorated with shuttered windows and a dark front door. On either side of the house, camellia bushes and holly trees provided lush greenery while flowers bloomed brightly in the landscaped yard: chrysanthemum, pansy, begonia, and foxglove.

A jogger rounded the street's corner at an easy pace. The residents were either away or inside, and no one noticed the jogger. Not that anything alarming was to be seen, for the jogger regularly passed that way.

Digitalis purpurea.

In the eighteenth century, an English herbalist made a concoction of twenty different herbs that promised to rid the body of unwanted fluids. A doctor named William Withering identified the concoction's magic herb as foxglove, and he began using it experimentally with patients who suffered from dropsy. Sometimes it worked. Sometimes it didn't. The dose spelled the difference between medicine and poison.

The jogger paused, kneeled over a shoelace, and surveyed both sides of the empty street. After removing small scissors from a pocket, the jogger dashed across the lush lawn to the flower bed.

Stay calm. Make sure you get enough.

The jogger quickly harvested green leaves from the blooming foxglove plants. Ten. Twenty. Thirty. The jogger placed the leaves in a plastic bag and then tucked the bag into a pocket.

These will help things along.

With a quick glance to verify no one was watching, the jogger returned to the street and soon disappeared around the next corner.

TWO

Krista Jackson woke to her alarm at five thirty a.m., dressed quickly in exercise clothes, and strolled into the family room. The boys were asleep and the dogs were asleep. This was the only time of day she could reliably have to herself. She sat on a second-hand rowing machine—purchased at a yard sale for thirty dollars—and played with her phone. Krista liked to listen to romance novels while she exercised, and her subscription to Audible was one of her few personal indulgences. Her salary as a communications officer with the Wintergreen Police Department, plus the occasional child-support payment from her unreliable ex-husband, afforded the basic necessities but didn't leave much for luxuries.

Forty-five minutes and three miles later, she rose from the rowing machine, perspiring and breathing heavily. That Lance Reilly was such a cad. How could a man with that much money be a lowlife but infuriatingly handsome and charming? Krista would have to wait a whole day to learn whether Lance successfully maneuvered himself into the bedroom of Daphne Jefferson, the young and beautiful marketing analyst who worked for Reilly's company.

Krista attended the coffee machine and had just pushed the brew button when David, their Great Dane, walked hesitantly in from the laundry room where he and Goliath slept. *Can I go out now?* he asked with his deep brown eyes. The coffee maker popped, and her Chihuahua, Goliath, scampered to the back door. The sun had risen, and soft light brightened the Rockfish Valley, where they lived. Krista spread the blinds at the window to inspect the backyard and the nearby pasture for deer. The field rose gently to the mountain base a hundred yards distant. Deer sometimes emerged from the forest to graze in the early morning, which drove Goliath absolutely crazy. The coast was clear, and Krista let the two dogs out to do their business.

She turned the television on with the sound muted and fixed cereal and a cup of coffee. The news broadcast dialed through local stories and the weather, nothing too exciting. She thought about her upcoming day on the mountain. Routine, she expected. Krista wished she could do more for the police department, but she didn't have the training. She remembered the fast and furious week during which she had helped Bill O'Shea and Mitch Gentry investigate the murder of Lou Thorpe. Now, *that* had been exciting. And her internet sleuthing skills had proven helpful. Bill O'Shea said as much himself.

Bill O'Shea. Thinking of him brought warmth to Krista's cheek. She had made an overt pass at Bill that he rejected as kindly as possible. Turns out, he had interests elsewhere. What was she thinking anyway? Though not unattractive and certainly a nice person, Bill was twenty years her senior if not more. She'd been lonely—that was all, and finding a new guy to hang out with in Nelson County was no small task. But she and Bill were friends now. He had come to watch the boys play football a few times. His new girlfriend, Cindy, the caterer, had come along too. At first, Krista sensed tension coming from Cindy, but not too much, and it dissipated as soon as Cindy realized Krista retained no romantic interest in Bill.

Krista was not interested romantically; however, she still longed for the excitement of that investigation, the thrill of the chase. Again, she wished she could add more value to the police department. Maybe her recent research into surveillance cameras would bear fruit. At a team meeting the prior month, Interim Chief Alex Sharp had asked for a volunteer to investigate the feasibility of placing cameras on the road into Wintergreen. Krista's hand had shot up, and Alex gave her the assignment. If she had some idle time today, she might finish the research and forward her summary to Alex. Should she include a recommendation? Why not? Crime was rare in Wintergreen, but there was an occasional traffic accident and the odd theft. A few thousand dollars in equipment would enhance their ability to keep the community safe.

From the bedroom wing of the small house came the sound of a toilet flushing. One of the boys was awake. The bus would come in forty-five minutes, and Krista turned her attention to assembling breakfast foods.

THREE

A few valleys over in the village of Lyndhurst, Wintergreen Patrol Officer Mitch Gentry sat at the kitchen table and watched Lulu make a smoothie for breakfast. He was already dressed in his uniform, but Lulu didn't have to be at work until 8:45 a.m., so she wore a long-sleeved T-shirt and pajama bottoms.

Mitch was still getting used to the house and the neighborhood. They were engaged to marry in three months and had moved in together the previous week. A lot of firsts for Mitch. First time living with a woman. First time living in a house that wasn't his childhood home. First time living in a more diverse neighborhood. That part seemed like a no-brainer to Mitch, as Mitch was white, and Lulu was black. There were still parts of Augusta County and Nelson County where an interracial couple attracted an extra glance from passersby. Not a big deal, certainly not for Mitch. But still, he noticed. When he and Lulu had driven to meet the rental agent for this house, they had gotten stuck behind a school bus making frequent stops. At one stop, a bunch of kids got off the bus. Two black kids approached one house, and two white kids approached the next house. Nearing the entrances, the two little girls, one black and one white, turned and waved at each other before going inside. That was the best sales pitch Mitch could imagine.

Smiling, Lulu brought her smoothie to the table.

"Why are you smiling?" he asked.

"You know Christi, the other hygienist I work with?"

"Yup."

"We got new software yesterday, and Christi is not good with the systems. She got this one patient's numbers all wrong."

"Oh, my goodness. I hope nobody lost the wrong tooth."

Lulu widened her eyes. "Not that bad, but close. Dr. Wainwright almost referred the patient for gum surgery, but then he realized Christi incorrectly entered the data."

Mitch sipped his coffee. "Talk about getting a bad upsell. What did the good doctor do?"

The dentist had asked Lulu to stay an extra hour to help Christi learn the new program, which Lulu didn't mind because she got paid for the extra time. They needed every dollar they could get.

Lulu and Mitch had first met in high school. After graduating, they broke up for a time when they attended different community colleges. While in college, they both had side jobs—she served in a restaurant, and Mitch worked at a warehouse. Then he attended the police academy, and she got her dental assistant's certification. After that, he moved to Richmond to work as a cop, and she moved to Harrisonburg to pursue a four-year degree in biology at James Madison University. She worked part-time right through graduation but still acquired a mountain of student loans. Since then,

Lulu had earned her dental hygienist certification, which enabled her to get a good-paying job, but she had higher ambitions.

"Do you want to see a movie tonight?" said Mitch. "The new Batman is showing in Waynesboro."

Lulu frowned. "I have to study for the Dental Admission Test. It's in three weeks."

"You need to take a break some time."

"I'm worried about the test. What if I fail?"

Lulu's facial muscles grew tense. Worry wrinkles formed at the corners of her eyes. Mitch hated to see her that way, so he stood, walked behind her chair, and gently massaged her shoulders. Her muscles were tight.

"You won't fail," he said. "You're the smartest person I know."

"But what if I do?"

He leaned to kiss her neck. "Then you'll retake the test in six months."

"Am I crazy? The four-year tuition is two hundred and fifty thousand dollars. That's a quarter of a million."

Mitch continued to work on her shoulders, and her muscles began to relax. His fingers ran down the sides of her arms. Lulu heaved a sigh and sampled her smoothie. Then he whispered in her ear, "It's just a number. Follow your dream, and we'll figure out the rest."

Mitch drove his white 2009 Ford F-150 down a two-lane road through Sherando and into a forest of oak and hickory trees. The sun remained behind the mountain on his left, but it had risen enough to cast the world in full sunlight.

He *was* worried about the debt. Jeez. A quarter of a million dollars on top of the loans she already had. And while Lulu was in the program, she wouldn't have time to work. His salary, a respectable amount but not a huge pile, would have to carry them both for four years. And then, with her degree in hand, Lulu had to find a practice or build her own, which could take years, decades even. Mitch had studied up on it. Lulu's great adventure would put them under for a long time. Well, at least they didn't have to worry about a house. Mitch had a different plan for that.

The forest opened on the right to a field owned by a nearby church. A pavilion with picnic tables waited patiently for weekend gatherings of the faithful. Mitch turned left on Reeds Gap Road and began a slow climb, his worries scattering in the face of Appalachian wonder. The incline steepened, and the road cut back and forth up the side of the mountain. Mitch took his foot off the gas to maneuver his truck through the sharp turns. The speed limit dropped to fifteen miles per hour, and Mitch obeyed it. He had seen many ditched vehicles waiting for a tow along this road.

Mitch reached the top of the mountain, rolled across the Blue Ridge Parkway, and began the steep decline down the other side. He glanced at the clock—seven thirty. Mitch would arrive twenty minutes before his shift started. Mitch was almost always early; he liked to get a feel for the action before heading out in a cruiser. What calls came in the previous night? Bear sightings? Loud parties? Murders?

Ha! Not likely. The only murder in Wintergreen during Mitch's three-year tenure had occurred a couple of months ago. They would not have another one anytime soon. But the memory of the investigation brought Mitch's thoughts to Bill O'Shea, the retired police detective who had helped with the case. Mitch had enjoyed working with Bill. The man knew a heck of a lot about police work but didn't flout his expertise as some guys would. Mitch wondered what Bill was up to. Must be nice to retire. Work your tail off for four decades and then take a long break.

FOUR

At six thirty in the morning in the mountain resort of Wintergreen, Bill O'Shea and Justin Quintrell paused at the corner of Fawn Ridge Drive and Blue Ridge Drive. Wind blew through the oak and hickory trees. The golf course's second green lay nearby. A maintenance truck drove past on Blue Ridge, and the driver waved.

"See you in an hour," said Bill.

"Yep."

Justin turned and began running back down Fawn Ridge. He was younger and needed a more strenuous workout to achieve his fitness goals. Justin was visiting his mother for a month before starting boot camp at the Coast Guard Training Center in Cape May, New Jersey.

Bill hiked up the trail that would take him along the fairway, past the tennis courts, and back to his condo building on the ridge.

Justin's mother, Cindy, was Bill's girlfriend. Girlfriend? Yes, definitely. Although they had not formalized their relationship in such a way, it was high time they did, and Bill took a mental note to raise the subject in his next one-on-one conversation with Cindy. That was the one drawback of Justin's extended visit—a significant loss of alone time with Cindy. But the visit was important to her, because joining the service represented a big step in Justin's life, and his schedule would soon become less flexible. And, as a bonus, Bill had gained a partner for his morning walks.

Back at his condo, he showered, dressed in catering attire, ate a quick breakfast, and took a cup of coffee onto his balcony. Silence hung heavy and comfortable, broken only by the intermittent chirping of small birds. Idle chairlift towers and cables ran up the slopes to where the Mountain Inn lay at the top of the valley. The crest of the hill across the wooded hollow rolled softly down from the right. Hidden ski runs cut sweeping lines through the forests. Off in the distance, a soft blue haze hovered over the rounded peaks of the Blue Ridge.

Stepping to the balcony rail, Bill leaned out and glanced at Cindy's condo building to the right. Lush greenery flourished at the edges of her balcony. More condo buildings lined the ridge to the left and right. He would have enjoyed lingering over coffee with his binoculars close at hand. According to a lecture he had attended at The Nature Foundation at Wintergreen, various hawks had begun their yearly migration and would soon be visible to casual observers. But he had to work. Cindy ran a catering business on the mountain, and Bill occasionally helped out. She had landed a wealthy new client who often hosted special events. That day, they would prepare and serve breakfast, lunch, and dinner for the new client and his guests.

Bill sipped his coffee and glanced down at the lawn behind his building. There he was, Bill's furry friend, the neighborhood groundhog.

"Hello, Mr. Chips."

Mr. Chips stood eighteen inches tall and calmly surveyed

his surroundings. Bill waved and said, "Wait there. I'll be right down."

After watching several YouTube videos of groundhogs interacting with humans, Bill had resolved to strengthen his friendship with Mr. Chips. He grabbed a well-ripened tomato from the countertop and hustled out the condo door and down the stairwell. Once outside, Bill hurried around the building to the left and paused. Mr. Chips remained standing near his burrow's entrance, and Bill's pulse quickened. He lifted the tomato and jiggled it from side to side to fire up Mr. Chips's taste buds. The YouTube groundhog family had shown a particular liking for tomatoes.

"Hey, what are you doing?"

Bill's eyes darted to Cindy's third-floor balcony, and the day seemed to grow a bit brighter. She was blond and in her late fifties, several years younger than Bill. With her hands on the balcony railing, she leaned forward and smiled. She had not yet dressed for work and wore a tank top and jeans shorts. One leg lifted playfully behind her.

He raised a finger to his lips. "Shush. I'm going to feed Mr. Chips."

"That'll never work."

Oh, ye of little faith.

Mr. Chips stood on his hind legs next to the hillside thirty feet away. He was angled to one side with his eye fixed on Bill.

Bill stepped gingerly toward the furry creature with the tomato extended as a peace offering. Bill scarcely breathed. He whispered, "Come on, boy. Here you go. Have a bite of this big juicy tomato."

When the distance was half-closed, Mr. Chips stood straighter, and his front legs pulled closer to his body.

"Easy now. Easy."

Bill shortened his stride and took two more steps. He was a dozen feet away now.

Suddenly, Mr. Chips' entire body tensed.

"No," whispered Bill. "No."

And Mr. Chips scampered into the hole of his burrow.

"Darn."

Cindy giggled. "I told you it wouldn't work."

"You're no help," said Bill. "Casting doubt from the peanut gallery."

"Don't leave that tomato lying around," she said. "Food attracts bears."

"I know."

"Maddie and I are almost ready. I've got to get dressed. Can you come over in ten to help us load the SUV?"

"You bet."

Cindy went inside her condo, and Bill strolled to Mr. Chips's burrow entrance. He leaned toward the hole and imitated the YouTube groundhog's call.

"Nuck nuck nuck nuck."

Bill leaned closer.

"Nuck nuck nuck nuck."

The hole remained dark. Mr. Chips was down there somewhere. How big was a groundhog burrow anyway? Bill considered the tomato in his hand.

What the heck. Might as well give it to him.

He dropped the tomato into the burrow, and it rolled out of sight.

"See you later, Mr. Chips."

FIVE

"Is that everything?" asked Bill.

Justin handed him a large dish of freshly baked quiche covered with foil.

"Yes. They'll be out in a minute."

Bill placed the quiche in a cardboard box and rearranged some items to minimize jostling on the drive to the client's home.

Maddie Katz and Cindy had begun preparations in Cindy's kitchen before sunrise. They made two large quiches, a coffee cake, and yogurt parfaits with fruit and granola. The four of them would remain at the client's home from breakfast right through dinner and dessert. Damian Susskind had a large kitchen with all the appliances and equipment Cindy needed to prepare lunch and dinner.

Cindy and Maddie exited the condo building wearing the same uniforms as the men: black pants and white shirts. Cindy hired Maddie Katz as an assistant several months earlier and had since told Bill she was pleased with Maddie's performance. Maddie was a talented apprentice in the kitchen, and although she lived a forty-five-minute drive from Wintergreen, she was always on time for work.

Maddie carried a large box of fruit, and Justin hastened to take it from her. She was a little younger than Justin, in her early twenties, stood five feet six, and had light brown hair and a slim figure.

"Thanks," she said. "That's heavy."

"No problem," said Justin.

Standing off to the side, Bill raised his eyebrows at Cindy, and she gave his arm a push. Bill had recently told Cindy that he detected a vibe between the young adults. Cindy had said he was imagining things, and that in any case, she wouldn't mind because she considered Maddie a good match for Justin.

How would she know?

Some people, including Cindy, believed they could assess a person's nature soon after meeting. But Bill's thirty-five-year career as a policeman in Columbia, South Carolina, had taught him otherwise. Many people were skilled at hiding their true selves. The mind was a strange and largely uncontrolled machine. He suspected that Maddie—like most people—harbored a secret or two.

Cindy drove, and Bill sat in the passenger seat up front. They followed Blue Ridge Drive for a quarter mile, turned right on Wintergreen Drive, and then turned left on Devils Knob Loop to climb toward the mountain's summit. Bill swiveled in his chair to observe Justin and Maddie. Justin's nose was buried in his phone, and Maddie watched the passing forest through the partially open window. Odd. Bill could not recall ever seeing Maddie on her phone. Did she even own a phone? Surely, she must. Everyone had a smartphone. As a police detective who spent decades trying to find answers to questions, Bill had developed an acute sense of curiosity.

"Hey, Maddie," he said. "I noticed you don't spend a lot of time on your phone. How do you manage that? Do you process it all at once?"

Maddie turned to Bill and smiled shyly. She had alabaster skin and hazel eyes. The breeze from the window blew a strand of hair across her face, and she pulled it behind her ear. "Oh, that. Yeah, I'm off the grid in terms of social media. A few months back, I realized I was, like, wasting hours a day on it, and I dropped everything."

"Everything?" said Justin. "Instagram?"

"Instagram. TikTok. Snapchat. Even the dating apps." Maddie laughed nervously. "All of it. Pulled the plug."

"Jeez," said Justin. "I don't know if I could drop Instagram."

"I get it," she said. "The first few days were kinda rough. I kept forgetting and would reach for my phone, but honestly, since then, I haven't missed it much. I still check for emails and texts, but I try to limit that to three times a day."

"Huh," said Justin. "Off the grid."

Justin's tone indicated great surprise, and Bill understood why. His own kids interacted with their phones every few minutes. Bill himself checked his phone at least once an hour.

Maddie caught Justin's gaze and shrugged. "I know. It's weird."

"Not at all," said Justin. "I should spend less time on my phone." And he shoved it into his pocket to underscore a newfound resolve.

SIX

Bill carried a tray of mimosas and orange juice onto the back deck of Damian Susskind's mountain retreat.

Whoa. That's one heck of a view.

The house was built onto a mountainside, with the deck jutting into the open air. The mountainside fell away to reveal the Mountain Inn, several ski trails, and two ridges that sloped down to the valley floor. Puffy white clouds floated in a mid-morning sky.

Earlier, Cindy had told Bill what she knew of her client and his guests. At the head of the table sat Damian Susskind, an extremely successful entrepreneur. In the 1980s, Susskind had opened Fair Game, a high-end sporting goods store in Charlottesville that had done well. Over the ensuing decades, he had parlayed his success into a chain of more than fifty stores across the Southeast. A barrel-chested man with a loud voice and a big head, Susskind had undoubtedly been an imposing figure in his younger years, but he had recently survived a severe heart attack followed by quintuple-bypass surgery. Though his words continued to exude confidence and swagger, his voice had lost its edge, and his face carried the worn look of an unhealthy person. He had selected a yogurt parfait for breakfast.

Bill offered him the tray. "Care for another drink?"

Susskind reached for a mimosa. "Thank you, Bill. Don't mind if I do."

Earlier, Cindy had introduced the catering team and explained the buffet menu of breakfast choices. Damian Susskind was evidently the kind of person who remembered names.

"Do you think you should?" said Angie Finch, the woman seated on Susskind's right.

"Yes, I do. A little champagne isn't going to hurt me."

Angie Finch was Susskind's personal assistant and Cindy's primary contact for arranging the event. In her mid-fifties, she was a slender woman who wore her auburn hair cut short. Finch kept her phone in her lap, and whenever Susskind leaned toward her to speak, she would make notes on her phone. Angie paid more attention to Damian than she did to all of the others combined.

Evan Hale sat on Angie's right and was in his mid-thirties. A tall, handsome man with an athletic build, Evan wore shorts and a long-sleeved green T-shirt. After working for Susskind's company in high school, he had risen through the ranks from stock boy to head of merchandising at the age of thirty. Hale had since left the company to open Burgers Galore, a casual dining restaurant in downtown Charlottesville. When Burgers Galore met with early success, Hale took a page from Susskind's playbook and opened another six restaurants over the next few years. Apparently, he was now considered a rising star in the Charlottesville business community.

When Bill offered Evan the tray, Evan smiled broadly and then said in a low voice, "I don't mean to be difficult, but is there any chance I could get a full-on champagne?"

"Of course," said Bill. "I'll bring a glass shortly."

"No worries," said Evan, standing. "I'll fetch it myself."

"Sure." Bill nodded toward the kitchen. "The glasses are on the counter, and the open bottle is in the fridge."

"Thanks."

Turning to the woman next to him, Evan squeezed her shoulder and said, "Care for champagne?"

"No, thanks," said Lacey Akin. "I'll have juice."

"Your loss," said Hale in a friendly tone, and his touch lingered on Lacey's shoulder for an extra beat.

Lacey giggled. Dressed in jeans and a colorful top, she had long blond hair that fell below her shoulders. Lacey was Damian Susskind's stepdaughter and his only living relative. She worked for the Charlottesville Department of Social Services and lived in the city, but for the next few days, she would stay at the retreat along with Damian and Angie Finch.

At the other end of the table, Maddie Katz brought Damian Susskind a cup of coffee. Her hand shook a little as she set the cup down. Damian said something to Maddie, and she laughed nervously. Angie Finch frowned at the two of them.

Bill next offered a beverage to Whit Whitlock, the man on Lacey Akin's right. "Care for a mimosa or orange juice? Or I can get you champagne."

"Better stick with juice," said Whitlock. "Need to stay sharp with this crew." He had been Susskind's attorney for many years. In khakis and a pale blue buttoned shirt, Whitlock was dressed more formally than the others. He had a kind face, a full head of salt-and-pepper hair, and watchful brown eyes. Bill guessed that Whitlock was in his mid-fifties.

Then Bill served Tanya Stafford, the last guest. Tanya had a healthy complexion, sparkling blue eyes, and light brown hair with soft bangs. In her thirties, Tanya sat erect and had strong arms. Similar to Evan Hale, she had begun her career with Fair Game at an early age and been rewarded for her performance with quick promotions. She was now chief operating officer and had run the company during Susskind's recovery from the heart attack and surgery. Seated on Damian's left, Tanya said something to him about the fall merchandise lineup, and he nodded his approval.

Damian then rapped a fork against a glass to get everyone's attention. "Thank you. I want to spend a minute on today's agenda. As you know, we go through this process once a year, typically around Thanksgiving. I've pulled it ahead this year given my recent, uh, health setback. I'll meet with each of you, including Angie, for about forty-five minutes." Susskind specifically acknowledged Angie with a nod, as if this year she was taking on a new role.

Angie Finch sat taller in her chair.

Susskind continued. "As usual, Whit will attend the meetings to take note of any decisions I make on the spur of the moment. I should complete the one-on-one sessions in time for us to have lunch at one o'clock. The afternoon is yours to enjoy as you will. The mountain facilities are at your disposal for golf, tennis, hiking, etc. We'll have cocktails at seven. Any questions?"

Evan Hale stood with a champagne glass in hand. He was easily six feet tall and had a strong upper body. "I'd like to make a toast." He raised his glass. "To Damian Susskind. Sportsman, mentor, businessman, and philanthropist. A great life. Thank you for everything you've done."

Those at the table raised their glasses for the toast, and

then Damian said, “Thank you, Evan. Kind words, but did I detect a note of finality concerning my achievements?”

“No! Of course not.”

“Okay. That’s good, because I assure everyone that I’m not done yet.”

SEVEN

After breakfast, the group split up. Susskind, Whit Whitlock, and Tanya Stafford walked into Susskind's large study and closed the door; Angie Finch and Lacey Akin went their own ways; and Evan Hale sat on the back deck to finish his champagne.

In the spacious kitchen, which adjoined the dining and living areas, the catering crew worked to put away leftovers, clean the dishes, and begin lunch preparations. Cindy planned to serve a leafy green salad, seafood bisque, and a variety of sandwiches.

Evan Hale entered the house through the sliding glass doors and asked if there was any more champagne.

"You bet," said Bill, and he fetched the open bottle from the fridge.

Evan stopped Bill from pouring at half a glass and then walked to stand across the counter from where Maddie prepared vegetables for the salad. He sipped champagne, and his eyes twinkled as he watched Maddie. He addressed his next sentence to her but said the words loud enough for everyone to hear. “Do you know the purpose of these meetings?”

From the stove, Cindy glanced over her shoulder and then returned to the task of sautéing seafood. Justin washed lettuce at the sink. Maddie sliced tomatoes.

“No,” said Bill, answering for all of them. Of course, the nature of the meetings was none of their business, but Bill would not stop Evan Hale from sharing.

“It’s extraordinary,” said Evan. “As you might imagine, Damian is wealthy. But other than Lacey, he has no natural heirs. Fair Game—the company—has been his family. Tanya and I started working at the Charlottesville store in the same year. We were in high school, and we worked hard. We stayed on with the company right through college and beyond. Over the years, Damian took notice of Tanya and me, and when we reached the age of twenty-two, he sort of adopted us. He invited us to stay here at the retreat anytime we wished and basically gave us whatever we wanted.” Evan raised his eyebrows and gazed through the sliding doors toward distant mountains. “Let me tell you, as a twenty-two-year-old who never had a lot of money, I took full advantage of Damian’s generosity. It was a blast.”

“I’ll bet,” said Bill.

Evan said, “But Damian’s generosity came with a price. As a surrogate parent, he felt entitled, and perhaps obliged, to provide us with direction on how to live our lives. Not on a daily basis, mind you; he wasn’t trying to become our father. After all, we’re not orphans. No, instead, he began to host annual get-togethers where he would formally give us what you might call a report card.”

“Report card?” said Bill. “You mean like a review of your performance at the company?”

Evan gave a slight nod, but then his head tilted to one

side. "Not exactly. More like a review of how we conducted ourselves in our free time. He gave feedback on our social habits, hobbies, and how we otherwise spent our time."

"I see," said Bill in what he hoped came across as a neutral tone, though the arrangement struck him as odd. Arguably, every young adult could benefit from a wise mentor's counsel. But would they listen? Some of life's essential lessons had to be learned the hard way.

Evan leaned across the counter and lowered his voice so it wouldn't carry beyond the kitchen. "When I was twenty-two, the lectures were no big deal. I appreciated the advice, and I *definitely* enjoyed the generosity, but now I'm thirty-five and have my own views about life. So it's kind of a bore." Hale's eyes narrowed, and he drained the glass of champagne. Then he stood straight and said, "But I still have to do it."

Bill wanted to ask why. Evan Hale had left the company and ran his own successful business. If he no longer wanted the counsel, why bother coming at all? But Bill resisted prying. Listening to a client's guest sharing his thoughts was one thing, but nosing into Susskind's personal affairs could hurt Cindy's business.

At the opposite end of the living area was the door to Susskind's study. In the next moment, the door opened, and Tanya Stafford appeared. She spied Evan from across the room and marched toward him, swinging her arms. Her face was red.

Evan saw her coming and turned from the counter.

"Do you know what that idiot has done now?" she said.

Evan flashed the others a tight grin and touched Tanya on the arm. "Take a deep breath," he said. "Remember where you are."

Tanya did as Evan instructed and began to calm down.

"I'm up next," said Evan. "Are they ready for me?"

Tanya's eyes shot back to the study door. "No. They're taking a short break."

"Okay," said Evan. He turned her toward the sliding door. "Let's go outside, and you can tell me all about it."

The caterers stared at each other for a moment, and then Cindy gave Bill instructions for making chicken salad.

A few minutes later, Angie Finch came into the kitchen and asked to review the lunch menu with Cindy. They huddled across the counter from where Bill cut freshly baked chicken breasts into cubes. A minute later, Whit Whitlock walked up and asked for Evan, who was still outside on the back deck with Tanya Stafford. Evan and Whit went into the study, and Tanya paced back and forth on the deck. Bill watched Tanya from the corner of his eye and concluded that she remained upset. After a few minutes, Tanya came inside, hurried to the counter, and interrupted Cindy's conversation with Angie Finch.

"I'm worried about Damian," Tanya said to Angie. "He seems tired."

Angie glanced at the caterers, told Cindy they could finish their discussion later, and then indicated to Tanya with a tilt of her head that they should move away from the kitchen. Before they were out of earshot, Angie said, "Actually, his cardiologist is encouraged. But he *is* still recovering."

Tanya tapped a finger against her temple to indicate she had concerns about his mental health as well.

Angie laughed and said something, but Bill could no longer make out their words. He glanced at Justin, who stood next to the sink with bulging eyes.

Cindy said, "Okay, guys, we're here to do a job, and our business has nothing to do with the client's business. Back to work."

"Yes, ma'am," said Maddie.

EIGHT

Damian and his guests ate lunch at the large dining table inside because the sun on the deck was now too bright. Damian sat at one end of the table with Angie Finch and Lacey Akin on either side. Maddie and Justin served beverages—sparkling or still water, a light white wine, and iced tea. Bill and Cindy served food and cleared the dishes later.

Bill served bowls of bisque one at a time to avoid spillage. He placed a bowl in front of Angie Finch, and she tweaked her nose at it.

"Can't you give me a smaller portion?" she said. "That's too much."

"I certainly can, but if I were you, I'd ask for a larger portion."

She turned her face toward him. "It's that good?"

"Best *I've* ever had."

"Oh, all right, then."

Angie Finch struck Bill as the sort of person who went out of her way to view the world in the worst light. Take a good thing and twist it around until it looks bad.

Tanya Stafford and Evan Hale conversed at the other end of the table. Whit Whitlock played with his phone.

Damian turned to his left and asked Lacey, “How are things at work?”

Lacey straightened her shoulders. “It’s become exciting. The city council and the city manager are stressed about the homeless situation. I’ve been assigned to a task force formed to research creative solutions.”

Damian nodded. “An age-old problem. What should we do with the poor? No easy answer, I’m afraid.”

Lacey began describing a new concept, and Bill walked out of earshot. He returned with bisque for Lacey a minute later.

Angie said, “So the idea is to create a public-private partnership that brainstorms solutions and attracts volunteers and donations.”

Lacey nodded.

“But who’s in charge?” said Damian.

Bill returned to the kitchen counter, where Cindy handed him another bowl of bisque.

“How’s it going?” she said.

“They’re solving the world’s problems.”

“I meant with the salads.”

“They scarfed them. Everyone except Whit Whitlock. He seems preoccupied.”

“Okay. Good.”

Bill served Damian next.

The entrepreneur shook his head. “I have my doubts, Lacey.”

“You could help by joining the governing committee. I’ll nominate you. The task force would be thrilled.”

Damian curled his lip. “I’m no good with committees. Not unless I’m the chairman.”

"It's a joint body. No one is in charge."

Damian shook his head as if he viewed public endeavors with a high degree of skepticism. "Let's switch subjects. Tell us of your romantic adventures. Any shining knights on the horizon? Dukes? A prince?"

Lacey's arms grew tense, and she pulled her hands into her lap.

Bill approached Tanya Stafford at the other end of the table.

On Tanya's right, Whit Whitlock tapped on his phone screen.

Evan Hale leaned toward Tanya.

Bill placed a bowl in front of Tanya, and Evan said in a low voice. "What are you going to do?"

Bill's instinct was to linger long enough to hear Tanya's answer, but that would have been inappropriate; nevertheless, as he stood and turned toward the kitchen, she said, "I'm a female executive on a rocket ship. I have options."

When everyone had been served salad and soup, Cindy asked Justin and Bill to join her in the kitchen. Maddie stayed near the table to handle requests. Cindy asked Justin and Bill for their observations. They both thought everything was in great shape. Cindy appeared nervous, and Bill gave her arm a reassuring squeeze.

"So far, so good," he said. "The food's fantastic, and I didn't spill the soup."

That earned him a chuckle.

After the soup course, Cindy discussed the sandwich options with the table. She explained that she, Justin, and Bill would take individual orders and serve while Maddie stood by to refill beverages. They also had fresh coffee.

Bill approached Tanya and Evan to take their orders but

stood to one side because they were in the middle of a conversation.

"What are you doing this afternoon?" said Tanya.

"Not sure yet. Lacey and I discussed going for a hike. Are you up for it?"

"Heck, yeah. What about Humpback Rocks?"

Evan noticed Bill standing nearby and stopped talking so that Bill could take their sandwich orders.

Across the table, Whit's cell vibrated, and he picked it up to examine the screen. From the other end of the table, Damian Susskind shot Whit an inquisitive glance. Whit nodded at Damian and stood.

"Whitlock speaking," the attorney said. "Hey, yeah, thanks for getting back to me."

With his phone at his ear, Whitlock stepped away from the table and slowly made his way into Damian's study.

Once the sandwiches were served, the conversation, which had been lively, quieted as everyone focused on their food. When the sandwich plates grew bare, Justin and Bill cleared the table, and Maddie took orders for dessert and coffee.

From the kitchen, where Bill paused for a drink of water before loading the dishwasher, he noticed Damian Susskind lean back in his chair. Damian suppressed a yawn and wiped a hand across his face. After loading the dishwasher, Bill walked into the dining area to see if there was anything he could do.

From the head of the table, Damian raised his voice so that Evan and Tanya would take notice. "What are you guys doing this afternoon?"

"We're hiking Humpback Rocks," said Evan.

Damian's gaze turned toward the floor-to-ceiling windows. Not a cloud marred the sky.

"Beautiful day for it," he said.

"Care to join us?" said Tanya sincerely.

But it could not have been a sincere offer. Bill had hiked Humpback Rocks. Though the trail was well-groomed, the journey to the top included a seven-hundred-foot climb in elevation, not a suitable outing for a man recovering from heart surgery.

Angie Finch touched Damian's forearm.

Damian smiled ruefully at Tanya and said, "Maybe another time. I'm a little tired. Let's step on the deck for a few minutes. Then I'll probably read awhile."

NINE

After lunch, Damian Susskind and his guests ventured onto the deck. Cindy and her crew worked to clean the dishes and begin dinner preparations. Forty minutes later, the two men had finished cleaning up and were relaxing at the breakfast table. Despite his earlier resolve, Justin played with his phone. Bill read a nonfiction book he had brought from home that related future applications of artificial intelligence. Cindy and Maddie chatted in the kitchen area.

At some point, boisterous laughter came from the back deck. The coffees had certainly revived the group. Bill spied Damian engaged in an animated conversation with Tanya and Evan. Angie, Lacey, and Whit were in their own cluster farther out on the deck. Bill returned to his book and read a few more paragraphs.

Then Damian Susskind strode into the kitchen with Angie Finch trailing behind him. "Cindy," he said, "will you please prepare refreshments for the trail? We're hiking Humpback Rocks. Brownies and some apples will do if you have them. And we need bottles of water."

Cindy blinked several times, glanced in Bill's direction, and then recovered. "Certainly. No trouble at all."

Bill could understand Cindy's reaction. Damian had undergone a transformation. Earlier, he had been ready for a nap. Now, he wanted to climb a mountain.

Angie tried to turn Damian gently to the side, but he resisted her.

"Do you think this is a good idea?" she said in a measured tone.

"Of course. Why wouldn't it be?"

"Dr. Varga advised you to take it easy. No rigorous exercise."

"Varga? Why should I listen to the mad Hungarian? What's the point of the surgery if I can't live my life?"

Angie wrung her hands. "Why not take a walk in the Nature Reserve? Why climb a mountain?"

"Because it's there. Look, Angie, I appreciate your concern, but I'm fine." Damian filled his lungs with air and raised two fists. "I feel great. I'm going to get dressed."

Damian made for the staircase leading to the second floor, and Angie turned to Cindy with a dazed look on her face.

"What just happened?" she said. "He's gone mad."

At that moment, Evan and Tanya came in from the deck.

"What's the matter with you?" Angie said sharply. "You know he can't do a hike like that."

Tanya raised her hands in exasperation. "It was a joke. I thought he was going to take a nap."

"It's not a joke," said Angie in a raised voice. "He could die on a strenuous hike."

Evan tried to calm the conversation. "Angie, please, relax. We're not taking Damian up Humpback Rocks." He rubbed his chin. "It must have been the coffee that revived him. We need another plan." Then he snapped his fingers. "I know. A bait and switch. Here's what we'll do. We'll drive down to where Laurel Springs Drive intersects with the Old Appalachian Trail. We'll tell him we've revised the itinerary and then take him to the overlook. It's less than half a mile from the road and an easy hike. Plus, the view is gorgeous."

Angie was mollified, but a chill ran down Bill's spine. The trail Evan referenced—once a part of the official Appalachian Trail—now ran along the perimeter of Wintergreen and passed by a rock ledge overlooking the Shenandoah Valley. Bill had been to that overlook several times. It was a beautiful sight, but Bill's fear of heights generally kept him away from such places. The last time he visited the overlook, he got down on his hands and knees before crawling to the edge.

TEN

An hour later, the young guests and Damian Susskind had left for their hike. Angie Finch took over Damian's study to do her work, and Whit Whitlock sat with his laptop on the living room sectional. Having finished most of the dinner meal preparations, the caterers took a break. Justin and Maddie went for a walk around the Devil's Knob summit. At the kitchen table, Cindy worked on her laptop, and Bill returned to his book.

Then Bill's cell phone rang. It was Alex Sharp, Wintergreen's interim chief of police.

"Hey, Alex."

"Sorry to bother you, Bill, but we have a situation."

"What's up?"

"Not sure. I'm still at the station. A call came in from the overlook off of Laurel Springs Drive. Apparently, it was a very short call. The cell service is bad there."

Bill sat straight in his chair.

Cindy's eyes darted to Bill's face.

"It seems that Damian Susskind has taken a fall."

"What?" said Bill. "Is he all right?"

"I . . . ah . . . I doubt it. The caller reported that Damian actually fell off the overlook."

Bill's mouth dropped. His mind involuntarily ventured back to the cliff's edge. It was a least a hundred-foot drop to the forest below.

"I can't believe this," said Bill. "I'm at his house right now. Cindy's catering for his guests."

"Seriously? Jeez. That's quite a coincidence. Anyway, I'm short-staffed. My investigator is on vacation this week, and Emily is out sick. Can you meet me over there and help us get organized?"

Emily Powell was Wintergreen's deputy chief and an experienced cop. But with Emily and the investigator both out of the office, Alex was the only manager around. Alex Sharp was a real estate broker who had worked the Wintergreen market for more than three decades, but he had no real police experience. When the previous chief of police quit suddenly to take a job out west, the board of trustees had asked Alex to step in.

"What about Nelson County?" said Bill.

"Shields and two deputies are on the way, but it will take them a while to get here."

Undersheriff Arnie Shields was second-in-command in the sheriff's office. Bill had met him on the Lou Thorpe investigation. Shields was a fine officer, but the sheriff's office was forty minutes away in the county seat of Lovingston.

"Okay," said Bill. "I can be at the trailhead in a few minutes."

"Don't tell anyone at the house, okay? We need to get the facts first."

"Yeah. Right."

Bill hung up. Cindy nervously touched the side of her neck.

"What is it?" she said.

He gave her an update and relayed Alex's request that they not inform anyone at the house.

"Is Damian all right?" she said.

"It doesn't look that way."

ELEVEN

Cindy drove Bill down Laurel Springs Drive to a point where a uniformed officer directed traffic around a growing number of vehicles parked on the side of the road. Two Wintergreen police squad cars were already there, along with Evan Hale's Land Rover, a Ford Escape, and Alex Sharp's pickup. Cindy stopped her SUV briefly, and Bill hopped out. Interim Chief Alex Sharp had just arrived, and the two men met at the trailhead.

The Old Appalachian Trail branched from the road in a southwesterly direction. Speckles of sunlight broke through the forest canopy high above them. The air smelled lightly of decaying leaves from prior seasons. Lichen-patched boulders the size of cars and tiny houses lay on the mountainside, discarded carelessly by an ice age's retreating glaciers.

Obviously anxious, Alex set a quick pace on the trail. He wore khakis and a light jacket, making Bill feel self-conscious in his catering outfit. The trail followed the contour of the mountain on a generally upward slope. The overlook was a little more than half a mile from the road, and they covered the distance in ten minutes. As they drew nearer, sunlight from the right brightened the forest.

Damian Susskind's guests—Tanya Stafford, Lacey Akin, and Evan Hale—stood in a quiet cluster forty feet from the overlook with an officer named Rodríguez. Their faces were drawn. Lacey looked pale.

Alex waved Rodríguez over.

"What's the story, José?" said Alex.

José pointed to where the trail continued south. "Officers Gentry and Hill went to search for a way to the bottom to see what can be done. EMS is on the way—should get here soon." José consulted notes on his phone. "It's not exactly clear what happened. The victim fell off the cliff—they all agree on that. But they were not together when he fell. The man—Hale—was standing back in the woods with Lacey Akin. Everyone agrees that Tanya Stafford and Susskind were out there on the rock."

An offshoot from the main trail broke through the trees and met the solid rock at the mountain's edge. The overlook itself was a ledge that ended abruptly in the open air. It stood alone now and peaceful, as if to proclaim its innocence—gravity deserved the blame. Wind blew up the mountainside and rustled the treetops.

"Here's the real problem," said José. "According to Lacey Akin, Tanya Stafford pushed Susskind off the cliff."

TWELVE

Mitch Gentry and John Hill hiked a quarter mile and then found a suitable place to leave the trail and venture farther down the mountain. Once off the beaten path, Mitch carefully studied the terrain before taking each step. The slope was steep, and the ground was covered with leaf litter from previous years. It wouldn't do to fall and break a bone here. The EMS team would have their hands full as it was, assuming Damian Susskind still breathed. After they had descended several hundred feet, Mitch cut right below the bottom of the cliff.

The rock was off-white and partially covered with moss and lichens. Mitch looked up but couldn't see the top of the cliff. Could anyone survive such a fall? The cliffside was steep but not smooth. Narrow ledges—six inches wide—appeared at random spots. Twenty feet up, a sapling clung tenaciously to a crevice. Mitch studied the rock wall and imagined a body bouncing down its side. He closed his eyes and took several deep breaths, but his breathing barely covered the sound of his heartbeats.

"We should get there soon," said Hill. "Don't you think?" His voice sounded edgy.

"Another hundred yards."

Mitch's shoes brushed through the leaves. Wind meandered into the shaded forest and chilled his face and hands. He wished he hadn't left his windbreaker in the cruiser.

A tall, thin man with dark hair rounded a corner of the wall ahead of them. Mitch startled.

Miracle of miracles.

The man had survived the fall. How was that possible? Wait. No. The man who had fallen was supposed to be older. This man appeared to be in his fifties. What the heck was he doing down here?

His name was Art Rossi, and when Damian Susskind fell, Rossi had been on the trail near the overlook. After the incident, Rossi had scrambled down the same route as Mitch and John Hill to see if he could help Susskind.

"I'm glad to see you guys," Rossi said. His hands shook.

"Is he alive?" said Mitch.

Rossi's grave face told the story.

Rossi accompanied them around the next corner, where they came upon Damian Susskind. Mitch would never get used to seeing a corpse. He had encountered three others in his career—two in Richmond when he worked there and then Lou Thorpe in Wintergreen. There was no question of saving Damian Susskind, for he had sustained life-ending injuries on the way down. Mitch's stomach felt queasy.

"Should we try to carry him up?" said Rossi.

Mitch admired Rossi's grit and desire to be a good citizen. Others would have stood to the side and done nothing. But in this case, there was nothing to be done except wait.

Hill took Rossi by the arm and led him away from the

victim. He entered Rossi's contact information into his phone, thanked him for his help, and told him he could take off.

Mitch glanced at the corpse again but quickly looked away. What an awful and sudden way to go. Damian Susskind had taken a wrong step and paid for it with his life. A rich man, from what Mitch had heard. Not rich now. One minute, he was on a pleasure hike, breathing the freshest air in the world, eyeing Mother Nature's beauty, and feeling the breeze's soft caress on his skin. The next moment, anxiety, terror, a tumble down the rocks, and then nothing. Mitch was young, strong, and confident, but he knew that even the healthiest of people could reach the end of their path without warning. He wished he had taken the time to kiss Lulu before leaving the house that morning. She had been in the back room, and he'd called to her from the hallway. They had exchanged *love you*s, and Mitch had left.

His radio crackled, and then Krista Jackson came on. EMS was fifteen minutes behind them.

"Did someone call forensics?" he asked.

"Stowers is on the way from Staunton," said Krista. Maybe she heard an edge in his voice, because she added, "Don't worry. She'll be there soon."

THIRTEEN

Alex sent Rodríguez out to the road to direct others in as they arrived. Then Alex and Bill conferred.

"We should try to get initial statements now," said Bill. "Memories are altered by reflection. First impressions mean something."

Alex nodded. "Makes sense."

"And we need to do them individually. Otherwise, they'll each be influenced by what the others say."

"You do it—take the statements. I'll mess it up." Alex could handle the administrative part of the job and the community relations, but investigative work was far from his line of expertise, and he wasn't afraid to own it.

Bill eyed Damian Susskind's guests. Lacey and Evan stood next to each other. Lacey's shoulders were tense, and Evan spoke softly to her. Tanya Stafford stood a little apart from the others with her arms crossed. Was she aware that Lacey had accused her of pushing Susskind off the cliff?

Bill said, "Take Evan and Lacey backward on the trail a hundred feet. Find them a rock to sit on. Try to get them to relax."

"Got it."

Once Alex had collected the others, Bill asked Tanya Stafford if he could ask her a few questions. She stood at least six feet tall—a few inches taller than Bill—and eyed his clothes with suspicion.

"No offense," she said, "but you're a caterer's helper. Why am I talking to you?"

"Reasonable question. I'm also a retired police detective from Columbia, South Carolina. Spent thirty-five years on the job."

"Substitute cop, huh? What an economy. Every job is going freelance."

Bill didn't know how to respond to that. Stafford had spoken in a relaxed and casual tone, but her hands were clasped tightly together. Who could fault her for the tension? Seeing something like that.

"What happens now?" said Tanya, still on the offensive. As a fast-climbing corporate executive, she was used to asking the questions.

"We're waiting for other law enforcement representatives. Folks from Nelson County and the state. Can you tell me what happened?"

Tanya examined his face, trying to read him. To be a successful leader in a company the size of Fair Game, you had to be good at assessing people. How would he stack up?

She shook her head. "It was quite strange. Damian jabbered the whole way from the road to here. I could hardly get a word in, and he made little sense."

"He was incoherent?"

"No, not like that. Damian kept saying he wouldn't let a simple thing like a heart attack slow him down. 'It's plumbing,' he said. 'We changed out the pipes, and I'm good to go.' And honestly, he sounded good too, right up to the end.

But he had sweat on his forehead, and his eyes flitted around."

"Did Damian know where he was?"

"Yeah, he did. He gave us a hard time for not taking him to Humpback Rocks. Said he would climb it tomorrow to show everyone that he was as strong as ever. But when we got to the overlook, everything changed." Tanya's eyes drifted to the overlook. One of her hands lifted hesitantly in that direction.

"What happened then?"

Tanya shuddered, and her eyebrows tensed. "He walked right to the edge. I said, 'Damian, come back from there.' But he wouldn't listen. He turned toward me with a smile, but then he grimaced horribly and clutched at his chest. I think he had a heart attack. I tried to reach for him, to pull him back from the edge. My hand touched his arm, but then he fell. In the next instant, he was gone."

Bill imagined the scene as Tanya described it, and hairs rose on his scalp. Her eyes remained at the overlook's edge as if she could still see Damian standing there. Perhaps she could.

Or maybe she had concocted that version for Bill's benefit. He remembered how angry Tanya had been when she came out of her meeting with Damian that morning.

"That must have been quite disturbing," he said.

Tanya shook her head as if to dispel the horrid recollection. "Yes."

"If you don't mind, I'd like to ask you about something that happened earlier in the day. After you met with Mr. Susskind this morning, you seemed upset."

Tanya pursed her lips. "Did I?"

"Yes. You approached Mr. Hale and expressed your anger. You called Damian an idiot."

Tanya frowned. “I don’t remember saying that.”

“Maybe I’ve gotten the words wrong, but you *were* angry. I’m sure of that. What made you so mad?”

Tanya breathed deeply and straightened her shoulders. She stood at her full height. “That was a company matter I’m not at liberty to discuss.”

Bill got a sense of how Tanya’s subordinates felt when she confronted them at the company. But he wouldn’t have been much of a detective if he let every suspect dismiss him at will. His expression convinced Tanya that she would need to elaborate.

She said, “Suffice it to say that Damian and I disagreed about a critical decision. Since having his heart attack and the surgery, he’s become less reliable in his thinking. It might have something to do with his medication, not his fault. Nevertheless, I’m the one who runs the company on a daily basis. When he comes up with erratic and unsound ideas, it irritates me.”

“I see. So it was a company matter related to strategy or tactics.”

“Yes. Exactly.”

Tanya’s mention of medication put another question in Bill’s mind. He had noticed a definite change in Damian’s mood after lunch. Damian was tired at the end of the meal, but later on, he had asked to join their afternoon hike. Bill asked Tanya whether Damian’s medication might account for his burst of energy.

She frowned and said, “I have no idea. I guess it’s possible.”

“Have you noticed those mood swings in Damian on other occasions?”

“No. Never. Before the heart attack and the surgery,

Damian was a rock. Never an unsteady moment. He had supreme confidence in his abilities, and why not? No matter what challenges he faced in life, his mind and body always delivered." Tanya's gaze returned to the overlook. "But not today."

FOURTEEN

When Bill had finished with Tanya, she asked whether she could call the office to check in. He okayed her request but asked that she not mention the accident until Nelson County had arrived and made their assessment.

Then Bill left to interview Evan Hale.

By the time he got to Alex and the others, an EMS team of two had arrived. While Alex gave the EMS team an update, Bill pulled Evan aside to get his statement. Evan asked if they could do it at the overlook. He wanted to see where Damian had stood before he fell.

Evan appeared shaken to the core by what had happened. On the way to the overlook, he related to Bill his close relationship with Damian Susskind. Unlike earlier in the day, when Evan had expressed misgivings about Damian's overbearing attempts to shape his behavior, Evan now showered his departed mentor with praise. The generous Damian had shared his wisdom, provided abundant opportunity for growth at Fair Game, and nourished Evan's entrepreneurial spirit. When Evan left Fair Game to seek his own fortune, Damian had wished him well. Now, Damian was gone, and Evan could scarcely make his mind believe it was true.

At the overlook, Evan ignored Bill's warning to stay back and marched to the precipice, as if fear of falling was far from his mind. In shorts and a long-sleeved T-shirt, Evan was athletic and graceful.

Bill grew dizzy at the sheer drop from the rocky ledge. Across the valley beneath them, the mountain's ridge sloped down and to the right into the Shenandoah Valley. Bill spread his legs wider for stability and inched toward the edge. He was still short of where Evan stood on the relatively flat stone.

"How could Damian have fallen from here?" said Evan. "I could do handstands and be perfectly safe." Then Evan commenced jumping. At first, his feet rose only a few inches, but then he bent his knees and leaped in place.

A wave of nausea swept over Bill, and he raised his hand toward Evan.

Evan jumped higher still.

Bill tried to call out but only managed a croak. Finally, he found his voice. "Please, stop doing that and come back from the edge."

Seeing that Bill was upset, Evan retreated from the precipice. "What's the matter?"

"Nothing serious. I do not enjoy heights."

Though Evan had been a single misstep from death moments earlier, he appeared unaffected. How could he be so fearless? Did youth bestow such courage? Had Bill been the same way decades earlier and only grown to fear death as he grew nearer? No, he had never been a reckless sort. He had taken his share of risks on the job, but that was the role of a police officer. Unlike Evan Hale, Bill had never sought danger without reason.

The two men retreated to stand beneath the branches of a small oak tree.

"Did you see Damian fall?" asked Bill.

"No," Hale hastily answered, as if it were important that Bill cross his name off the list of witnesses. "Lacey and I were engaged in a conversation and lagged behind Damian and Tanya. We got to there on the trail and paused a moment." Hale pointed to a spot a short distance away. "I wasn't even looking toward the overlook. Then suddenly, Lacey's face grew concerned, and she flinched. When I turned this way to see what concerned her, Damian was already gone. I rushed to Tanya, and she said that Damian had fallen."

"What happened then?"

A tremor shook Evan, as if he didn't care to remember the moments following Susskind's fall. "We were in a state, I'm afraid. I pulled Tanya back from the edge, and the three of us stood about here. I considered going down to search for Damian, but I knew no one could survive that fall, and Lacey was beyond upset. I managed to calm her and then called 911. I had a terrible signal, and the call dropped after thirty seconds. Then I couldn't get a signal to call the house."

Bill glanced at the overlook. How would he have reacted in the same situation? Could someone survive such a fall? Doubtful. Still, he would likely have hiked down the hill to make sure. Lacey may have been upset, but she was not in danger.

At that moment, Mitch and John Hill were at the bottom dealing with the aftermath of the fall. Bill did not envy them. Standing next to a corpse was an unpleasant task. Fortunately, the EMS team would reach them soon.

"Did you notice anything else of interest?" said Bill.

"Like what?"

"Anything at all. Could you hear what Tanya and Damian were discussing?"

Bill was fishing, of course. Officer Rodríguez had reported that Lacey said Tanya pushed Damian off the cliff. Bill wanted to know whether Lacey had told Hale the same thing.

"No," said Hale. "They were too far ahead. But it sounded as if they might have been quarreling."

"What would they have had to argue about?"

"I don't know. Tanya told me earlier that she had gotten angry with Damian over a company decision he was considering." Hale hastened to add context. "But that was not unusual. Damian was like that. He would throw out crazy ideas all the time. He called the process continual brainstorming, and he often did it to see how the listener would react. I had coached Tanya to play along with Damian when he got like that, but she had a hard time not shooting down ideas she considered ill-formed."

Bill frowned. In his youth, Damian Susskind had been an imposing figure with broad shoulders and strong legs, but his physique had deteriorated significantly. Tanya Stafford was a strong woman, and she could have pushed Damian off the cliff if the notion struck her. Standing next to the edge, had she come upon a brilliant idea of her own? The answer to all future arguments with Damian? One quick shove.

"Did anything else about Damian's behavior strike you as odd today?" Bill asked.

Evan cocked an eyebrow. "Odd? I don't believe so. Why do you ask?"

"After lunch, when Damian said he would join you and the others on a hike to Humpback Rocks, everyone was surprised. You said the coffee must have revived him and that the group should take him here instead."

"Yes, I recall saying that."

"Do you think coffee could have induced such a dramatic mood swing?"

Evan shrugged. "Coffee doesn't do a thing for me, but it affects people differently."

Which was true. Bill liked coffee, but if he over-caffeinated, his nerves grew jangled. Still, Damian's behavior didn't seem like the result of a caffeine high. Upon reflection, it seemed to Bill that Damian had consumed a more potent stimulant of some kind. But for the moment, Bill kept those thoughts to himself.

"Did Lacey tell you what she saw when Damian fell?" Bill said.

Evan waved a hand dismissively and said, "You'd better ask Lacey."

FIFTEEN

On the way back to Alex and the others, Bill and Evan passed the state forensic specialist named Kayla Stowers. Bill had met her briefly on the Lou Thorpe investigation. Stowers was a petite woman and had straight brown hair. They exchanged brief greetings, and Bill pointed toward the overlook.

Undersheriff Shields from Nelson County had reached the group along with a deputy. Arnie Shields and Bill shook hands and stood apart from the rest of the group. Arnie was a short, thin man with brown hair graying at the temples.

"Good to see you, Bill. I understand Alex had you take initial statements."

"Yeah. I have notes for you, but you'll want to interview them yourself." After Bill filled Arnie in on what he'd already learned, Arnie suggested the two of them meet with Lacey Akin next and that Bill lead the conversation since he had better context.

Lacey's round face had begun to recover some of its color, and Bill could objectively say she was beautiful. She was medium height with a shapely figure. Her dark brown eyes were now tinged pink.

Evan had put his arm around Lacey's shoulder to provide comfort. Tanya stood stiffly to one side.

After asking Lacey if they could talk for a few minutes, Bill led Lacey and Arnie on the trail in the opposite direction from the overlook. The path sloped downward gently. When they reached a wide spot out of the others' earshot, Bill stopped.

Lacey glanced nervously back toward the overlook. "Is it possible that Damian survived the fall?"

Bill exchanged a knowing glance with Arnie. Alex had told them that Mitch confirmed over the radio that Susskind did not survive.

"He's dead," said Lacey. She looked at the ground. "Isn't he?"

"I'm afraid so," said Bill.

Lacey drew a ragged breath, and her chin trembled. A tear formed in her eye, and Bill put a hand on her arm.

He knew from experience that a distressed person could often be distracted by a question. "Can you tell us what happened? Start with the drive over from the house."

Lacey sniffed but then straightened her shoulders. "We came in Evan's Land Rover. I sat in the front with Evan. Damian and Tanya were in the back. Damian grew irritated when he realized we weren't going to Humpback Rocks. Tanya told him we would do this hike first and then see how we felt, but he was still mad." Lacey's gaze was drawn to the trail headed back toward Laurel Springs Drive. Her eyes grew wider.

Arnie exchanged looks with Bill.

"Did Damian's behavior seem unusual this afternoon?" Bill said. It was a leading question, but Bill had witnessed

Damian's mood swing firsthand, and he wanted Lacey's take on the matter.

"Not really. But then I never knew what to expect from Daddy." Lacey stopped, and her eyes darted to Bill. "I mean Damian. He's my stepfather. Damian always liked it if I called him Father or Dad or Daddy. I rarely did. I guess it doesn't make much difference now either way."

"What happened when you got to the trailhead?" said Bill, to nudge Lacey on to the next part of the story.

"We began hiking, with Damian and Tanya ahead of Evan and me. Damian energetically marched to show off his fitness, but Tanya stayed with him stride for stride. They were still arguing."

"Could you make out their conversation?"

"No."

"Do you have any idea what they were discussing?"

Lacey paused a moment, then bit her lower lip. "Probably something about the company. They were always debating business tactics. After his heart attack, Damian stopped going into the office every day—doctor's orders. But whenever he saw Tanya, he wanted to talk shop."

At that moment, an overweight man appeared around a corner in the trail back toward Laurel Springs Drive. Bill recognized him as Soren Larsen, the state medical examiner. Before continuing with Lacey, Bill waited for Larsen to reach them. The ME stopped briefly to get directions from Arnie and continued on his way.

Bill knew they would not move Damian Susskind's corpse until the ME had a chance to examine him, which would take another half hour at least.

"Did you see what happened on the overlook?" asked Bill.

"Yes, I did." Lacey repeatedly nodded as if to reassure them of her confidence. "I told Officer Rodríguez."

"Can you tell us again?" said Bill.

Lacey's eyes were hesitant, as if she'd prefer not to, but she gave them a quick nod after a moment.

"Evan and I were behind them, and we stopped in the trees short of the overlook to finish our conversation."

From his interview with Evan Hale, Bill knew the location Lacey referred to, and as Lacey continued, he imagined himself standing there with a clear view of the overlook.

"Tanya and Damian had ventured out onto the rock, still arguing," said Lacey. "Evan wasn't looking in their direction, so he didn't see it. The two of them struggled like they were engaged in a tug-of-war. Damian tried to step away from Tanya. From where I stood, I couldn't see how close they were to the edge. Then Tanya shoved Damian, and he stumbled and fell to his knees. I thought he would be okay, but then he rolled off the cliff."

A stiff breeze blew through the treetops above them. Bill recalled the noise of the wind at the overlook.

"Are you sure they were arguing?" he said.

"Yes."

"Were they shouting or talking loudly?"

"Shouting, I think. But maybe they were just talking loudly."

Arnie frowned.

Bill said, "When Tanya pushed Damian, what was it like? Demonstrate on me as if you were Tanya, and I were Damian standing at the edge."

"You want me to push you?" Lacey asked, clearly uncomfortable now.

"Yes. Close your eyes and try to remember precisely what Tanya did at the overlook. Then do it to me."

Lacey did as Bill bid her. After a few moments with her eyes closed, she opened them and gave Bill a solid shove.

"Okay," said Bill. "Thank you. What did Tanya do then?"

"I'm not sure."

"Close your eyes again."

With her eyes shut, Lacey took several deep, calming breaths. "First, Tanya shouted. No, it was more like a shriek. Nothing intelligible. Then, Tanya got on her knees and crawled out as far as she could, as if to confirm that she had successfully pushed Damian over the side. By that time, I had screamed. Then Evan led me onto the overlook. But Damian was gone."

"Thank you. Arnie, got any more questions?"

Arnie said he was good, but then he asked Lacey if she would take him to the overlook and show him where she was standing. The three of them returned to the group, and then Lacey led Arnie forward on the trail.

Bill knew Arnie would want to ask his own questions. This homicide—accidental or otherwise—was in Nelson County's jurisdiction. The Wintergreen police, and Bill, would help out when asked, but it was the sheriff's call at the end of the day.

Several things about Lacey's statement bothered Bill; the most significant was how Tanya acted after she pushed Susskind off the cliff. Tanya had shrieked, then knelt to search over the side, as if desperately hoping Damian had only fallen to a ledge below. That didn't strike Bill as rational behavior for a killer. No, by instinct, a murderer would first turn around to check whether anyone had seen her do the deed.

SIXTEEN

At the bottom of the cliff, Mitch and the others waited uneasily a short distance from the corpse. The EMS team of two had arrived, officially confirmed that Susskind was dead, and then the four of them waited together. They jabbered about random stuff—their families, sports, the coming fall season—anything but the fellow human who would never say another word.

The sun had begun its descent, and its light filtered through the trees at a sharp angle. They had another thirty minutes of good sunlight. Jeez. They'd have a heck of a time getting Susskind out of here in the dark. Mitch hadn't thought to bring a flashlight from the squad car.

Then the state forensics specialist arrived. Although assigned to the Roanoke office, Kayla Stowers often worked from her house in the nearby town of Staunton. Mitch had met Stowers on the Lou Thorpe case. Kayla knew her trade well and told the others to move farther away from the corpse. She snapped photos of Susskind from different angles and then spent ten minutes studying the rock wall, as if trying to discern how Susskind had come to land where he did. She took photos of the wall from various angles and distances and asked Mitch and the others a few questions. After one last tour of the scene, Kayla hiked back up the hill to examine the place from where Susskind had fallen.

Mitch checked the time. Fifteen minutes had elapsed. The four of them began discussing the fading light. If the ME didn't arrive soon, they'd have to send for flashlights.

Would the chief try to bring Bill O'Shea into the investigation? Probably not. It seemed a straightforward accident, not much investigating to do. Still, Mitch would like to get Bill's take on it. Should he have done anything other than what he'd done? Mitch entered a few notes on his phone, so he could remember what to ask Bill the next time they met.

Then, thank goodness, the medical examiner arrived. Soren Larsen stood a little over five feet tall and was overweight. For a man with a macabre profession, Larsen was a jolly sort of person. He shook hands with each of them and spent several minutes on small talk. Then he examined the corpse from several different angles.

"Watch that first step, hey boys and girls?" said Larsen.

Nervous laughter from the group. The young woman, who was an EMS first responder, managed a genuine chuckle.

Larsen knelt and rolled Susskind's corpse to the side to check underneath the body. Then he came back to the group and addressed Mitch and John Hill. "Do you have any other details concerning what happened?"

"Not a lot," said Mitch. "We arrived ten minutes after he fell. The chief was right behind us."

"There's a whole crew at the scene now," said Larsen. "Shields from Nelson County, a deputy, and that other guy you've got up here. What's his name? Shea?"

"Bill O'Shea?" said Mitch.

“That’s him,” said Larsen. He eyed the corpse once more and then sighed. “Not a lot of mystery here. What a nasty way to go.”

John Hill said, “At least it was quick.”

“Yeah,” said Larsen. “All right, guys. Let’s get him out of here.”

SEVENTEEN

Four men stood on the overlook in the fading light to confer: Undersheriff Arnie Shields, Wintergreen Police Chief Alex Sharp, the medical examiner Soren Larsen, and Bill O'Shea. Lacey Akin and Evan Hale sat together in the nearby woods. Tanya Stafford stood by herself, typing on her phone. The others were hiking out to the road with the corpse.

The sun had fallen below a distant ridge to the left, creating a brilliant mix of oranges and reds. To the right and behind them, the sky was a crystal blue adorned with the night's first stars.

"What's your take, Bill?" said Arnie.

"It's a classic case of she-said–she-said." Bill went through his notes from interviewing Stafford, Akin, and Hale. Tanya Stafford thought Susskind had sustained a heart attack and fallen. Lacey Akin accused Tanya of pushing Susskind off the cliff. Evan's statement added no value since he missed seeing the critical moment.

Arnie rubbed his hands together, his face creased by a deep frown.

Bill knew Arnie was wrestling with what to do next. It was Arnie's call to make. Charging Tanya with murder was a big deal, but Lacey had made a serious accusation. Would Lacey's testimony hold up in court? Doubtful. Stafford would hire a skilled lawyer.

Arnie turned toward the medical examiner. "Will you perform an autopsy?"

"What for?" said Larsen. "He fell off a cliff."

"If he had a heart attack, that would bolster Stafford's story," said Arnie.

Larsen said, "On the other hand, maybe Stafford noticed he was having trouble and helped him along with a push."

Arnie's frown grew more profound. "That sounds like a stretch to me."

Larsen shrugged.

Autopsies took time, and Larsen was responsible for a large region of Virginia. His office undoubtedly handled multiple deaths every week. He didn't have the time to perform an autopsy on every corpse. Nevertheless, Bill believed Larsen was stalling. Larsen wanted Arnie to thank him for assisting the investigation and maybe earn a few credits for the goodwill account. Out here in the rural counties, everyone was short of resources. A lot got done through relationships with other jurisdictions. But in case Larsen was actually trying to wriggle out of the work, Bill decided to cast his vote.

"There's another reason to perform an autopsy," Bill said. The other three looked at him, and Bill explained the mood swing he had witnessed in Susskind earlier. "It's possible he ingested something that altered his mood."

Alex said, "You believe someone gave him something? Or he took it himself?"

Bill lifted his hands. "I have no idea. All I know for sure

is that he was ready for a nap after lunch. Thirty minutes later, he wanted to climb Everest."

Arnie turned to Larsen and put his hands on his hips as if to say, *What excuse are you gonna give now?*

"Yeah," said Larsen. "We'll do an autopsy. First thing tomorrow."

Larsen took off, leaving the three of them standing on the overlook. The breeze had picked up. The men stood a good ten feet from the edge, but Bill rechecked the distance to be sure. He was chilled now and ready to go somewhere warm. Oddly enough, he was also hungry.

"What are you going to do?" Alex asked Arnie.

Arnie said, "I don't have much choice. I could call the sheriff, but I already know what he would say." Arnie's gaze returned to Tanya Stafford.

How many times had Bill brought a suspect in for questioning during his career? A hundred? Two hundred? He was glad to be retired. Taking someone in came with the territory, but it was seldom fun. Did Tanya know that Lacey Akin had accused her of murder? Probably not.

"Under the circumstances," Arnie said to Alex, "I believe we should get everyone out of Susskind's house and seal it for now. Can you handle that?"

"Yeah. Sure."

"A couple of people are staying there," said Bill. "Angie Finch and Lacey Akin for sure. And maybe Whit Whitlock."

"Let them take a few overnight things," said Arnie, "but watch them pack. It's probably overkill, but at this point, we don't know exactly where we stand."

Arnie left to talk with Tanya Stafford. Bill tried to read Arnie's hand gestures. *Just a formality. The sheriff would like a word or two.*

Tanya stiffened, then her head tilted, and she said something. At one point, she turned toward Lacey and Evan.

Her eyes were shooting bullets.

EIGHTEEN

At Alex's request, a large group gathered in the living room of Damian Susskind's retreat. All of Damian's guests were there, save Tanya Stafford. Evan and Lacey were well aware of the grim facts, but Angie Finch and Whit Whitlock knew only that the hiking expedition was long overdue. Krista Jackson had come from the Wintergreen police station. The catering team of Cindy, Justin, and Maddie Katz had remained on site. When Bill entered the room, Cindy gave him a questioning look. He returned her query with a slight shake of his head, and Cindy stared at the floor.

Alex was gracious and brief in revealing what had happened. Bill's gaze was drawn to Angie Finch and Whit Whitlock, the two closest to Damian who were unaware of his death. Angie drew a quick breath, pulled her hands to her face, and then slowly fell apart. Krista Jackson hurried to Angie's side to provide comfort. When Whit Whitlock heard that his long-term client had died suddenly, his posture stiffened and the blood drained from his face.

A while later, the initial shock began to wear off, and Alex explained that the police were securing the house for now, so everyone would have to leave. If anyone needed to take a few things with them, Krista or Alex would have to oversee that process.

"Where is Tanya?" asked Whitlock.

Evan Hale's eyes moved to Alex. Lacey Akin stared straight ahead with her arms at her side.

Alex handled the question well. He explained that because Tanya had been standing near Damian when he fell, the sheriff wanted to meet with her personally. Alex didn't mention Lacey's accusation.

Angie Finch and Lacey Akin wanted to pack a few things. Evan Hale owned a condo on the mountain. Whit Whitlock was staying at the Mountain Inn and had only brought his briefcase. Krista helped Angie and Lacey with their packing, and Alex gave Whitlock's briefcase a cursory inspection. Cindy asked Bill if they could take the food they had prepared, but Bill said they'd better not.

"I don't know what we'll eat," she said.

"We'll think of something."

Alex and Bill were the last to leave the house. Alex had already instructed on-duty officers to check on the house every hour, and he now asked Bill if they could meet for coffee in the morning to discuss what else needed to be done.

"Sure," said Bill.

"Will the sheriff arrest Tanya Stafford?" asked Alex.

Bill pulled on his ear. "I doubt it. Not based on Lacey's statement. But let's see what the autopsy turns up."

NINETEEN

The first thing Cindy did after they reached her condo was open a bottle of wine.

"Sheesh," she said, pouring a healthy glassful. "What a day."

Cindy moved to the next glass and kept pouring. On the fourth glass, Maddie Katz stopped Cindy when the glass was less than half full.

"I have to drive."

"I forgot," said Cindy. "You could sleep on the couch if you like."

"No, thanks. I need to get home."

Maddie's words gave Bill the impression that an urgent task waited for her at home. Feeding a pet. Taking care of a loved one. Mysterious evening rituals. He was curious but resisted the temptation to pry.

Cindy's condo was a mirror image of Bill's. The kitchen was on the right in the main room, while the living space and furniture were on the left. Two bedrooms were at the end of a short hallway.

Bill and Cindy sat on the love seat in the living area,

while Justin and Maddie sat on opposite ends of the sofa. Justin's long legs extended beneath the circular coffee table. Maddie sat upright with her knees together and held the wine glass in her lap.

Cindy turned toward Bill, and her foot nudged his calf. She pestered him to provide details from the scene of Susskind's death. He shared what he could but left out the specifics of Lacey Akin's accusation and the discussion of whether to conduct an autopsy.

"Why did Tanya Stafford have to go Lovingston?" Cindy asked with a note of suspicion.

"Alex covered that," said Bill. "She was nearest to Damian when he fell, and the sheriff wanted to hear what happened from Tanya firsthand."

"But you said Arnie Shields was at the scene."

"Yes, but you know how hierarchies work. Arnie is the undersheriff, and the sheriff is the sheriff."

Cindy frowned, unsatisfied with Bill's answer.

"The whole thing is spooky," said Justin. "I've been to that overlook. It's a sweet view, but I'll never go again without thinking of Mr. Susskind falling off the side."

Maddie sat still with her hands gripping the wineglass. She stared at the wine, and it appeared to Bill that her mind was miles away.

Justin turned toward Maddie. "Have you ever stood on a cliff and wondered what it would feel like to fly?"

Maddie rotated her head slowly toward Justin. Had she even heard the question?

"Are you suggesting he jumped?" said Cindy.

"It's possible," said Justin.

"But he was rich," said Cindy. "Why would a man with that much money take his own life?"

"He had a weak heart, didn't he?" said Justin. "Maybe he

got depressed because he couldn't do the things he used to do. There's no better place to off yourself."

"That's silly," said Cindy.

Bill addressed Justin. "I agree with your mother. Humans are wired to fight for survival. Even when sick, most people cling to life for as long as possible."

The room grew silent. Cindy had opened a sliding glass door for fresh air, and the wind whipped onto the balcony. Bill studied Maddie. Her gaze remained locked on her wineglass, and he grew concerned for her.

"Are you all right, Maddie?"

Maddie sat straight, and her eyes darted to Bill. "Yes, I'm okay. It's just that I need to get home." She stood and hurried to take her glass into the kitchen.

Justin said he would escort Maddie to her car, and the two young adults left. Cindy suggested to Bill that they go onto the balcony. The sun had set behind them, and a thousand stars shone in the dark sky. Bill looked toward Mr. Chips's burrow entrance, but the groundhog had long since retired.

Cindy touched Bill's hand. "I believe Justin is attracted to Maddie."

"I agree."

"Do you think they're kissing in the parking lot?"

"I doubt it," he said. "Maddie didn't seem to be in the mood."

"Just as well. I don't know what could come of it. He goes to Cape May next week, and then he'll be off to God knows where."

"Yeah. Long-distance relationships are difficult to sustain. How well do you know Maddie?"

"Reasonably well. She's a nice girl, a good worker, and knows her way around the kitchen."

Something about Maddie Katz struck Bill as off, but he

couldn't decide what it was. She had acted nervous when serving the guests on Susskind's deck that morning. Bill had decided she was intimidated by Susskind's larger-than-life gregariousness, but her lack of attention moments earlier hinted at a different emotion—fear. The nearness of death could do that to a person. He'd seen it many times.

"I'm sick about the food," said Cindy. "What will happen to the mahi-mahi? It'll keep in the fridge overnight but won't taste as good. Will they let us in tomorrow?"

"I don't know. Maybe."

It depended on what came from the autopsy report. Bill recalled how Damian Susskind marched into the kitchen after his miracle revival on the back deck. Could coffee have triggered such a transformation?

Justin returned shortly, and they made sandwiches for dinner. Bill had recently been spending the occasional night at Cindy's condo, but they had agreed that he would sleep alone at his place for Justin's visit. It was too early for Cindy to disclose the full details of their relationship to her son. Bill didn't mind—he would settle for any kind of relationship with Cindy.

After kissing her goodbye at the door, he walked outside and turned right toward his condo building. Then his phone buzzed. It was Whit Whitlock—Damian Susskind's attorney. Whit was at the Mountain Inn and asked whether Bill might join him at the Edge for a beer and a short conversation.

"What time?" said Bill.

"Anytime tonight that works for you," said Whitlock. "Or we could meet tomorrow for coffee."

"As it happens, I'm free now. I'll be there in fifteen minutes."

TWENTY

Bill parked in the lot below the Mountain Inn and then walked through the lobby to the brick patio out back. The Edge restaurant lay a hundred yards behind the inn's main building. Tall fir trees bordered the walkway, and Bill passed a courtyard with picnic tables on the right. A man and woman exited the square carrying a large pizza box. On their way back from having dinner at the Edge, a young family passed by. A girl about three years old held her father's hand —she seemed tired and happy. Off to the left, the resort's main ski run sloped down toward the valley. Bill crossed the wooden bridge that led to the restaurant, and a woman came through the door. The woman wore her blond hair styled in layers that touched her shoulders. She was tall and moved with a lively step. Bill guessed she was in her late forties. She had a round face, sparkling eyes, and smiled as if she'd heard great news.

"Good evening," said Bill.

"Thank you. Beautiful, isn't it?" She lifted her arms toward the sky. "The stars are spectacular."

Her enthusiasm was infectious, and Bill found himself

smiling. At the door, he turned to glance at the woman again. She swung her arms in unison and clapped her hands with every other step.

Inside the restaurant, Bill found Whit Whitlock ensconced in a window booth. The Edge was decorated like a classic ski lodge, with varnished wooden tables and antique skis and poles mounted high on the walls. Though the restaurant could seat a hundred patrons, less than two dozen customers were present. Over at the bar, a man and a woman watched a late-season baseball game on a flatscreen television.

Bill approached the table, and Whitlock stood and offered his hand to shake. "I'm glad you could join me. Thank you for changing plans on short notice."

Whit had an unremarkable figure, medium height, average weight, and rounded shoulders. He had a thick mustache and wore a ready smile despite the day's circumstances.

"I had no evening plans," said Bill. "Your invitation was welcome."

"Excellent." The attorney indicated with a hand that Bill should take the opposite bench seat, and then he waved at a server. "Let's get you something to drink."

Whit Whitlock had evidently just finished eating. A piece of lettuce and a few French fries were all that remained of the meal. The server cleared the plate and took Bill's order for a Vienna Lager from Devils Backbone. Whitlock pointed at his beer glass for a refill.

"I'm sorry for what happened today," said Bill. "I gather you worked with Damian for a long time."

Whit laid one arm across his belly and held his chin with his other hand. Then he heaved a sigh. "It's a sad day indeed. I worked for Damian and Fair Game for over twenty years. He was my biggest client, by far, and my firm's biggest client as well. When you work for someone that long, you get to know them. We were never personal friends, but still, I knew him, and he knew me."

Whit's gaze drifted off as if he was contemplating the many years he had regularly spoken with Susskind. It must feel uneasy for him to think he would never talk with Susskind again. What effect would Damian's death have on Whit's livelihood? Not good, in any case.

"What did you want to see me about?" said Bill.

Whitlock came back to the present. His eyebrows bounced, and then he said, "Evan Hale mentioned that you took statements from witnesses at the overlook today."

"Yes, that's correct. I'm a retired police detective. Alex Sharp is the acting chief here in Wintergreen. He's new to the game and asked me to help out."

"I see. Makes perfect sense. In your professional opinion, how will Damian's death be investigated?"

Bill scratched his cheek. As a police detective, he had stuck fast to one rule regarding the flow of information: It was better to receive than to give. Still, Whit was waiting for an answer, and he appeared to be a nice person so Bill would respond, albeit with an answer that provided little helpful intel.

"It will be investigated as an accidental death."

"Of course. I can see you're uncomfortable with my question. Please be assured that I am not motivated by idle curiosity. I am the executor for Damian Susskind's will, and as such, I must verify that Damian's death involved no impropriety."

Bill nodded as if everything now lined up in his head. "I have no reason to believe the death was anything other than accidental. Do you?"

Whit frowned. "On the contrary, I can't imagine that it

was anything else. I wasn't there, of course, but I'm certain Damian fell due to a clumsy step." But then Whit raised one eyebrow. "I suppose there is another possibility. You must have heard that Damian recently suffered a serious heart attack. He nearly died, and the cardiologist had warned him to take it easy. He could have sustained a second attack at the overlook that caused him to lose his footing."

Whit leaned back and raised his head as if to ponder this new thought.

Bill remained silent.

"The more I consider it," said Whitlock, "the more I favor this heart-attack scenario. Damian was athletic, not one to lose his footing, but he didn't live a healthy lifestyle. He was a bigger-than-life type who welcomed risky endeavors, the kind of person who keeps running right through the bitter end. And the stress? Off the charts. His doctor recommended meditation, which was a joke, I assure you. Damian would have sooner died than sit and listen to his breathing for thirty minutes. Not happening."

Bill knew well the sort of person Whit described. There were plenty of Type A personalities in Columbia's police department. Several had died from heart attacks before they could retire. Maybe they should have tried meditation. Bill had never sought the headaches and stress that came with promotion. He liked detective work for what it was—seeking clues, talking with all kinds of people, and figuring out suspects' motivations. Still, Bill had recently read that meditation could help anyone manage their thoughts. Perhaps he should give it a try.

"Don't get the wrong impression," said Whit. "I had tremendous respect for Damian. In the middle years of his career, he was a comeback genius. No matter how many times the business knocked him down, he kept coming back for more. Unfortunately, that success shaped Damian's outlook on all aspects of life for longer than it should have. Despite his age, he never learned how to take his foot off the gas. Even after the quintuple bypass surgery, Damian believed he had forever to live and could do whatever he chose. Obviously, he was wrong."

"What sort of relationships did Damian have with Evan Hale and Tanya Stafford?" asked Bill.

Whit bobbed his head as if trying to decide how to answer the question. "In my experience, his relationship with them resembled that of most rich men and their offspring. In other words, part fantasy and part nightmare."

Bill frowned. "I don't follow."

Whit rubbed his hands together as if he were about to broach an unpleasant topic. "He played games with their emotions. I hate to say this, but I believe Damian enjoyed torturing those close to him, watching them suffer."

"But they're adults," Bill said. "He had no control over them."

Whit shrugged. "All three of them—Evan, Tanya, and Lacey—stood to inherit large sums of money."

Money. Time and again, people contorted their lives over money. Well, now that Whitlock was on a roll, Bill should shake him for whatever he could.

"How much money?" he said.

"I'm not at liberty to divulge that information."

"Get me in the neighborhood for the total pot. What was Damian's net worth? Ten million?"

"Goodness, yes."

"Twenty million?"

Whit blinked several times and said, "Bill . . . Is it okay to call you Bill?"

"Of course."

"Thank you. Call me Whit. Bill, you need to use your imagination. Much bigger."

"Fifty million?"

Whit pointed his index toward the ceiling.

"One hundred million?"

"Now you've gone too high, but not by much."

Okay, so Damian Susskind was worth a lot. Call it eighty million dollars. And each year, Damian manipulated Lacey, Tanya, and Evan like a puppeteer. Oh, I love you this year—you'll inherit thirty million. You've been childish and reckless—I've cut your slice to five hundred thousand. The game could drive strange behavior for people who cared about money—and honestly, who wouldn't care about thirty million dollars?

"Evan mentioned something today that I found disturbing," said Whit. "He said Lacey accused Tanya of pushing Damian off the cliff."

Whit waited for Bill's confirmation. Colleagues had described Bill's face as unreadable at moments like this. "I can't discuss statements."

"Of course, but in any case, I wouldn't believe such an accusation for an instant. This was an accident. Tanya and Damian often disagreed, and they had sharp words this morning, but she would never dream of harming him."

"What did they argue about this morning?" said Bill.

"It was a company matter."

"That's what I understand. Could you be more specific?"

The server brought their beers. Whit sipped his and then eyed the glass with satisfaction. "The local breweries make some excellent craft beers."

"Don't they? Wintergreen is fortunate to have so many breweries and wineries nearby."

As if to underscore Bill's statement, the attorney smacked his lips, then said, "Let's see, where were we?"

"You were relating the argument Tanya had with Damian this morning."

"Right. To understand their disagreement fully, I need to give you some background."

"Take your time. I have all night."

"Tanya and Evan began working for Fair Game as interns —Fair Game has always hired interns from local schools. Damian personally tracked interns' performance and hired those who did well as permanent employees. Tanya and Evan both proved to be good workers, and Damian liked them, so he nurtured their careers with the company by bringing them to corporate executive meetings to take notes and run errands. Soon, he began bringing them up here to Wintergreen. Eventually, it occurred to me that they had become like surrogate children for him."

Whit paused to attend to his beer.

"What about Lacey?" said Bill.

"Lacey was ten years old when Damian married her mother. Unfortunately, Lacey's mother became ill and died five years later. Damian and Lacey always had a good relationship, but she is closer to her own father, who lives in Richmond."

Bill worked the numbers in his head. Lacey had come into Damian's life through his marriage to her mother at around the same time that Tanya and Evan became interns for the company. Bill guessed that the three of them had known each other through the Damian connection for over fifteen years, plenty of time to form their own interrelationships.

Whit continued. "Evan and Tanya both did well at Fair Game. They were bright and worked hard, and Damian promoted them into positions of responsibility. I always figured that Evan had a slight advantage over Tanya because he was a man in a sporting goods company, but it was Tanya who grew to love the outdoor sports of hunting and fishing. In any case, I thought Evan would succeed Damian as CEO whenever Damian decided to step down."

"But that didn't happen."

"No, Evan had his own ideas. When Evan announced he was leaving Fair Game to form Burgers Galore, I expected Damian to explode, but he surprised me by encouraging Evan to pursue his destiny."

"Did Lacey ever work for Fair Game?" Bill asked.

"No, Lacey doesn't care much for the business world. She studied liberal arts in school and eventually became interested in social issues."

"And Tanya stayed with the company this whole time?"

Whit nodded and slowly turned the beer glass with his fingers. "Which brings us to the argument she had with Damian this afternoon. Tanya continued to progress in the company. She worked tirelessly, sixty to seventy hours a week, and with each passing year, Damian gave her more of the company to manage. Eventually, she became the chief operating officer. Then last year, Damian announced to the board of directors that he formally supported Tanya as heir apparent to the role of CEO."

So far, so good, thought Bill. *But there has to be a sad face in this tale.*

"But then Damian had the heart attack," said Whit. A puzzled expression came over Whit's face. He stared at his glass as if he might find an answer in the clear amber liquid. "The heart attack affected Damian. I suppose a near-death experience often changes people's outlooks on life. In any case, he told me in confidence that he had decided to hire an experienced retail executive to take his place instead of putting Tanya in the top slot. He still believed in Tanya but said she needed another five years to be ready."

"Oh," said Bill, and he recalled Tanya stating to Evan Hale earlier that she was a female executive with options. "Is that what they argued about today?"

Whit rubbed his hands together, stalling for time because he didn't want to answer the question. "I don't know for sure. I was with them when they discussed his will, and Damian didn't mention his succession plan then. But after our conversation, I went to the restroom, and Damian asked Tanya to stay for a minute. I suspect he told her at that point because she was angry when I saw her next."

Tanya had certainly been angry when she came out of Damian's study that morning. Hmm . . . what had Tanya said to Evan Hale? "Do you know what that idiot has done now?" In Bill's mind, Tanya argued with Damian as they hiked through the woods. She tried to change Damian's mind, but he was stubborn, and she grew angrier by the moment. Standing next to the overlook's edge, Tanya's anger turned to fury, and she gave him a good shove. That was all it took.

"I'm afraid I may have given you the wrong impression," said Whit. "I don't for a minute believe that Tanya pushed Damian off the overlook. She wouldn't do that. It was an accident."

"You're probably right," said Bill.

"Even so, I imagine they'll perform an autopsy."

"Why would they do that?" asked Bill, though he already knew the answer.

The lawyer responded to the question as a lawyer would. "It's logical. The sheriff will want to know if Damian had a second heart attack. If he did, that would go a long way to proving Tanya's innocence."

"I suppose it would," said Bill.

Whit then brought the conversation back to where he started, asking Bill to share the investigation's ongoing status so Whit could execute Damian's will expeditiously. Bill reassured Whit that he would share what he could, and the conversation moved on to other topics. Whit asked about Bill's family, and Bill related that he was divorced with two grown sons. Bill asked the same question in return, and the attorney explained that he lived with his sister and had never been married. Whit's face brightened, and he reached for his phone.

"I suppose MaryEllen is why I've never had time to find the right partner. She has autism spectrum disorder. Don't misunderstand me—MaryEllen is a high-functioning individual—but she needs help with some of life's more complicated tasks. Here, let me show you her picture."

Whit was obviously proud of his sister. The article he shared was from a Charlottesville news website. MaryEllen had been named a local clothing store's Team Player of the Month for three months in a single year. She held the position of senior associate, and the photo showed a middle-aged woman with a bright smile, blue eyes, and curly brown hair.

Bill considered the photo. "She's pretty."

Whit nodded, stared at his phone again, and then put it away. "She's quite independent when it comes to most aspects of life. For example, I'm staying here tonight, and MaryEllen will be perfectly fine on her own. In fact, my earlier excuse for not having found the right partner is unfair. The truth is I'm an awkward person."

Bill frowned. "I doubt that. I don't find you awkward at all. Of course, I've never been on a date with you."

Both men laughed, but Bill instantly regretted his words. For all he knew, Whit was gay, and the last thing Bill wanted to do was make him feel awkward.

If Whit was uncomfortable, he certainly didn't show it. He said, "They say it's never too late for love, and in my case, the outlook has brightened. I've begun seeing a new woman, and she says she likes me." Then he rapped his knuckles on the table.

"Good for you," said Bill.

Whit asked if Bill cared to have another beer, but Bill was tired and begged off. He reached for his wallet, but Whit insisted on paying. Bill got up to leave, and Whit said he'd left some papers at Damian's house that had to do with the will. Would he be able to get them the next day? Bill promised to mention the matter to Alex Sharp, then he left the Edge.

Outside the Mountain Inn, a three-quarters moon shone high in the sky. The wind had grown quiet, and in the dark and nearly empty parking lot, Bill could hear his footsteps. He was lucky to have retired in such a peaceful community. But then an owl hooted from a nearby tree, causing Bill to jump. Some distance away, a second owl hooted in response.

Hoo? Hoo?

Of course, it was his imagination, but it certainly seemed to Bill that the owls were insistent. They wanted an answer.

TWENTY-ONE

In the early morning, Cindy poured a cup of coffee and strolled onto her balcony dressed in jeans and a sweater. The sun had crested the mountains on the left and cast a warming golden light on the ridge of condo buildings where she and Bill lived. The beauty of the moment stole her breath away. Every Wintergreen sunrise was an original, and she hurried back inside to fetch her camera. As an amateur photographer, Cindy always kept an eye open for the perfect shot.

She took several snaps, and then motion caught the corner of her left eye. In the next building over, Bill was on his balcony. He lived on the same floor as her, but the downward slope of the ridge brought him twenty feet below her level.

Bill gave her a wave and then pointed in the direction of the groundhog burrow at the lawn's edge between their buildings. The groundhog—whom Bill had named Mr. Chips—stood quietly nibbling on leafy greens he had picked from the grass. Lazy thing. As far as Cindy could tell, Mr. Chips did little other than eat and lounge all day.

Cindy's cell phone rang. It was her ex-husband, Kevin, a

realization that filled Cindy with conflicting emotions. She cared for Kevin and considered him a friend, albeit a friend who knew her like no other ever could. Still, knowing she was about to speak to a man who had shared her bed for twenty-five years only moments after greeting her new romantic interest made her feel distinctly awkward. Without waving goodbye to Bill, she strode inside the condo.

"Good morning, doll," said Kevin.

"Kevin, I've told you before, enough with the terms of endearment. It's absurd."

"I'm sorry. Slipped out. Old habits and so forth. It won't happen again."

Empty promises. They were a rarity with Kevin for their first twenty years, but then he changed. He remained a good father, listened to the kids, participated in their activities, and helped them whenever they asked. But the attention he paid her slowly faded over the years. When they first got together after college, he could hardly keep his eyes, or his hands, off of her. By the end, he couldn't maintain his end of a conversation for more than a few sentences. Ironically, after the divorce, when he could no longer be with her at all hours of the day, he became more attentive. For example, he now recklessly slipped terms of endearment into his greetings.

"How are you?" he said with genuine feeling. "How is your visit with Justin coming along?"

"Quite well until yesterday, when we lost a client under horrid circumstances." Cindy related the previous day's events, which Kevin naturally found most concerning. After assuring him repeatedly that she and Justin were fine, the conversation moved on.

"So," he said, "how's the short cop? What's his name?"

"He's not short, and it's none of your business." Justin

must have described Bill to Kevin. Cindy took a mental note to give Justin a hard time about that later.

"Is he six feet tall? If not, then he's short."

Cindy's face grew warm. Darn Kevin. Though Kevin was tall, well over six feet, she had never heard him belittle someone else's height. He only did that to tease her. Screw him.

"He's taller than me," she said. "We fit nicely together."

That shut Kevin up. She could almost feel him sulking through the phone line.

"Why did you call?" she asked.

"The Coast Guard. It's a terrible move."

When Justin had first discussed his plan to join the Coast Guard with his father, Kevin had expressed enthusiastic support. Whatever Justin wanted to do was good with him. But apparently, Kevin now had second thoughts.

"I disagree," she said. "This move will give Justin focus and teach him valuable skills. You said you were supportive."

"I went along with it at first, but now I've had time to reflect. Think of all the boys who attended high school or college with Justin. None of them has gone into the military. He'll wind up with a bunch of blue-collar kids who barely made it out of high school."

"That's not so bad. Would you rather he tended bar for the rest of his life?"

"Wait," said Kevin with panic in his voice. "Is Justin there? Can he hear you?"

Cindy realized that she had raised her voice. Though she and Kevin had disagreed many times, they had always kept their arguments away from the children. She nervously peered down the hallway toward Justin's bedroom. The line under the door remained dark, and she breathed a sigh of relief.

"No, he's still asleep."

Kevin picked up right where they'd left off. "Justin will grow tired of bartending soon. We should push him toward graduate school."

"He has no interest in graduate school," Cindy said in a voice barely above a whisper. "This is a good stepping-stone for him."

"Stepping-stone to where? Name one person of substance who served in the Coast Guard."

Though Cindy didn't know of any names right off, she was sure there were many. If she'd been sitting at her laptop, she would have searched for them.

"Well?" he said.

"I don't know of any right now."

"See? That's because they don't exist. Now, how can we change his mind? That's why I called—to come up with a plan."

"I'll do no such thing. It's Justin's decision. But feel free to share your opinion."

"I most certainly will, but it will have more impact if we present a united front."

"Nope. You're on your own."

"Why not? It's the ex-cop, isn't it? He's a vet. Don't let your boyfriend screw up our son's life."

Cindy's head nearly exploded. It took every ounce of her resolve to keep from shouting. On a nearby shelf was a photo of Justin and his older sister when they were six and eight years old. Cindy blinked several times and began to calm down. Then she said, "This conversation is going nowhere. Goodbye." She hung up before he could get another word in.

She marched onto her balcony and tightly gripped the railing. Normally, she would inspect the full planters for flowers that required attention, but she barely noticed them.

She stared straight ahead but didn't see the gorgeous valley either. That darn Kevin. How dare he? What impudence. What gall.

And the worst part was, she had her own doubts about Justin serving in the Coast Guard. She turned toward Bill's balcony, but he had gone inside.

When Cindy lived in northern Virginia with Kevin and the children, she had worked as the regional manager for a nationwide chain of restaurants. She oversaw twenty-three stores with millions in sales and hundreds of employees. In that position, she had met most of the company's senior executives. The bigwigs. CEO. SVP of Marketing. SVP of Operations. The top executives had all gone to fancy schools for MBAs or law degrees.

She couldn't think of a single one who had served in the military, let alone the Coast Guard.

TWENTY-TWO

With a big ripe tomato in hand, Bill skipped down the stairs in front of his condo building and turned left to go around the side. Fifty feet away, Maddie Katz climbed the stairs to Cindy's building. Maddie noticed Bill, stopped, and stepped to the railing with her upper body leaning in his direction.

"What are you doing with that tomato?" she asked.

"I'm going to feed Mr. Chips."

"Who?"

He pointed at the groundhog, who continued to eat leafy greens near his burrow entrance.

"Can I watch?" she said.

"Of course."

Maddie hurried down the stairs and then came to Bill's side. Instead of her catering uniform, she wore jeans and a long-sleeved T-shirt.

Bill said, "I didn't know if you'd come to work today given that the event is off."

"Cindy asked me to help her with some baking. She's decided to do that instead."

When her catering business was light, Cindy sometimes made desserts for resale through various shops in the Rockfish Valley.

"I don't know if she really needs me," said Maddie, "but I sure could use the money."

"No doubt you'll be a great help."

"What's up with the groundhog?"

Bill related the YouTube groundhog family story and said he was determined to hand-feed Mr. Chips.

"Why do you call him Chips?"

"Not Chips. Mr. Chips."

When Bill turned toward the burrow, Mr. Chips noticed and dropped his greens to stand straight. Bill explained that when the groundhog stood erect and proper that way, he reminded Bill of a university professor, hence the nickname Mr. Chips. Maddie still seemed confused, so Bill told her of the literary character who bore the same name.

"How do you plan to feed him?" said Maddie.

"Walk right up and give it to him."

"Have you tried that already?"

"Yesterday."

"How did it go?"

"Not so well. Mr. Chips ran inside, and I dropped the tomato down his burrow."

Maddie then told Bill that her father fed squirrels in their backyard. They ate snack foods out of his hand: potato chips, pretzels, popcorn even. The trick was in the training. You could chase squirrels all day and make no progress. You had to hook them first with a free sample.

"Free sample?" Bill said.

"Yep. The first thing you do is hold that tomato up and jiggle it so he'll notice."

Bill did as Maddie coached.

"Then, we stroll toward Mr. Chips until he gets nervous. About twenty feet away, I'd guess."

The two of them proceeded in that fashion to the prescribed point. As if on cue, Mr. Chips straightened his posture and appeared as if he might scamper off.

"Now, put the tomato on the ground where he can see it, and then we'll slowly back away."

Bill and Maddie retreated to the sidewalk and observed Mr. Chips and the tomato for a full minute. Nothing happened.

"It's not working," said Bill.

"Give it time."

It took two more minutes for Mr. Chips to make his first move. He searched his surroundings for danger, then dashed forward a third of the distance to the tomato, where he stopped to check for signs of a trap. A minute later, he closed the remaining distance by half. And then a short while later, he sprinted to the tomato, stuffed it in his mouth, ran back to his burrow, and disappeared down the entrance.

"Holy hemlock," said Bill, his face beaming. "It worked."

Maddie nodded as if she'd never had a doubt. "Every day, move a little closer to Mr. Chips before laying down the tomato. If he ever runs away, don't give it to him. He'll make the connection quickly. When you can get to about five feet from him, crouch down so he doesn't feel threatened, and hold the tomato out for him to take. One day he'll do it."

They stood three feet apart on the sidewalk. Maddie's sleeve tattoo was mainly hidden under her brown T-shirt. She had been quiet the previous day after Damian's death, but feeding Mr. Chips brought a smile to her face.

"Do you live with your parents, Maddie?" he asked.

"I do now. I went to college for a year in Harrisonburg, but college didn't agree with me."

Bill nodded. College was not the right path for everyone. He had never attended college, and life had worked out well for him. So far.

Maddie said, "I lived with roommates for a few years, which was fun but expensive, so I moved back home to save money."

No way to know for sure without prying, but Bill would bet the sleeve tattoo had come during the roommate years.

"Good plan," he said. "It's good to save money, plus you get to watch your father feed squirrels."

Maddie giggled, but only for a few seconds, then she stopped as if to correct herself. She eyed Bill as if trying to sort him out. "Justin told me you used to be a policeman."

"That's right. I retired."

"You don't seem like a policeman."

Maddie had formed an impression of a stereotypical police officer somewhere along the way. The problem came with the job. Most people only interacted with the police in situations that involved conflict. It might be as simple as a traffic citation, but it was a rare cop who could write a ticket and come across as the good guy.

"Cops come in all shapes, sizes, and colors," he said. "Just like every other job."

"I guess."

It would take more than one groundhog-feeding session to change Maddie's impression. But, if she kept working for Cindy, he might get the chance.

"I'd better get to work," she said.

Bill nodded and said he'd see her later.

She walked away, and Bill thought, *She's twenty-three, maybe twenty-four.*

Bill envied Maddie's father for getting the chance to live with his daughter again. Bill's two sons were twenty-three and twenty-five: Brandon worked as a junior accountant back in Columbia, and Matt was a freelance graphic artist living in Savannah. People described a boomerang child experience as a bad thing. But they were wrong.

His cell phone buzzed. It was a text from Alex Sharp.

I'm ten minutes from the Mountain Inn.

Bill typed his response. **Be right there.**

TWENTY-THREE

Bill and Alex grabbed coffees at the shop inside the lodge, strolled onto the back patio, and sat at a picnic table with a view of the mountains sloping down toward the Rockfish Valley. Bill's condo building was high on the ridge to the left. A slight breeze blew across the upper reaches of the ski slope, and Bill was glad he'd thrown on a windbreaker.

Alex blew into his coffee, and steam rose from the cup.

"I had a beer with Whit Whitlock last night," said Bill. "He invited me to join him at the Edge."

"Do tell."

"Yep." Bill related what he'd learned from Whitlock, including the possible motive for Tanya Stafford to push Damian off the cliff.

Alex cocked an eyebrow. "It seems a drastic step to take over a job."

"I agree. But people have been killed for less. Did the sheriff keep her in jail overnight?"

"No. Arnie gave me the scoop this morning. Tanya's story never changed one bit, and the sheriff has doubts about her guilt. They asked her to remain in Nelson County for the moment. Arnie says if she runs, they'll know she did it."

Bill nodded. He silently agreed with the sheriff's decision. The sheriff and the prosecuting attorney had likely conferred and concluded they had a weak case against Tanya Stafford. Better to give her some rope. And they needed to see the autopsy results first anyway.

Alex continued with his update. Arnie Shields expected to receive the preliminary autopsy results that morning. Until that came in, they would keep Susskind's house closed.

Bill relayed Whitlock's request to retrieve papers having to do with Damian's will from the house.

"I'll mention it to Arnie," said Alex. "That's his call to make."

Bill nodded. It occurred to him that they would likely never know for sure whether Tanya had given Damian the fatal shove. If the autopsy said Damian had suffered a heart attack, it would lend credence to Tanya's version of the story, but she still might have helped him take a fall. If he hadn't suffered a heart attack, he might still have stumbled and fallen on his own. Either way, it was inconclusive, which was no big surprise in the larger scheme of life. Somewhere between eight and ten thousand people died in the US every day. Many of those deaths occurred under uncertain, mysterious, or even suspicious circumstances. But if the prosecuting attorney couldn't make a case, the true cause of death would remain a mystery, perhaps for all time. Which was part of the job. If you couldn't deal with uncertainty, you shouldn't become a homicide detective.

"Do you expect this investigation will turn into a big deal?" said Alex.

Bill lifted a hand and let it fall again. "I doubt it, not unless compelling evidence comes to light. Arnie will ask some more questions, the sheriff will kick it around in his head for a while, and the medical examiner will eventually sign it off as an accidental death."

"But it *is* possible that it'll turn into something else. Something bigger."

"Yeah, sure."

"In which case, I want to hire you to help Wintergreen do our part."

Bill frowned. "Why would you do that? You've got Connor Johnston. Let him do the investigating."

"I told you. He's on vacation. Actually, that wasn't the complete truth. Confidentially, Connor is interviewing for a job in Memphis."

"Seriously?"

"Yeah. Apparently, a lot of experienced detectives are retiring, as you did. Investigators like Connor can name their price. No way I can fill this job overnight, so if this investigation turns into something, I want to hire you as a consultant."

"You're the interim chief, Alex. The board may not like you bringing a resident onto the payroll."

"I already talked to the board. They love the idea."

"I retired for a reason. I don't want to work anymore."

Alex took a slow sip of coffee and then smiled. A twinkle formed in his eye, like he was in on some sort of secret.

"What?" said Bill.

"Come on. You love this stuff. Besides, you said yourself this investigation probably won't amount to much." Alex put his cup to the side, leaned toward Bill, and began counting on his fingers. "First thing, I won't make you come to any meetings unless they pertain to the investigation. Second thing, no paperwork. We'll handle all of that. And lastly, I'll make Mitch Gentry and Krista Jackson available if you need any help. I know you like those two."

Bill rubbed his chin. Alex was good at reading people, a skill he'd undoubtedly picked up selling real estate for thirty years. Before making his decision to retire, Bill had read up on the subject. Every advisor said the same thing. You had to retain a purpose for your life. It was fine to quit working for money, but if you sat around all day eating snacks and watching television, you'd grow fat and weird in a short while. He had the part-time work helping Cindy out, but that still left him with time on his hands. Of course, there were plenty of volunteer opportunities in Wintergreen and Nelson County that he had yet to explore. But he could certainly spend a few hours on an investigation, and it might be fun.

"Yeah, all right, if this turns into anything, I'll try to help."

"Awesome. I knew you'd say yes."

TWENTY-FOUR

After Alex left for the station, Bill relaxed with his coffee on the brick patio. High on the ridge, yellow and red leaves were interspersed with all the green, an early sign of the changing season. He'd never seen Wintergreen fall colors other than in the promotional photos that promised a fantastic show. Not long to wait now.

"May I join you?" asked a woman with a shaky voice.

It was Angie Finch, Damian Susskind's personal assistant.

Bill stood. "Please, have a seat."

Angie was a slender woman with auburn hair and eyes wounded by grief. She moved with efficiency but without athleticism.

He guessed that Angie had stayed overnight in the Mountain Inn. It had to be awful to lose a person she'd known well and lose her source of income at the same moment. What would become of her?

"I'm sorry," he said, "about Damian."

Angie replied with a quick nod, as if she didn't trust herself to speak.

Bill let her sit a few moments in silence. He sipped his coffee and then realized she didn't have a drink. He asked if he could get her something, but she declined.

"How long did you work for Damian?" he asked.

"Five years." It seemed that Angie would add nothing to her direct response, but then she said in a rush, "But it was more than a working relationship. We were lovers."

"Oh."

"In fact, we were engaged to be married."

Bill was dumbfounded. Goodness. He blinked several times, uncertain of what to say next.

"Gosh, I'm terribly sorry. I had no idea."

"That's all right. You couldn't have known; it wasn't public information."

"Even so, let me underscore my earlier condolences."

"Thank you." Angie took a tissue from a small purse and wiped her nose. "You were at the overlook yesterday after he fell. Did you learn what happened? I haven't heard anything."

Bill was still trying to process Angie's revelation. How horrible. Her fiancé, the man she loved, left the house to go for a short hike and never returned. What answer could he possibly give her that would help?

"I'm afraid he ventured too close to the edge. It was an accident."

He didn't know for sure that it was an accident, but putting more uncertainty in Angie's mind would *not* help.

Angie stared straight ahead, but Bill doubted she observed any of the natural beauty.

She squinted and then said, "That makes no sense. Damian was sure-footed even after his heart attack. I don't remember him ever stumbling. He never even stubbed a toe."

"Maybe Damian wasn't himself. Did you notice anything unusual about his appearance or behavior yesterday?"

Her nose twitched. “No, he seemed normal. Except for the meetings. Those meetings with the three kids were always a source of stress.”

“I can imagine,” said Bill, for no other reason than to say something. He doubted the meetings were as stressful for Damian as for the other participants.

“He was particularly upset with Evan and Lacey,” Angie snapped. “They’re obviously still carrying on.”

Bill chewed his lip. He hadn’t known that Evan and Lacey were in a relationship. Although, when Damian and the others hiked to the overlook, Evan and Lacey had lagged behind the other two. Angie was still upset. Her hands shook. Bill didn’t want to upset her further, but he was also intensely curious.

“Did Damian have a reason to disapprove of their relationship?”

“He didn’t need to have a reason.” Angie sneered. “He was their benefactor!”

Bill lifted his hands. “Of course, you’re right.”

Angie turned toward him and made chopping motions with her hand as she spoke. “So many people around Damian didn’t appreciate what he did for them. Evan. Lacey. Tanya. And charities. And other people too. Like that Rachel Dunn, for example.”

“Rachel Dunn?”

“Yes. She’s a scheming hussy, that one.”

Bill knew Rachel Dunn. He’d met her during the Lou Thorpe investigation. Earlier in her life, Rachel had been a high-priced escort for movers and shakers in DC. She had moved to Wintergreen at Thorpe’s behest. But Bill didn’t realize that Rachel was still around. He’d always assumed that she’d run from Wintergreen as fast as possible.

"What was Damian's relationship with Rachel Dunn?" he asked.

Angie screwed her lips into a skeptical bunch. "Masseuse. But she aimed for more, and I know that for a fact. Not that she got anywhere. Damian loved me."

So, not only did Rachel Dunn still reside on the mountain, but she was still up to her old tricks, riling people up with one of the oldest and meanest emotions of all. Jealousy.

Bill wondered if Rachel still lived off of Black Rock Drive. He was of a mind to go over there and press her for some intel. Why not? He might learn something useful.

But first, he had to wind up his conversation with Angie Finch. What could he say that wouldn't set her off again? Steer clear of the overlook, that's for sure. Filling her mind with questions concerning what had happened would lead to no good. After some consideration, he decided to remain silent. What Angie needed more than anything was time to process the terrible loss life had dealt her. Time healed all wounds. He'd read that once on a slip of paper from a fortune cookie. It was worth more than the meal.

They sat awhile without saying anything. Perhaps Angie finally noticed the beauty of the morning, for her breathing settled, and her hands grew still. When she finally spoke, she apologized to Bill for losing her temper. Then she left.

TWENTY-FIVE

Mitch Gentry steered around a tight curve on Reeds Gap Road and glanced at the dashboard clock. He was running five minutes late, but he hardly noticed. Mitch had not slept well. Images of Damian Susskind flashed through his mind every time he drifted off. They bothered him still.

Where was Damian Susskind now? Was there an afterlife or nothing at all? As a child, Mitch attended church with his mother regularly. The preacher said that he should rely on faith to answer the tough questions. And for the most part, Mitch did. But still, there were times on the job—like when he and Officer Hill were minding Susskind's corpse below the overlook—when questions crept into the corners of Mitch's mind.

Mitch came to the top of the hill, crossed over the Blue Ridge Parkway, and pulled to a stop in the parking lot near the Appalachian Trail. He shook his head to chase the negative feelings away, then took a deep breath and thought of Lulu and their life ahead. Would they have children? Would they grow old together? No way to know for sure, but he felt good about his chances. Lulu had such a beautiful smile.

Fortunately, he and John Hill had not had to wait long before others had arrived on the scene to keep them company. The EMS team. The forensics specialist. The medical examiner. They'd each performed their tasks, and then they'd taken turns carrying Susskind up the hill.

Mitch frowned. Something bothered him about his recollection of the previous day. Like he'd allowed a small task to go undone. Forgot to lock the door. Left the oven on. To find the loose end, he replayed his interactions with each party at the scene in reverse order. But he got all the way back through the EMS team without a wrinkle. Earlier, it was just the two of them, him and John Hill. They had discussed one of John's DIY projects. He was building a treehouse for his kids.

Wait. Wait. There was someone else. A man had come down from the overlook to see if he could help Susskind. His face was pale from the shock of seeing the corpse. What was his name?

Mitch used his cell phone to call John. It was John's day off, but he remembered the man's name. Art Rossi. John had logged Rossi's contact information in his report.

When they carried the corpse near the top of the overlook, Mitch had noticed a discussion going on between Alex, Undersheriff Arnie Shields, the medical examiner, and Bill O'Shea. Bill read from notes on his phone. But had anyone taken Rossi's statement?

Mitch called the office to get direction from Alex. Krista Jackson answered, and Mitch filled her in.

"Just call Bill O'Shea," she said.

"Why Bill?"

"I guess you haven't heard. Alex stopped by my cubicle a

few minutes ago. He has hired Bill in case the accident investigation turns into a bigger thing. And here's the kicker—you and I are to give Bill whatever support he needs."

"No bull."

"Yeah. Isn't that great?"

TWENTY-SIX

Two seconds after Bill rang Rachel Dunn's doorbell, his cell phone buzzed. It was Mitch Gentry.

Wonder what he needs.

Footsteps approached the door from inside. Mitch would have to wait.

Rachel was in her mid-forties, tall and fit, with long blond hair. She matched Bill's image of a yoga instructor. Her eyes showed no recognition for the few first moments, but then she gave him a tight grin.

"Bill O'Shea," she said. "Aren't I the lucky one?"

Bill tipped his head. "Rachel, I never thought I'd see you again. Without Lou and the others around, I figured you had made off for bigger stakes long ago. Not that I cared much, to be honest. But I guess you found a new turkey to pluck, and a richer one at that."

Rachel was barefoot and dressed in black leggings and a long-sleeved white workout shirt. She crossed her arms on her chest. "You say the sweetest things, Bill. But truthfully, I don't know what the heck you're talking about."

He chuckled. "You'll never change. Always the last to know."

She sighed. "Come on in. Have a sparkling water. I seem to recall you like those. You can tell me what's going on, and I'll try to help you if I can." Rachel turned, strolled down the hardwood hallway, and turned right into the kitchen.

Bill knew the way.

She made sparkling water with her machine, dropped in ice cubes, and grabbed a fresh lime wedge from a cutting board on the counter. Rachel always had fresh lime wedges around.

He followed her into the living room, where floor-to-ceiling windows overlooked a stunning view of a ski slope and mountains in the distance. Rachel's townhouse was built on the edge of the run. Through the windows on the right, Bill spied the balcony of a neighboring townhouse. An older man sat under an umbrella on the wooden deck and watched birds through binoculars.

"How are you and Mr. Fields getting along?" Bill asked.

"We've made peace. Actually, we've become friends. Robert's handy with home projects. Plus, he's lonely because he doesn't get out much." Rachel grinned mischievously. "I give him a freebie once in a while."

"A freebie?" Bill could feel his face growing warm.

"A massage," she responded in the tone of a reprimand. "Your mind is in the sludge. That's my business now. I'm a masseuse."

"Uh-huh," said Bill, aware that he had spoken in a voice laced with skepticism.

Anger flashed in Rachel's eyes. "You think you're the good guy, don't you, Bill? You walk around all casual, cracking jokes, everybody's friend, but deep down, you're as judgmental as the next person. Even more so because at least they're open about it, whereas you disguise your biases under a veneer of tolerance. Well, guess what, there really are second chances. Some people turn things around so they can feel good again. I'm trying to do that, and I don't care two hoots in hell what you believe because it won't help anyway. I'm the only one who can change me."

It was quite a speech. The sort of words Bill didn't hear every day. And they carried a ring of truth. Second chances. The cop's life had turned many an optimist into a skeptic, and he had to count himself among them. He'd witnessed too many broken promises. Too many shattered dreams. But Wintergreen was a special place, a long way from a dark city filled with concrete and metal and anger. Maybe up here, things were different. Maybe he should try to start this conversation over.

"So, how does that work exactly?" he said. "The massage business."

Rachel turned her head to the side. She had seen a lot in her life, and Bill guessed she had given up on crying long ago. But her expression did appear somber.

Bill took a seat on the couch. "I'm serious," he said. "What's the deal? People come here to your place?"

She chewed on her lower lip and read his eyes. Then she sat in the armchair across the coffee table. "Most of my clients are older, in their seventies or eighties. A majority of them are women. Some live alone, and I'm a bright spot during a long week. A few clients come here, but for the most part, I go to them. It's easier for them that way."

Bill raised his hands. "Now, don't go off on me here, but to be clear, there's no funny business. Right? No happy endings?"

She shook her head without hesitation. "No happy

endings. No one's even asked for one, but I would shut them down if they did. Those days are behind me."

"And you can make a living at it up here?"

"Yeah, for the most part. Some months are better than others, but I have a lot of savings." Her eyes roamed around the room. "I took out a loan to buy this place, but it's not a big loan. And my living expenses are modest."

"Good for you." And he meant it.

"Why did you come to see me?" she said. "Surely it wasn't to discuss the massage business."

He laughed and so did Rachel, making him feel a little better.

"No, actually, it's about one of your clients."

Her eyebrows furrowed, and her lips made a flat line. "Damian Susskind."

"Yes."

"I heard he was killed. It's awful, but I thought it was an accident. Why are you involved?"

Bill rubbed his hands together. "Truthfully, I'm here on a whim. I had a conversation with Angie Finch, and she mentioned your name. By the way, she's not a fan of yours."

"Angie Finch."

By Rachel's tone, Bill gathered neither woman cared much for the other.

"Yes," said Bill, "she and Susskind were engaged to be married. She's shaken up about it."

Rachel scowled. "Engaged? She told you that?"

Bill nodded. "Yeah. Her exact words were, and I quote, 'We were engaged to be married.'"

"Oh," Rachel said. "Now, I understand. The operative word there is 'were.' They *were* engaged briefly, but Damian broke it off after his heart attack."

"She said they were lovers."

Rachel shrugged. "Now, that part is true. I'm sure—right to the end. But as for the engagement, well, a heart attack followed by a quintuple bypass tends to focus a person's mind. Damian told me all about it."

Huh. While Angie had not technically lied to Bill, she had misled him by insinuating that she and Damian were engaged at the time of his death. Maybe she chose to mislead herself as well.

Bill didn't wish to set Rachel off again now that she'd calmed down, but at the same time, he retained a sliver of skepticism concerning her methods.

"Why would Damian Susskind reveal such intimate details to you?"

"You'd be surprised what people will reveal when they're half-naked and relaxed on a massage table. I don't even have to ask questions."

"I suppose so."

"Angie was having a hard time dealing with the end of their engagement. Damian told me he might have to fire her, that she was not performing at her best level."

"What a nice guy."

"Oh, I don't know. He was probably blathering at that point. He even suggested that I take on the position, but I nipped that notion before it had time to flower. I'm sure he would have paid well, but he didn't want me for my skills in office management. And I like my new business."

Would Rachel have felt the same way if she'd known Damian was worth eighty million dollars? Even a thin slice of that pie would pay for this place several times over. Bill reprimanded himself for entertaining the question. Such a cynic. Give her the benefit of the doubt. Believe in the new Rachel. She appeared genuinely enthused about her gig.

"Did Damian Susskind reveal any other interesting details on your massage table?"

Rachel pinched her lower lip. "Not that I recall. I guess he didn't tell me much after all." She paused to dredge her memory for a few moments and then lifted a finger. "One tidbit. Last week, I showed up for our appointment, and he seemed depressed. I asked him what was bothering him, and he said Lacey had grown angry with him. I asked him why they disagreed, but he didn't want to discuss the matter further. He said little during the rest of the session."

Damian Susskind had all that money, but he couldn't keep bad stuff from happening. Bill had read an article once about a high-tech executive who did well and made a gazillion dollars. Despite the new riches, the executive never upgraded his house—he and his wife stayed in the same three-bedroom rancher in a bland suburban neighborhood. When asked by a reporter why they hadn't moved, the man said, "We're happy here. Why would we go somewhere else?"

Rachel knew nothing else of interest related to Damian Susskind, but Bill didn't rush off. He and Rachel drank their sparkling waters and discussed life in Wintergreen. Neither of them had spent a winter on the mountain, and they were curious to see what it looked like with no leaves and covered in snow. They might never be close friends, but they could be friendly. And the last thing Bill wanted was an enemy in the community.

Outside Rachel's house, Bill returned Mitch Gentry's call.

"What's up?" he said after Mitch answered.

Mitch explained that another person had been at the overlook the previous day when Susskind fell. A fellow named Art Rossi.

Bill thought for a minute and then said, "Okay, here's what we're going to do."

TWENTY-SEVEN

Bill and Art Rossi each came in their own cars, and they parked on Laurel Springs Drive where it intersected with the Old Appalachian Trail. Art Rossi drove a red Ford Escape and was a thin man perhaps a few years younger than Bill. He wore jeans, a khaki shirt, and hiking boots. Bill introduced himself and asked Rossi what he'd seen at the overlook when Susskind fell.

Alex Sharp, Mitch Gentry, and Krista Jackson arrived in a squad car a few minutes later.

After everyone had assembled, Bill said, "Let's go out there and try to reenact the scene."

The group said little on the ten-minute walk to the overlook. Once they entered the forest, thick foliage blocked much of the sun's light and warmth. Rocks and roots littered the trail, and Bill watched the ground to keep from stumbling. His hands tingled with excitement. He had a hunch about something, but the only way to know for sure was to revisit the overlook.

First, the five of them walked out on the rock.

"Mitch," said Bill, "you'll be Damian Susskind. You stand out at the edge."

Mitch, fearless as usual, marched right to the lip of the precipice.

Bill's eyes widened, and he raised his hands. "Not *that* close. Yeah, pull it back a yard or two. That's good. We don't need two corpses."

Alex Sharp stood on Bill's right and examined the scene. The Old Appalachian Trail ran parallel to the overlook, and two smaller connecting paths angled to the rocky ledge from opposing directions of the main trail.

Bill continued with his instructions. "Krista, you'll play the part of Tanya Stafford. Stand a yard from Mitch on the forest side. Yep, that's good." Bill turned to Art Rossi. "Is that right?"

Rossi scratched his neck. "Possibly." Then he turned to eye the connecting path that led to the right. "But I have to stand where I was to get a good feel for it."

"Okay," said Bill. "Mitch and Krista, stay here."

Art then led Alex and Bill to a spot thirty yards away on the right-side connecting path.

"I was standing here," said Rossi.

Bill glanced back toward the overlook. He had a clear view of Mitch and Krista near the edge. But could he rely on Rossi's memory?

"How do you know you were standing right here?" Bill asked.

Rossi pointed to a small tree next to the path. "I stopped to take a photo of this American Chestnut."

Bill frowned. Hardwood sapling. Green leaves. The forest was filled with them.

Perhaps Rossi saw the question in Bill's eyes, because he explained further, "I've never seen an American Chestnut in this area. Notice the canoe-shaped leaf with the forward-hooked teeth along its edges? It's a distinctive pattern. And the trees never grow above twenty feet because of the blight."

Bill and Alex exchanged looks. Art Rossi knew a lot more about local flora than Bill.

Pointing toward the overlook, Bill said, "Is that where they were standing?"

Rossi scrunched his eyebrows. "Not initially. The man reached the edge first, and he faced the valley. Then the woman approached him from the path."

Bill called instructions to Mitch and Krista.

"Then the woman called to the man," said Rossi. "He turned toward her, and they exchanged harsh words." Rossi nodded his conviction. "They were arguing."

"Okay," said Bill, and he gave Krista and Mitch additional direction.

"Then the man reached out as if he would touch her face."

"What do you mean," said Bill, "like hit her?"

"No, a gentle caress, like a parent would touch his child. But she pushed his hand away. She was angry."

"What happened then?" said Alex.

Rossi scarcely breathed. He kept his eyes fixed on the overlook. "The man stiffened. Like he'd been shocked or something. Then he clutched his chest with both hands. She reached for him, but his knees buckled, and he started falling. She stepped toward him, but it was too late." Rossi shuddered. "If he'd fallen toward her, he would have been fine, but he fell out and away. And then he was gone."

"She didn't push him," said Alex.

Rossi shook his head vehemently. "No, just the opposite. But there's no way she could have saved him, not with the way he fell."

Bill spent the next five minutes playing director for Mitch

and Krista's reenactment of the scene. After each run-through, he'd check with Rossi for adjustments. When Rossi indicated that the scene accurately recreated what had happened the previous day, Bill asked Rossi to stay put. Then Bill and Alex moved up the trail to where Lacey Akin had said she stood when she witnessed Tanya Stafford push Damian.

Leaves from a branch hovered above the path to the overlook. A slight breeze blew, and the branches' leaves obstructed their view. Two tree trunks bordered Mitch's figure at the edge.

Alex frowned. "It's not that easy to see from here."

"I agree," said Bill, and then he called for Krista and Mitch to proceed.

Krista approached Mitch, and he turned to face her. They argued. Mitch reached to touch her face, and she swatted his hand away. From that angle, Krista partially blocked Bill's view of Mitch, and he couldn't discern Mitch's movements. He knew that Mitch stiffened only because of their rehearsal. Krista's arms reached toward Mitch, and then Mitch fell to his knees to imitate Damian's fall.

"Oh," said Alex, "we need to see that again."

"Run through it again, guys," called Bill. "And amp up the argument."

Bill and Alex watched the reenactment three more times, conferred, and concluded that a reasonable person might think Tanya had pushed Damian off the cliff. Particularly given that the two of them had been arguing.

But Rossi had the better view, and he made a credible witness because of his impartiality and his recollection of details like the American Chestnut.

The five of them returned to Laurel Springs Drive, and Alex thanked Rossi for his assistance. After Rossi left, the others stayed to sort out the next move. Mitch's radio crackled with a call from the office, and he stepped away.

It wasn't nanotech research. Lacey Akin had misinterpreted what she saw at the overlook, and Rossi's testimony cleared Tanya Stafford of suspicion. Alex asked if Bill would come back to the office to help him bring Arnie Shields up to speed.

"Sure thing."

Mitch walked up and addressed Alex. "That was Kerry. She's been trying to get you."

Alex pulled out his phone. "The signal stinks here. I have half a bar. What did she want?"

"The autopsy results are in, and the ME wants to talk."

TWENTY-EIGHT

Alex Sharp and Bill joined a video call in the station's conference room. Arnie Shields appeared to be sitting in an office. A photo on the credenza behind Arnie showed a young boy holding a large fish by its gill. Soren Larsen, the state medical examiner, wore a casual buttoned shirt and was sitting in what Bill guessed was a forensics lab. They had already gotten through the preliminary chitchat.

Then Larsen said, "It's difficult to determine what killed the victim—cardiac arrest or blunt force trauma from the fall. But he was definitely in the middle of a heart attack that would almost certainly have killed him by itself."

"Even if he had a heart attack," said Arnie, "that doesn't prove Tanya Stafford didn't give him a shove."

"Yes," said Alex, "but Bill and I have some new information."

Bill went through the statement they'd gotten from Art Rossi that cast serious doubt on Lacey Akin's accusation. Arnie, Alex, and Bill debated the question a bit and were closing in on an accidental death conclusion.

"I don't want to keep you guys from gift-wrapping this

thing," said Larsen, "but the autopsy did reveal other findings of note."

"Oh," said Arnie, and he lifted his hand. "Soren, please continue."

Larsen explained that the autopsy uncovered three substances that may or may not have straightforward explanations. First, blood content indicated the victim had consumed three to four alcoholic beverages an hour or two before his death.

Bill tried to recollect what Damian had consumed at lunch. Maybe a glass of wine, but no more than that. So when did he drink the rest of the alcohol?

"Second, his heart failure was likely brought on by something called digitalis toxicity."

Bill sat straight in his chair.

"What's that?" said Arnie.

"This is rare," said Larsen, clearly engaged in the unusual nature of this particular autopsy. "Digitalis toxicity is typically related to the consumption of digoxin, a medication that doctors used to prescribe for some heart conditions." Larsen shook his head. "But I haven't seen this in years. Most cardiologists would now prescribe other, improved medications. You'd have to ask the victim's doctor to find out more."

Arnie said, "Alex, can you guys run down the doctor?"

"Yes, we've got that."

"Let's assume he had such a prescription," said Bill. "What would cause the toxicity?"

Larsen explained that patients should only take digoxin in prescribed amounts. Patients had been known to take too much—either accidentally or intentionally—and cause themselves harm. Heart failure was uncommon but not without precedent.

"Could someone else have given it to him?" said Alex.

Larsen frowned. “Yes, hypothetically. I’ve never heard of that happening, but someone could have ground up pills and put the substance into a beverage.”

No one spoke. Perhaps they were pondering the same questions as Bill. He recalled the guests who had dined with Susskind. Could one of them have intentionally slipped a powder into his coffee?

“What was the third substance?” said Arnie.

“MDMA,” said Larsen. “The party drug sometimes referred to as Molly or Ecstasy. It’s a recreational drug commonly taken to induce effects of altered sensations, increased energy, and pleasure.”

Arnie’s thick eyebrows scrunched so deeply they nearly formed a unibrow.

Alex said, “Hold on. You’re telling me Susskind had booze, Molly, and this digi-whatever in his system simultaneously? What kind of party was he throwing, Bill?”

But Bill scarcely heard Alex. On the day before, after lunch and having coffee on the back deck, Damian had marched inside and announced his intention to climb Humpback Rocks. He had asked Cindy to prepare snacks. Now, the transformation made sense. Damian had consumed Molly. Or had someone given it to him along with the digitalis?

Bill asked Larsen why someone would intentionally poison another person with a cocktail mix of digitalis and Molly. The ME shook his head and said it served no purpose he could see other than wishing the intended victim a good time on their way to a heart attack.

Arnie and Alex asked Larsen a few more questions but learned nothing else of interest. Now that they had the autopsy results, the state forensics team would begin a more focused search of the house. The presence of Molly in Susskind’s desk or prescription digoxin in his medicine cabinet would explain how he had come to consume those drugs.

The forensics team would crawl all over the house. They would pay particular attention to the dishes, searching for traces of the target substances. But Bill knew they wouldn't find anything because the dishes were all clean. He had washed the coffee cups himself.

TWENTY-NINE

"Let's get some lunch," said Bill. "I'm starving."

"What about barbecue?" asked Mitch. "I've got Blue Ridge Pig on speed dial."

"Perfect."

They were driving down the mountain in a Wintergreen squad car. After the call with Soren Larsen, Alex had pulled Bill, Mitch, and Krista into the conference room to plan the next steps. First, Krista had called Angie Finch and gotten the name of Damian Susskind's cardiologist, a Dr. Varga, who ran a practice in Charlottesville. Krista then arranged for Bill and Mitch to visit Varga that afternoon.

By the time they reached Blue Ridge Pig on Route 151, the sandwiches were ready. Mitch asked if they should eat in the car on the way.

Bill frowned and said, "No. The job is hard enough without indigestion. Let's sit here and eat for ten minutes."

They sat at a wooden table inside the small dining area. Photos and knickknacks from decades past decorated the walls. Blue Ridge Pig had been there for quite some time.

Bill had chosen the pork barbecue sandwich, and he dove

in. He believed the Carolinas produced the best pulled-pork sandwiches on the planet, but he had to admit Blue Ridge Pig's entry was a contender for the prize. And the potato salad? Whoa. That *was* tasty.

Mitch took a monster bite of his sandwich, chomped it quickly, and swallowed it down with a healthy belt of iced tea.

"So," he said, "our current theory is that Susskind consumed Molly and prescription meds, chased them with alcohol, and then had a heart attack at the overlook."

Bill sipped his Diet Coke. "I suppose so."

"But Susskind was in his sixties, right? I can't see a guy that age doing Molly."

"I don't know. You never know what's going on inside another person's head. Did you ever try it? Molly?"

Mitch popped several potato chips into his mouth and crunched them while he stared at Bill. "What is this? True confession?"

Bill shrugged. "When I was young, I smoked pot a few times, but Molly wasn't a thing then. I'm curious."

"Lulu never wanted to try drugs. She was always serious about work and studies. I experimented a little with other stuff but never tried Molly."

Bill wasn't surprised. Mitch and Lulu were into the outdoor scene. Hiking. Camping. Fishing. He tried to imagine Mitch dancing at a rave, crazed with Molly. Nope. Like trying to jam a football player into a ballet company.

After lunch, they cruised north on Route 151 past breweries, cideries, and wine-tasting rooms. On US 250, they drove east through sprawling estates and then hopped onto Interstate 64 toward Charlottesville.

Dr. Varga's office was in a research park near the University of Virginia. In the lobby, Bill waited his turn at the counter. Several of those who sat in lobby chairs stared at Mitch. When in his uniform—standing six feet tall and weighing over two hundred pounds with a lot of muscle—Mitch tended to attract attention.

"How y'all doing?" he said.

They all smiled.

"Fine," said one.

"Good, thanks," said another.

A minute later, a nurse ushered them into an examination room, gestured toward plastic chairs, and said the doctor would be in soon.

Bill took a seat. Mitch stared at a poster promoting a rock concert from the sixties.

"I never much liked going to see the doctor," said Mitch.

"Live long enough, and you'll get used to it."

Dr. Varga came in a moment later and shook their hands. Varga was a small man with gray hair and glasses. He spoke with a slight accent, perhaps Eastern European, but he was fluent in English and used slang in his speech. Bill guessed he had lived in the US a long time.

The physician's assistant had already told Varga they were there to discuss Susskind's death. When asked about Susskind's general condition, Varga said, "It was close to a miracle that he survived the heart attack and the bypass surgery. I hate to rely on a cliché, but he really was a ticking time bomb." Varga crossed his arms and sighed, as if he hated to lose a patient under any circumstance. "I understand he was hiking and fell off a cliff to his death."

"Witnesses believe he suffered a heart attack right before he fell."

Varga pushed his glasses up. "It's entirely possible. I would have preferred Damian to recuperate another month before any strenuous activity. I told him he still had a weak heart, but he didn't want to hear it. Damian was a carpe-diem sort."

"Did you prescribe him digoxin?" said Bill.

Varga frowned instantly. "No." He picked up a tablet he had brought and swiped a few screens. "He was on cholesterol medication and a blood thinner, but not digoxin. Why do you ask?"

Bill explained that the autopsy results indicated the presence of digitalis toxicity.

Varga pulled his head back. "Digitalis! Oh no, not from his meds." He glanced down at the tablet again as if to double check. "How on earth did he get digitalis toxicity?"

"We were hoping you could tell us," said Bill, then he lifted a hand of caution. "Bear with me while I ask a hypothetical question. Let's assume for a moment that someone wanted to cause Mr. Susskind harm. Would it be possible for them to grind up digoxin pills and mix it with something he ate or drank?"

"Could someone induce Damian into cardiac arrest by poisoning him with digitalis? Is that what you're asking?"

"Hypothetically."

"Yes," said Varga without hesitation. He nodded. "There'd be no guarantee that it would work, but in Damian's condition and with enough digoxin, it would likely do the trick." Then Varga eyed the ceiling as if he were reconsidering his answer. "But if that were their intention, they wouldn't need digoxin pills. They could grind up foxglove."

"Foxglove?" said Mitch. He glanced at Bill. "The flower?"

"That's right," said Varga. "Digitalis comes from foxglove. Doctors have used it for centuries to treat congestive heart failure, a disease they used to call dropsy. Essentially, the heart grows weak and can't pump blood the way it should. Digitalis stimulates the heart, which helps, but it's a tricky medication. It certainly was in the old days. Give the patient too much, and it could lead to heart failure."

"So foxglove could be used as a poison," said Mitch.

"Yes. Apparently, it *was* used as a poison on occasion in past centuries. But I've never heard of it being used that way in my career."

Neither had Bill. In his decades as a homicide detective, he had encountered many means of taking a person's life. He had even come across poison a few times. But foxglove? Never.

Bill told Dr. Varga that the autopsy also indicated Susskind had recently consumed alcohol and the party drug MDMA. Did he have an opinion on what effect the combination would have?

Varga shook his head. "I'm no expert on MDMA, but I know it doesn't mix well with other substances. That combination strikes me as extremely dangerous, certainly for a heart patient."

~

Outside, leaning against the squad car, Bill and Mitch traded their views.

"So, it looks like murder," said Mitch.

"Yes, unless another doctor prescribed him digoxin, which seems unlikely. In any case, we'll know soon what the forensics team finds at the house."

Bill had reached this conclusion in Varga's office, and now his mind was racing ahead. Someone had slipped digitalis into Damian's food or drink in the hours before his death. Each of his guests—not only those at the overlook but also Angie Finch and Whit Whitlock—was a suspect. And the list didn't end there. Every member of the catering crew had the opportunity to poison Damian. Justin. Maddie. Cindy. Even Bill himself. They were all suspects.

"And the MDMA?" said Mitch. "That part makes no sense."

"Maybe the murderer slipped it in for good measure? Or to create confusion? It's a head-scratcher."

Mitch's cell phone rang, and he answered. He glanced inside the squad car. "Yeah, we're out of range."

Bill assumed that whoever called Mitch had been trying to reach him on the radio.

Mitch listened, then his eyes rose to Bill. Mitch's eyebrows bounced.

"Okay," he said to the caller. "We're on the way." After hanging up, Mitch said, "That was Krista. Arnie Shields is at the station. We're to head back." Mitch rubbed his neck, bothered about something.

"What?" said Bill.

"Arnie wanted to make certain that you come."

Bill had a good idea of what that was all about.

THIRTY

On the way back to Wintergreen, Bill got a call from Alex.

"I'm in my office," said Alex in a low voice. "Arnie's in the conference room with, ah, some folks, but I slipped in here to give you the scoop."

Bill's shoulders sagged. He had a feeling that Cindy, Justin, and Maddie were in for a long afternoon.

"The forensics team is at the house. They're just getting started. But after ten minutes, they called Arnie and told him they had found no MDMA or prescription digoxin in any obvious places. Arnie believes that means Damian didn't take the stuff himself."

"I agree," said Bill. "Someone else slipped it to him."

"Arnie says we have to question the catering crew."

"Uh-huh. Yeah, I get it."

"Cindy and Justin have been here for half an hour. Maddie's on the way and should arrive any minute."

Bill thanked Alex for calling and spent the rest of the ride back to Wintergreen in silence. They retraced their path through the beautiful horse farms and cow pastures and the cute little town of Nellysford, but Bill didn't notice the scenery.

Back at the office, Bill spent an hour in a small room with a sheriff's deputy and an investigator from the state police. It was another first. Over the length of Bill's career, he had never sat on that side of the table, and it felt distinctly uncomfortable. But they were polite and professional, and he supposed it helped that he knew what they were trying to find out.

They focused mainly on the hours leading to lunch, lunch itself, and the group's time on the back deck before leaving for the hike. Someone told them they could ignore the breakfast period, possibly the medical examiner. As they asked more questions, Bill reassembled the details of the day's events in his mind.

Had any of the catering crew taken water or something else to Damian's office in the hours leading to lunch? "No, we were focused on lunch preparations." Who poured the waters for lunch? "Justin." Who served coffee and tea? "Maddie." Who poured the wine? "Maddie." Who served the food? "Cindy and I." Who plated the food? "Cindy plated the food in the kitchen." Who served the whiskey on the back deck?

"Wait, what whiskey?" Bill asked.

The sheriff's deputy was a big man with a big head and a thick mustache. He exchanged looks with the state investigator, a big woman with a deep voice.

"We found whiskey glasses on the back deck," she said. "Some of them contained remnants of alcohol. I take it you don't remember anyone serving whiskey?"

"No, the only alcohol we served was champagne at breakfast and wine with lunch." Bill tried to recall the action on the back deck after lunch. He and Justin washed dishes, and

Cindy prepared a marinade for the mahi-mahi. Where was Maddie? He couldn't remember but had no recollection of her going out to the back deck. There would have been no need for her to do so because a coffee and tea station in the dining room allowed clients to refill their cups and glasses on their own.

Bill shared his recollections with the interviewers, and the state investigator took notes on her tablet.

"Maybe someone put digitalis in the whiskey," he said.

The investigator's eyes slid toward the deputy. "That's one possibility."

But she didn't enumerate the other scenarios, of which there were many. Justin might have slipped the digitalis into Damian's wine glass, or Maddie could have spiked his coffee. Maybe Cindy mixed some into his bisque, but how would she know which bowl to spike with poison?

Bill felt himself being excluded from the investigation, and for a good reason. He was now on the suspect list, and the investigators would no longer share their hypotheses. Alex might pull him off the investigation altogether. Arnie might insist on it.

By the time Bill came out of the interview room, Cindy, Justin, and Maddie had already left the station. Alex asked Bill to cool his heels while he and Arnie chatted with the state investigator. The three of them plus the sheriff's deputy disappeared into the conference room, and Bill wandered over to Krista's cubicle. Mitch sat in an extra chair, and the two of them watched Bill approach.

"What's happening now?" said Mitch.

Bill studied the closed door of the conference room. "They're deciding whether to kick me off the investigation."

"What?" said Krista.

"I was on the catering team. I'm a suspect now."

"That's ridiculous," said Krista.

"Rule number one," said Bill. "Follow the facts wherever they lead you."

A few minutes later, Alex and Arnie Shields came to get Bill and pulled him into Alex's office.

Arnie took a deep breath and rolled his tongue around the inside of his mouth. He eyed Bill and said, "You know what's going on, right?"

"Yes."

"The state investigator wants you off. I told her you were helpful on the Lou Thorpe thing. She doesn't care about that, but I can overrule her for now. Tell me, you ever meet this man Susskind before yesterday?"

"No."

"What about the rest of the catering team?"

"Cindy has worked for him on other events. Maddie might have helped as well. I doubt Justin's ever met him."

Arnie nodded and said, "Okay. So it appears that someone poisoned Susskind. Do you agree?"

"Yes," said Bill.

"Justin and Maddie had ample opportunity to put poison in his beverage, so we'll poke around in their backgrounds. You can't be any part of that."

"I understand."

"Alex wants your help, so you can do your thing, interviews and so forth, with the luncheon guests. Make sense?"

Bill nodded. "It's your deal, guys. Whatever you want. I'll punch out anytime."

"Not yet," said Alex. "Not yet."

~

The seven of them crowded into the conference room: Arnie Shields and his deputy; Alex, Krista, and Mitch; the state investigator; and Bill. They discussed where they stood and what they needed. Ideas went back and forth. They had a puzzle with a lot of missing pieces. Did the killer know Damian would hike to the overlook? Why did the killer give Susskind MDMA along with the digitalis? How did the killer poison Susskind? Did the whiskey play a role?

"The forensics team will send the whiskey remnants to the lab for testing," said the state investigator. "Also, we have food scraps from the trash. Unfortunately, all dishes, cups, and utensils were thoroughly cleaned." The investigator looked up from her tablet long enough to throw Bill an unfriendly glance, as if it was his fault that the catering crew had done their job.

His cell phone buzzed again. Cindy had texted him several times. **What the heck is going on? Please call me right away.**

Under the table, he typed a response into his cell.

As soon as possible.

Alex observed that Susskind might have taken MDMA on his own but been poisoned by the killer.

The state investigator shook her head. "Awfully big coincidence. And the forensics team hasn't found any MDMA."

"Maybe he took the last of what he had," said Alex.

"Yeah," said the investigator. "Maybe."

Eventually, the conversation came around to assignments. Bill thought he knew how this would land. The state investigator had other cases and other responsibilities. She was there to lend a hand and coordinate with the other state agencies, but she had no time for groundwork. Arnie and his deputy had other casework as well. The sheriff's department was responsible for safeguarding all of Nelson County, almost five hundred square miles. The sheriff's thin staff got a lot of action as it was. Alex volunteered to allocate most of Mitch and Krista's time to the investigation, and no one complained.

"We need motive," said Arnie Shields. "Assuming someone killed Susskind, why did they kill him?"

Bill shared what he'd learned from Whit Whitlock the previous night—several people stood to inherit a great deal of money now that Susskind was dead.

"And the catering crew?" said Arnie. "What motive would they have?"

"We should search for a connection between them and Susskind," said the state investigator. She scanned the notes on her tablet to recall the names. "Justin. Maddie. Cindy." Then she paused for effect. "And Bill."

Alex said, "Krista and Mitch will focus on finding unknown connections between the victim and the catering crew."

"I'd suggest you research the MDMA scene as well," said Arnie Shields. "I gather anyone with access to foxglove could make digitalis, but MDMA is a different story. We wrestle with drugs here in the county but not so much MDMA. That's more of a city thing."

Mitch raised his hand. "I'll get smart on that subject."

They agreed that Arnie, Alex, and the state investigator would have twice-daily conference calls to share updates, and the meeting broke up.

After the county and state folks left, Bill asked Alex for a minute in his office.

"I don't believe that Cindy or Justin or Maddie had anything to do with this," said Bill. "What possible motive could they have?"

"I agree. But we still have to run the drill, right?"

"Of course. As for me, I'll focus my attention on the guest list. They have all kinds of history that could spin into a motive."

"All right," said Alex. "Go to it."

In the next moment, Krista came to the door carrying her laptop.

"I found it," she said.

"Found what?" said Alex.

"Foxglove."

She turned her laptop around for them to see. The tall flowering plant had green leaves at the bottom topped by a long stem bursting with purple and white bell-shaped blooms.

"That's it, huh?" said Bill.

"Yes," said Krista. "A killer in a pretty costume."

THIRTY-ONE

Sitting in his car outside the police station, Bill made two calls. The first was to Cindy. She was abuzz with excitement over their police interviews. But she also had the uncomfortable feeling that they were now suspects. What did he know about it?

"Are Justin and Maddie there?" he asked.

"Justin is. Maddie went home."

"Okay. I'll be there soon, and we can talk. I need to make one stop."

"Why? Why can't you come now, for Pete's sake?"

"It's almost five. Have a glass of wine."

"Don't patronize me," she barked. "I spent ninety minutes being interrogated by cops."

Cindy was not herself. Not too surprising, now that he gave it more than a moment's thought. This kind of stuff was no big deal for Bill. A murder investigation. Kind of like getting a haircut. But most everyone else only encountered murder in books or videos—he needed to cut her a break.

"I'll be there as soon as I can."

But he still made the second call. Angie Finch answered

on the first ring. Was she still at the Mountain Inn? Yes. Would it be possible for him to stop by now? Yes, meet her in the lobby near the fireplace.

After parking, Bill climbed the steps to the inn and strolled past the front desk to the lobby. The lobby furnishings were suitable for accommodating small groups. A man in an upholstered chair on the right leaned over his laptop. Three women in casual clothes sipped coffee around a table. After searching the rest of the room, Bill found Angie Finch sitting on a sofa opposite the unlit fireplace. She held a closed paperback on her lap and stared at a blank wall. He wondered how long she'd been there and whether she had read many pages.

Angie noticed him, and Bill said, "Don't get up." He sat in a chair next to the sofa and asked how she was getting along. She said she was fine, but he could see the truth. At Damian's retreat the previous day, Angie had flitted about to demonstrate her command of Damian's world, but with his demise, her energy had fled. She sat still with legs together, shrunken in both personality and physique.

"Have you eaten today?" Bill asked.

"Yes. After we met earlier, I had a coffee and a pastry from the shop." She tipped her head at a coffee cup and a half-eaten pastry on a side table.

"The Edge will open soon," he said. "You should get dinner. You'll feel better."

"Thank you. I will." But her words carried no conviction. "Did you want to ask me something?"

Bill didn't want to tell Angie the police suspected someone had poisoned Damian. Still, as Damian's assistant, she knew things that could assist the investigation, so he had little choice in the matter.

"Were you aware of the specific medications Damian was taking?"

She nodded with conviction. "Of course. I managed his prescriptions. I picked them up at a pharmacy in Waynesboro."

"Did one of his doctors ever prescribe digoxin?"

"No." Angie rattled off the medications Susskind had taken. "Why do you ask?"

Bill rubbed his hands together. There was no way around it. "The autopsy results indicate that Damian had a heart attack on the overlook. That may be why he fell. The lab tests detected the presence of a substance called digitalis, which can cause heart failure."

Angie frowned. "How did this digitalis get into his system?"

"We don't know. The medication digoxin is one possibility."

She shook her head. "No. It had to be something else."

"Okay." Bill hoped to get to the next question before Angie could add up the numbers, but she was quick.

"Wait, are you saying someone poisoned Damian? That's it, isn't it?"

Angie's voice rose as her mind leaped to this new conclusion. Bill glanced around to see whether anyone had heard her, but the others in the room paid Bill and Angie no mind.

"We don't know yet, but it's possible."

Angie squinted at the unlit fireplace. Bill sensed she was trying to figure out who had poisoned Damian.

"I have another question," he said. "The tests also found the presence of a recreational drug called MDMA. Did Damian ever take something like that?"

"I've read about this drug. It's a party drug, right? Young people take it at clubs."

"Yes, sometimes. The intended effects are feelings of elation and high energy. It can also distort the senses. Maybe you didn't notice it, but yesterday, it seemed that Damian had a burst of energy after lunch. I suspect that was caused by the MDMA."

Angie looked away. "Damian never took MDMA in my presence. Maybe whoever poisoned him gave him that too." Her hands fidgeted with the paperback. She fanned her thumb across its side. "But . . ." Her eyes filled with pain. "After the heart attack and the operation, Damian grew tired more easily. He hated that. Damian said his life was being stolen from him. And then one night after dinner, he magically transformed into his old self. He was laughing and carrying on. I was surprised but also pleased. It happened a few more times in the past couple of weeks. And at one point, I thought perhaps Damian was taking something."

"Okay. Let's assume for the moment that Damian was taking MDMA. Where would he have gotten the drug?"

"I have no idea. Of course, he knew many people but none that I would have thought took MDMA."

Bill decided to drop the subject. Maybe Damian took MDMA for fun. Maybe he didn't. But the digitalis killed him, and conceivably, everyone at the retreat had the opportunity to lace his food or drink with poison.

Motive was the key at this point. Murder required the guilty party to leap from the logical world to crazy land. Who had a reason so powerful that it turned their mind to evil? Bill mentally reviewed the list of suspects. First, he dismissed the catering crew. They knew Susskind only as a demanding client who paid his bills. No motive in that arrangement. Then Bill ticked off the names of those who sat around Damian's table. Stafford. Hale. Akin. Whitlock. And Angie.

"I want to clarify something you told me earlier," he said. "When you mentioned that you and Damian were engaged, did you mean you were still engaged when he died? Or was it something else?"

Angie glared at Bill briefly but then sighed. "We ended our engagement after his bypass surgery. It was hard, but frankly, that was the only path that made sense. Damian was thumbs up about his health in public, but privately, he had serious doubts, and he shared those with me. He might be close to death, and if so, why marry again? I agreed with him. Not at first, because I loved him and wanted to be his wife, but I came around."

Bill was skeptical of Angie's version of the story, but he wouldn't challenge her if the story made her feel better. Still, she might have been angry at Damian. Furious, even. How much did she stand to inherit? When they were engaged, had they discussed a pre-nuptial agreement? And if so, did the will now reflect that understanding? Whitlock had been tight with the details so far. Whatever the answer, Bill doubted money would stir Angie to murder Damian. Then again, a jilted woman was capable of just about anything.

THIRTY-TWO

Bill glanced at his phone on the way back to his car. The chat with Angie had only taken a few minutes, but Bill worried that he should have skipped the interview and seen Cindy first. Women were hard to figure out. What did a few minutes matter? Dumb question. In certain situations, and with some women, minutes mattered a great deal.

He drove up Wintergreen Drive, passed the Founder's Overlook, and got an idea for an opening line that might earn Cindy's smile. It would only take an extra minute and could make all the difference.

After pulling into the Café Devine parking lot, Bill hustled past the life-size Black Bear statue and into the shop. Kim Wiley stood next to the register, and he waved at her on his way to the wine racks.

"Hallelujah," she said. "Bill O'Shea. It's been so long I thought you were dead."

"Don't start that, Kim. I was here on Sunday."

"I don't think so."

Kim was of medium height and had a headful of curly brown hair that bordered on frizzy. She was the proprietor of

Café Devine and a local gossip. Whenever Bill stopped by for coffee or wine, he left knowing more about who was doing what with whom.

"Do you have any Châteauneuf-du-Pape?" he asked.

"Next shelf up and to the left two or three slots. I have forty-dollar, fifty-dollar, and seventy-dollar choices."

Bill examined the labels and scratched his head. This was not a seventy-dollar occasion. Forty dollars or fifty dollars? He gave the decision another five seconds and then reached for the higher-priced option. He placed the bottle next to the register, but Kim showed no inclination to hurry his transaction along. Instead, she stood two feet back from the counter with her arms crossed. There was no one else in the shop.

"Word has it you're helping Alex with the investigation into Damian Susskind's death."

Jeez. Word traveled fast on the mountain. "Who told you that?"

Kim shrugged. "Everyone's yakking about it. Biggest news since the Lou Thorpe murder."

He'd ask Kim to identify everyone if it would do any good, but she would just give him another vague answer. Kim protected her sources like a veteran newshound.

"Okay," he said, "it's true. I'm acting as an advisor to Alex. No big deal. Krista Jackson and Mitch Gentry are doing the heavy lifting."

"Sure."

"And since you brought it up, do you have any relevant tidbits?"

"I might." Kim stepped to the register and rang up his wine.

No point in trying to rush Kim; she'd get to it in her own time.

"I'm sure you remember Rachel Dunn," she said.

"I do."

"And given your role in the Susskind investigation, I guess you've also met Evan Hale and Lacey Akin."

"Good guess."

"Here's the tidbit you're after," said Kim. "Rachel Dunn and Evan Hale are a thing."

"What now?"

Kim nodded. "Yep. A thing. Rachel has a reputation on the mountain, and many people I know keep an eye out for her. Last week, Evan and Rachel rode down the mountain in his convertible. Her hair was loose and flying back like you see in the commercials. Later the same day, another friend of mine spied them at Pippin Hill Winery south of Charlottesville, all cozied up and sipping wine. I understand they sat quite close together."

"That's interesting."

"I thought you'd say that. Now, here's another something you should know. Evan Hale is a playboy known for dallying with more than one woman at a time. For months now, people have said that Lacey Akin has finally tied Evan down. He's in love with her. She's spending a lot of nights at his condo in the Ledges complex right across the street. And so forth. Then the Rachel thing comes up. Turns out, he hasn't changed after all."

"That's interesting."

"You said that already. So, what's it mean?" asked Kim.

"I don't know. But thanks for the tidbit."

"You're welcome. Say hello to Cindy for me."

"You bet."

On his way out to the car, Bill ground his teeth.

That scoundrel Rachel Dunn. She had lied to him again.

THIRTY-THREE

Bill knocked on Cindy's door and listened. He discerned an English accent coming from the television, probably the BBC World News show Cindy recorded every day. Hurried footsteps approached, and the door swung open.

Cindy's eyes signaled irritation at first, but then he lifted the bottle of Châteauneuf-du-Pape.

"I come bearing gifts."

Her eyes softened. "I'm sorry I snapped at you earlier."

"We've all had a hard day."

He stepped toward her, and they hugged. Her hand touched his neck and sent tingles down his spine.

Cindy took the bottle from him. "Let's open that bad boy."

Justin entered the living area from the hallway, and Cindy offered him wine, but he declined, saying he planned to go for a run later. Through the floor-to-ceiling windows, the sky was losing its sharpness as the daylight waned. Dark clouds advanced from the east. The three of them sat at the dining table and discussed the day's events.

Similar to Bill's experience, the detectives had asked

Cindy and Justin detailed questions concerning the food and beverage service. Who served what to whom? And when?

"They went through the lunch service several times," said Justin. "It was hard to remember the specifics. But the more questions the detectives asked, the more I was able to recreate what happened."

"I know what you mean," said Bill. "The mind is a strange machine."

Justin was a tall young man with long arms and big hands. His brown hair was short on the sides but long on top, and Bill suspected the Coast Guard would give him a haircut.

"Why were they so interested in the lunch service?" asked Cindy.

Bill brought them up to speed on the autopsy results and the investigating team's suspicion that someone had given Damian a substance to induce a heart attack.

"He was poisoned?" said Justin.

"Most likely."

"So," said Cindy, her voice resolute, "I was right. We're suspects now. That's what the questions were all about."

Bill raised his hands to urge caution. "Suspect is a harsh-sounding word, but technically, yes. Everyone in the house had the opportunity to slip something into Damian's food or drink, so we're all suspects, even me."

Justin adopted a thoughtful expression. "It all makes sense now. They kept asking about the coffee and the tea. Who poured the coffee, Maddie or me? Maddie poured the coffee. I filled water glasses. Did I pour water at the table? I fixed glasses of water before anyone sat down, then poured refills at the table. Maddie did the same thing with the coffee."

Cindy wanted to know what sort of poison the killer had used. Digitalis. Bill explained that the digitalis could have come from a prescription medication or the common foxglove plant.

"Yes," said Cindy. "I knew foxglove was poisonous."

"You did?" said Bill. He peered through the window at the rows of plants on Cindy's balcony. None resembled the photo on Krista's laptop.

"I know a lot about plants," said Cindy. She shook her finger at Bill. "You'd better be careful."

Justin recoiled. "You don't have foxglove here, do you?"

"No, but I have other stuff that would make your stomach turn. So you'd better be good too."

Bill asked whether Cindy or Justin had noticed anything unusual at Susskind's house unrelated to the catering. Cindy was an observant person and often saw details Bill missed. First, they discussed Evan Hale's statements concerning the annual reviews with Damian Susskind. Then Cindy noted, as Bill had earlier, that Damian acquired a burst of energy after lunch.

"Here's something," said Justin. "The detectives asked whether I had served whiskey on the back deck. I didn't even know they had whiskey out there."

"I had forgotten that," said Cindy. "They asked me about the whiskey too. But I didn't see it either."

"How did we all miss that?" said Bill.

Cindy tapped a finger against her chin and then said, "There's another door that opens onto the deck. It must go into the study. I'll bet Damian brought the whiskey out from his office. He might keep glasses back there as well."

Bill tried to recreate the view from the kitchen onto the back deck in his mind. From the sink, he'd had a clear view of the wooden table where they served breakfast. After lunch, Angie and Lacey Akin had sat at that table a while to have coffee. But there was another table out of view on the left.

Had Damian served his guests whiskey at that other table while Bill did the dishes? Had the killer poisoned Damian's whiskey? If so, the forensics tests should detect the poison.

"Maddie seemed a bit shaken after the interviews," said Cindy.

Justin pushed his lips out. "She seemed okay to me."

"She's only twenty-four," said Cindy, before turning to Bill. "I invited her to hang with us until you came back, but she said she'd better get home."

"That makes sense," said Bill. "I'm sure her parents are anxious about the whole thing."

"How long will the investigation take?" Justin nervously twisted a ring on his finger. "I'm due in Cape May next week. Is this going to screw up my schedule?"

Bill reminded himself, once again, that murder investigations unsettled normal people. The single word murder—when used in the context of an actual person and an actual crime—tended to raise tension in a room.

"Murders don't happen randomly," Bill said. "The people around Damian's table knew him well. The four of us on the catering team knew him only slightly, if at all, so the investigators will focus on Damian's guests, not us. You'll make it to boot camp on time."

Justin nodded. "Yeah, okay."

"Can you influence the investigation?" Cindy asked Bill.

Bill cocked an eyebrow. "What do you mean?"

"I assume Alex asked you to help out like he did last time. You're all hanging together, the sheriff's department, the state police. You guys are all cut from the same cloth. Can't you just tell them we're innocent?"

Cut from the same cloth. Bill had never heard that expression used in the context of the police force. He'd never considered police officers a homogenous group. He'd known many cops: short, tall, good, and bad. Many cultures. Many colors. Cindy was wrong, of course, about all cops being the same, but perhaps he was guilty in the same way with other groups of people. Professors, for example. They were long-winded, a bit clumsy, and leaned left politically.

"Yes," he said, "Alex asked me to help out, but no, I can't influence the investigation. We have to let it take its course."

Cindy frowned but didn't object.

Justin said he wanted to get his run in before it grew dark.

"Didn't you work out this morning?" said Cindy.

"Yes." Justin smiled as if he were pleased with himself. "I'm trying to work out twice a day." He lifted two enthusiastic fists. "I have to get in shape."

"Oh," said Cindy, her voice falling. She glanced outside. "Better take a windbreaker. That storm's coming in fast."

After Justin left, Cindy and Bill took their wine out to the balcony and sat on outdoor barstools. The wind had picked up. A shadow of rain fell between clouds and the earth many miles away.

"Are you okay?" he said, touching her arm.

"Why shouldn't I be? Justin's leaving for four years, and you're investigating a murder."

It was a reasonable answer, but Bill sensed there was more under the surface. Several months earlier, Cindy had asked him to relate his experience of serving in the military with Justin. Bill hardly considered himself an expert, as he had done his four-year army stint many years ago. But he was the only veteran Cindy knew, so Bill had talked with Justin and shared his views of the pros and cons. Justin had weighed the decision for a few weeks, checked out the various military branches, and settled on the Coast Guard.

Despite Bill's concern that something was bothering Cindy, he didn't question her further. Sometimes, it was best to keep your mouth shut. He watched the advancing storm and tried to enjoy his wine, but the nagging sensation of unfinished business stuck with him. And judging by the tension on Cindy's face, he had wasted fifty dollars.

Cindy said she didn't feel like having much for dinner, maybe a sandwich. Bill took the hint and said he had some bills to take care of at home. They ended the visit on a more positive note—at the door, she thanked him for the wine and gave him a warm kiss.

After a quick dinner, Bill strolled onto his balcony to watch the approaching storm. Wind rushed up the mountain and eerily moaned as it fought for entrance to closed windows and doors. Lightning flashed in the Rockfish Valley.

Bill's cell rang. Interim Chief Alex Sharp. He walked inside so he could hear.

"I thought you'd want to know," said Alex. "More forensics results came back. They found no traces of MDMA or digitalis in the whiskey glasses."

"Huh." Bill was surprised.

"They did a more thorough search of the house but still haven't found a trace of either drug. There's no way to be sure, but the state investigator we met today believes it was in the coffee or the tea."

"Does she? Okay. Did anyone mention how many whiskey glasses were on the back deck?"

"No. But I can check in the morning."

"Thanks."

Alex asked Bill what he planned to do the next day. Bill related his conversation with Kim Wiley and said he would start with Rachel Dunn. After that, he would pursue his standard routine. Hassle people with questions they might not want to answer. Make a nuisance of himself. Try to find a killer.

THIRTY-FOUR

After dinner with Justin, Cindy sat on her covered balcony and watched the approaching storm. Rain soaked the Rockfish Valley. Wind buffeted the condo's siding, crept onto the balcony, and wreaked havoc with her hair.

Justin had been an adventurous toddler. Constantly climbing out of his crib. Playing with the neighbor's pit bull. Trashing his room.

Maybe she and Kevin should have encouraged Justin to pursue a different major. What good was English? He should have taken computer science courses. Those kids made a fortune, and it wasn't too late. Kevin believed they should push Justin away from the Coast Guard and toward graduate school. Maybe Kevin was right.

Cindy had a week to work on Justin if she wanted to change his mind. With her and Kevin presenting a united front, Justin might choose a different course. Then again, Justin already had a lot to consider. His training. Maddie. The darn murder investigation.

Her stomach had been twisted in knots all day. A regular

customer had planned to host a large dinner party in two weeks, but when Cindy called her that afternoon to confirm the menu, her customer had postponed the event. Did that have anything to do with the investigation? If word spread that Cindy and her team were suspects, it could ruin her business.

It was absurd to suspect Justin or Maddie. Absurd. What could they possibly have to do with Damian Susskind? They were practically children. They didn't know anyone of any consequence.

And Bill. He seemed almost cavalier about the whole thing. The police had questioned her Justin. Her toddler. And Bill was like—don't fret. It'll be over soon. Of course, it wasn't Bill's fault, but couldn't he do something?

Lightning cracked on the ridge across the hollow, and Cindy flinched. Rain swept up the mountainside and reached her building. Drops pelted her bare feet, and she moved her chair farther back on the balcony.

Justin liked Maddie, no question. After dinner, he had called to check on her. When Maddie answered, he had hustled back to his room to have a private conversation. Five minutes later, Justin hooted with laughter. Maddie made him laugh. A good sign. Or was it? If he were sticking around for a few months or a year, they would become an item. Cindy was sure of it. But with Justin running off to Cape May, what chance did they have? Little to none. Frankly, Cindy was conflicted about the matter anyway. Maddie was a nice girl, but she hadn't even finished college. Was she the right woman for Justin?

Candidly, Bill had not attended college either. He was intelligent. He knew something about a lot of subjects. History. Philosophy. Science. But he had acquired his education the old-fashioned way, by reading books. He was considerate and fun most of the time. And she found him casually handsome, as opposed to romance-novel gorgeous.

She found Bill's past life as a policeman both mysterious and exciting, as he had investigated many murders and chased many criminals. Her chest felt light. Cindy had to admit her tangential involvement in the Lou Thorpe investigation was an absolute thrill.

Lightning flashed near the chairlift on the right, and then a boom sounded, rattling the windows of her condo. The sky was a dark gray trending toward black. Rain fell in torrents, and she could no longer see the valley. Wind blew rain onto the covered balcony, and she lifted her legs higher on the chair.

A murder investigation. Exciting, yes, but was that kind of excitement a good thing? It was fun with the Lou Thorpe case, but it was far too close this time. She had prepared the victim's final meal. No big deal for Bill. He was a retired cop. Once a cop, always a cop? Nothing to it. This was the world he had lived in for a long time.

But was it the world for her?

THIRTY-FIVE

The storm blew through overnight and left in its wake a startlingly bright day.

At seven o'clock, Mr. Chips was nibbling fiercely on greens near his burrow, and Bill took another ripe tomato down to test Maddie's method. Once again, he held the red fruit aloft and wiggled it to attract the groundhog's attention. Bill then crept until he was fifteen feet away and laid the tomato in the grass. Mr. Chips scrutinized Bill's every move, but he didn't scamper off. Furthermore, after retrieving the tomato, rather than disappearing down his burrow entrance, Mr. Chips stayed topside and proudly gnawed his treasure down to the seeds. Then he licked his paws.

A warm feeling grew in Bill's chest, and he smiled. Wintergreen was quite a home.

Bill drove to Rachel Dunn's house at eight o'clock, intending to catch her before she hurried off to an appointment. But when he rang the bell, no one came. He waited for a minute and then rang the bell twice again. Could she have left the house already? No, her white BMW sat parked in the driveway. Perhaps she was meditating and didn't wish to be disturbed. Or listening to loud music through earbuds. Bill cupped his hands around his eyes and placed his face against the side glass panel. The hallway and living room appeared unoccupied, but a light shone from the kitchen onto the hallway floor. He examined the living room. To the right of the couch, a picture window revealed a sliver of the back deck. What was that? A lounge chair? Yes, and on top of it lay a bare leg and some sort of wispy robe.

Bill stepped away from the window, and his heart rate jumped. Rachel was lounging on the back deck. Sheesh. His initial instinct was to get in his car and drive away. But as was always the case with investigations, time mattered a great deal. Damian Susskind had died more than thirty-six hours earlier. Soon, it would be two full days. And then three. Memories would fade and become jumbled and unreliable. Motivations would change.

He descended the front steps and took a path leading around the right side of the house. The hill sloped downward, and the house rested on square support columns. Bill came to a wooden stairway that led to the back deck. Soft jazz music played from speakers. He backed several feet away from the stairway and called, "Hello. Ms. Dunn?"

No answer.

He raised his voice. "Hello! Rachel? Are you up there?"

The music's volume lowered. "What? Did someone call?"

"Yes, Ms. Dunn. It's Bill O'Shea. I'm on the ground."

After what seemed a long time, Rachel's head and shoulders appeared over the wooden railing above him. She wore sunglasses, and her hair was pulled back. Her robe, or negligee, or whatever, was see-through. With her forearms rested on the railing, Rachel interlaced her fingers and smiled tauntingly.

"Is that you, Bill? What on earth are you doing down there?"

"Um, I tried the doorbell, but you couldn't hear me over the music. Could I possibly get a few minutes of your time?"

Rachel leaned back and glanced down at her body, hidden from Bill's view.

"Sure, come on up."

"Thanks." But Bill's imagination ran away with him. What was Rachel wearing under the negligee? He found the question both exhilarating and absolutely terrifying. What was he to do? She remained in the same place, smiling at his discomfort. "Rachel?"

"Yes."

"Are you fully clothed?"

She chuckled, torturing him. "What's your definition of fully clothed?"

He stepped onto the first stair but then stopped. "I don't want you to feel uncomfortable."

She shrugged and then glanced down at her body again. "I'm perfectly comfortable."

Bill squeezed the stairway railing. Was she ever not at ease? His stomach churned. "Yes, I can see that. I guess it's me—I'm the problem."

Rachel waved a hand in dismissal. "Relax. I'm suitably covered."

The robe was flimsy and sheer, but she wore a beige sports bra and black shorts underneath it. The notion of her lounging half-naked had been a fabrication of his mind.

"Something to drink?" she said. "Coffee?"

"No, thanks. I've had plenty."

Rachel gestured at a round table covered with an umbrella, and they settled into neighboring chairs. Bill took a deep breath. The sun was well above the distant ridge, and he was glad for the umbrella. The grassy ski run was less than a stone's throw from the back deck. A small hill covered with old-growth hardwoods separated this ski run from the next one over.

"Goodness," she said. "Bill O'Shea visits two days in a row. I feel special."

The anger he'd held for Rachel the previous day had vanished with the sunbathing mystery, and now he tried to reignite it.

"You weren't truthful with me yesterday," he said.

Rachel frowned. "Says who?"

"You said you had no romantic interest in Damian Susskind—"

"I didn't."

"When in truth, you had your eyes set on his younger acquaintance, Evan Hale. The burger king."

Rachel studied Bill's face. She bit her lip.

"Don't try to deny it," he said. "You've been seen cavorting with Hale all over Charlottesville." Bill purposefully exaggerated his intel to get Rachel's reaction.

She snorted. "Cavorting. Where do you get these words? I went out with Evan a few times, but what of it? You didn't ask about Evan Hale yesterday. Not that it's any of your business who I see. You've become overly nosy."

"Yesterday, we believed Susskind's death was likely an accident. Now, we're not sure."

Rachel straightened her shoulders. "What do you mean?"

Bill explained that Susskind had ingested suspicious substances that might have led to his death. Subsequently, the police had expanded their effort into a full-blown investigation. Rachel paid rapt attention. Bill further explained that Damian had spent the day with those closest to him before he fell, including Evan Hale, Lacey Akin, and others.

"You told me you had no interest in Susskind," said Bill. "I believed you. Then I heard that you and Hale were close. So, I stopped by to see what else you know."

"There's not much to tell."

Rachel acknowledged that she and Hale had been out socially a few times in Charlottesville. She had first met him on the mountain at the Edge.

"I go to the Edge by myself occasionally for the human interaction," she said. "I have a glass of wine and a salad at the bar and chat with whoever is there. Some nights, it's just the bartender and me. One night, it was Evan Hale. Evan lives in Charlottesville but also owns a condo up here. He seemed kind of fun, so I said yes when he asked me to go wine tasting."

Bill guessed that Rachel was in her mid-forties, perhaps a decade older than Evan Hale, but she could pass for thirty-eight. The motive of jealousy crossed Bill's mind. Both Damian and Evan had known Rachel.

"Did Evan ever discuss Damian?" asked Bill.

"Not that I recall. He might have mentioned Damian in passing."

"Did Evan know you were Damian's masseuse?"

"No, that never came up. Honestly, we didn't see each other enough times for it to amount to anything."

So much for the jealousy motive. But since Bill was already there, he might as well ask a few more questions. "What sort of man is Evan Hale?"

Rachel shrugged. "He likes to party, and he likes women. However, it soon became clear that he wanted a no-strings, hookup-centered relationship. I wasn't interested, so I stopped answering his texts."

"What about drugs, specifically MDMA. Did he use MDMA or talk about it at all?"

"The subject of recreational drugs never came up. Evan may have tried MDMA at some point in his life, but not with me. We did a winery, live music at a bar, his burger place, and a restaurant. Nothing crazy."

Time to wrap it up. Bill thanked Rachel for her help. She said no problem and offered her contact information.

"If you have any more questions," she said, "next time, you can text ahead."

He promised he would, and then Rachel surprised him by escorting him to his car. She must have spent a lot of time in her bare feet because she crossed the gravel driveway without missing a step.

At his car, she appeared pensive. "Why did you mention MDMA? Was that one of the substances Damian ingested?"

"Yes. Why? Did you remember something?"

"Nothing to do with drugs," she said. "Something else. In my former line of work, I developed a sixth sense about men and money. I still notice details. What restaurant do they choose? Do they study the prices before they order? How fast do they reach for the check? These signals are subtle but telling. When I was out with Evan, I offered to pay for drinks a few times. He always said no, but he considered the option first. Bottom line, I got the impression Evan might be strapped financially."

Bill nodded. "That's interesting. Thanks."

He started back down Black Rock Drive but then pulled off to the side long enough to call Krista and get Evan Hale's cell number. Whit Whitlock had not shared the details of Damian's will, but it was reasonable to assume that Evan Hale would inherit a substantial sum. And money made a fine motive for murder.

THIRTY-SIX

Bill parked his Mazda at the Devils Knob Golf and Tennis Center and checked his phone for the time. Evan Hale had a tee time in half an hour but had said he was happy to meet beforehand. Bill spotted Hale at the driving range and strolled over to watch the young man hit perfect shots with ease. For the first time in his life, Bill was now taking golf lessons, and he found the act of swinging a club quite tricky.

If I could hit shots like that, I'd play the game three times a week.

Oak trees swayed in the light breeze. The range was wider than a football field and three times its depth. Two turkey vultures circled low over the forest beyond the range.

Hale noticed Bill and immediately came over to shake hands. He was physically fit in a balanced way, not overly muscular like the weight room fanatics nor pencil thin like the long-distance runners. Hale had finished his warmup and suggested they grab a coffee on the clubhouse patio. While waiting for their coffees, they discussed the weather and other light topics. Hale had the likable aura of a successful sales executive. When Bill spoke, Evan maintained eye contact and gave Bill the impression he was listening to every word.

After the server brought their drinks, Evan said, "I understand the investigation into Damian's accident is ongoing. How may I help you?"

Bill noted that Evan used the word accident instead of more sinister words like homicide or murder. Bill was of a mind to throw him a little off balance.

"We have a mutual acquaintance," said Bill, as if to continue the small talk. "Rachel Dunn."

Evan raised an eyebrow and took some time to sample his coffee again.

"Yes," he said. "I don't know Rachel well, but we've seen each other socially a few times. Why did you bring her up?"

"No particular reason. I saw Rachel earlier today, and she asked about the investigation. As you can imagine, it's a big story on the mountain. She mentioned that she knew you casually." Bill shrugged. "Not a big deal."

Evan nodded that he now understood.

"Tell me about your business," said Bill. "Gourmet burgers, right?"

Evan delivered a well-rehearsed answer. After working for Fair Game for fifteen years, he had decided to steal a page from Damian's playbook and build his own company. There were plenty of cheap burger joints everywhere, but the citizens of Charlottesville, and other affluent markets, desired a higher-end experience with their beef patties. Specifically, they wanted craft beers, wine, and cocktails; a menu that catered to special dietary considerations; and table service. His store on the downtown mall had turned a profit in its third month, and from that moment, Evan had focused his efforts on a long-term rapid-growth strategy.

"How's that working out?" said Bill.

"Great. Fantastic. We have twenty stores up and running with another ten in the pipeline."

"Congratulations. I'm in awe of anyone who can run their own business, particularly in the restaurant game. It's such a brutal industry. Are all the stores performing as well as the one in Charlottesville?"

Tension entered Evan's eyes. "They're ramping up nicely. But, of course, Charlottesville is a unique situation, the perfect market. The other stores have not hit that home run yet, but they'll get there." The confidence in Evan's voice waned.

Bill lifted his hands in a *what do I know* gesture, then said, "I understand the capital required for a rapid business expansion can strain investment funds. How's the balance sheet?"

Evan narrowed his eyes. "Why? Did Rachel say I was in financial trouble?"

"No. I'm just curious. Besides, how would Rachel know if you were? I thought you only knew her casually."

"That's true." Evan bobbed his head slightly, thinking. "Confidentially, if I had to do it over again, I would moderate the expansion. The bank is pushing me around a bit. But I've been in worse scrapes."

"I'm sure you have." It was a throwaway statement. Bill wrestled with where to take the conversation. Secrets were like hidden fruit in a tree. Sometimes, if you shook the trunk, the juicy facts would fall out.

Evan sat quiet, waiting for Bill's lead.

"I guess a nice inheritance from Damian Susskind would placate the bank."

After laughing as if Bill had told a good joke, Evan said, "Is that what you think? That I stand to inherit a fortune? Maybe you believe I murdered Damian."

"Did you?"

Evan scowled. "Don't be absurd. I told you on the overlook that I wasn't standing anywhere near Damian. If anyone killed him, it was Tanya. She was with him."

"Why would Tanya kill Damian?"

"I'm not saying she did, but she did have a reason. She was angry that morning because Damian had told her he would hire someone else to lead the company."

"Is that what they were arguing about on the way to the overlook?"

"I'm sure of it."

Evan Hale had now confirmed the motive for Tanya that Bill first heard from Whit Whitlock. But Tanya had not pushed Damian—they had confirmed that with Rossi. Whoever poisoned Damian had planned their move well in advance, which argued against a motive acquired only that morning unless Tanya carried MDMA and digitalis around in her purse.

Bill explained that the police no longer suspected Tanya of pushing Damian. Instead, they now believed Damian had a heart attack brought on by poison.

"Poison!"

"Yes, the autopsy revealed that Damian ingested a combination of substances shortly before his death—alcohol, MDMA, and something called digitalis."

A look of horror gripped Hale's face. "What? That's incredible." Hale rubbed his hands together roughly and stared at the table, mulling Bill's new information. "The alcohol makes sense. We had whiskey on the back deck. If someone poisoned Damian with the other stuff, they might have put it in the whiskey."

"Have you ever known Damian to take MDMA?" asked Bill.

Evan frowned. "MDMA? That's the party drug, right? No, I'd be surprised. Although it's not out of the question. I know he smoked pot in college, and he told me he'd once taken mushrooms." A hint of nostalgia entered Evan's eyes. "Damian was like that, bigger than life. Bragging about stuff. Making grand proclamations of what he would do. It's hard for me to believe he's gone."

For a moment, it appeared that Evan would tear up. As was typical with murder cases, whoever had killed Susskind likely knew him well. And the murderer might now be feeling remorse over ending the great man's life.

"Tell me about the whiskey," said Bill.

Evan sighed. "Damian loved whiskey. He had a huge collection in his study. That afternoon, he insisted we try an esoteric scotch he had recently discovered. I'd never heard of the stuff."

"Do you remember the brand?"

"Braemore."

Bill took a mental note that the forensics team should find this whiskey bottle and test its contents.

"Tell me whatever details you can remember concerning the whiskey tasting."

Evan took note of the seriousness with which Bill had asked the question. "Damian, Whit, and I tried the whiskey. Tanya did too. Angie and Lacey don't care for whiskey, so they begged off."

"Who poured the whiskey?"

Evan gnawed on his upper lip. "I'm not sure." He turned his head to the side. "No, it was Damian. Definitely. He poured huge slugs into rocks glasses from his study. No one drank all of what he poured. It was too much. We had a few sips. But the Braemore was good stuff. I remember that."

The whiskey tasting session had happened while Bill and

the rest of the catering crew were washing dishes after lunch. Had someone poisoned the whiskey? And if so, how had they managed to get the poison into Damian's glass?

"Did Damian say where he'd found the whiskey?"

"No. I don't recall him mentioning it. It wasn't a noteworthy event. He'd done the same thing with other special brands."

Evan glanced at his watch and then signaled the server for a check. "I should probably get going."

"Definitely. I don't want to disturb your round. One more question, if I may. Describe your relationship with Lacey Akin."

Evan's eyebrows furrowed, but then he smiled. "You're good at this stuff, aren't you? Prying into other people's lives."

"I should be. I've had a lot of practice."

"Lacey and I have become involved romantically. I've known Lacey casually for decades. For the longest time, she was far too young for me to be involved with, but we were always friends. We used to ride horses together down at Rodes Farm. The romance thing is a recent development."

Kim Wiley had said Lacey regularly spent the night at Evan's condo. On the hike to the overlook, Lacey and Evan had lagged behind Damian and Tanya. Perhaps they paused along the way to share a kiss. Maybe that's why Evan had not seen Damian on the overlook—Evan had focused on other attractions.

"Would you characterize your relationship with Lacey as serious?"

Evan pushed his lips out. "It's hard to tell with these things. We enjoy each other's company. I know that much."

Bill decided he didn't like Evan Hale. Kim had described him as a playboy known for seeing more than one woman at a time. Of course, sometimes Kim's gossip was of little value, rumors based in fact but blown out of proportion in the retelling. But in this case, Kim's intel was legit. At the same time that he was seeing Lacey regularly, he had tried to lure Rachel Dunn into what she described as a no-strings, hookup-centered relationship.

As if Hale could read Bill's mind, he said, "Do me a small favor?"

"If I can," said Bill.

"Don't mention to Lacey that I've seen Rachel Dunn socially. Rachel and I were barely even casual friends, and I haven't seen her in weeks."

"I don't see how it would come up," said Bill. It wasn't a promise. Not even a commitment, but Evan seemed to take it that way.

"Thanks."

Bill accompanied Evan downstairs to where Evan had left his golf bag. Bill turned to go, and Evan said, "I'd like to clear up one thing, an incorrect assumption you've made."

"What's that?"

"In our review conversation the other morning, Damian told me he intended to shift most of my inheritance to charity. Unfortunately, the amount he planned to give me wouldn't satisfy the bankers."

After the interview, Bill sat in his car and considered Evan's reference to his inheritance. Whit Whitlock hadn't mentioned that Damian intended to give money to charity. Then again, Whitlock had kept the details of Damian's will to himself.

Bill phoned Alex to give him a briefing and suggest that the forensics team test the bottle of Braemore for traces of the poison. Responding to Bill's earlier question, Alex reported that they had found four whiskey glasses on the back patio.

“Four,” repeated Bill, a bit disappointed, because the answer tossed one of his scenarios in the dumpster. He had thought the killer might have laced Damian’s glass with poison and then whisked it away to hide the evidence.

“Yes, four glasses. Each of them had some whiskey residue. They tested each separately, no poison.”

Bill then checked in with Krista Jackson. Had she managed to contact Tanya Stafford as they discussed earlier? Yes, the good news was that Tanya had taken the day off and did have time to meet Bill. She was spending the day fly fishing in Stoney Creek. He could meet her there.

Bill wanted to ask Krista if she had learned anything from her background research on Justin Quintrell and Maddie Katz. But Bill had promised Alex he’d steer clear of the background checks due to his conflict of interest. Still, Krista would let him know if she found anything. Wouldn’t she?

THIRTY-SEVEN

Bill turned right on Blue Ridge Drive at the end of the clubhouse driveway. A woman in gray leggings and a sleeveless pink top ran on the footpath to the right. She was tall and clearly an experienced runner, for she made easy work of the hill's incline. He drew closer and recognized Lacey Akin.

Bill rolled down the window and pulled alongside her.

"Hello."

Lacey stopped. She leaned toward the car with her chest heaving and a puzzled expression.

"It's Bill O'Shea. We met on the overlook after Damian fell."

"Oh. Hi."

Bill glanced in the rearview mirror. A truck climbed the hill behind him. Whatever. They could wait.

"Sorry if I startled you," said Bill. "Alex Sharp asked me to help him with the accident investigation."

The truck beeped its horn at Bill, and he waved out his window for the driver to pass.

Frowning, Lacey watched the truck pull up beside Bill.

The truck stopped, and the driver made a rude hand gesture.

Bill frantically dug the shield Alex had given him out of his pocket and thrust it toward the other driver. Bill again waved for the driver to move on, and the truck roared up the hill. Then, looking at Lacey, Bill said, "Could I ask you a few questions?"

"Now?"

"Um." And it occurred to Bill how ridiculous it was for him to stop Lacey on the roadside. Sometimes he pushed things too far. "No, whenever you're done. If it works for you."

Still breathing heavily, Lacey glanced up the hill and then back at him. "I'll be finished in twenty minutes. Can you meet me on the Mountain Inn's patio?"

"Sure."

Bill felt slightly embarrassed, but it wasn't the first time he'd made a fool of himself. And it wouldn't be the last. Down at the Mountain Inn, he picked up two bottles of water at the snack shop and waited for Lacey on the patio. When she came, perspiration shined on her forehead, and she happily accepted his peace offering of water. They sat in colorful Adirondack chairs that overlooked the ski run.

After a long drink, Lacey asked, "Have the police arrested Tanya?"

Bill folded his hands on his lap and said, "No, they haven't."

"Why not?"

Bill explained that he believed Lacey had indeed seen Tanya push Damian off the cliff. However, another witness had come forward and claimed otherwise. After a careful reenactment at the scene, the police concluded that Lacey had observed an optical illusion created by the players' relative positions. The wind blowing through overhanging leaves may have exaggerated the illusion.

"An illusion?" she said.

"Yes."

Lacey sipped water and stared into the distance. "It's possible. I know what I saw, or at least what I think I saw, but it's true that I didn't have a clear view." She sat back to consider this new possibility.

Bill waited patiently. Until Lacey moved on from her earlier beliefs, his questions would make little sense.

"I'm relieved," she said. "I've always liked Tanya. Now that you've told me Damian fell by accident, I feel much better."

"But there is a complication," he said. Bill then related the autopsy results and the conclusion that someone may have intentionally poisoned Damian.

Tanya's eyes widened as the implications became clear. "Oh." She drew her head back. "That's why you stopped me. You're trying to figure it out. Who could have done it and all that stuff?"

"Exactly."

"Does that mean I'm a suspect? Should I hire a lawyer? But I don't know any lawyers except for Whit."

"I can't give you legal advice. But we're still in the early phase of the investigation. Damian may have ingested the digitalis accidentally, though that appears unlikely."

"So it's possible that Tanya killed Damian after all."

Apparently, Lacey still considered Tanya the prime suspect.

"Yes," said Bill, "but anyone who dined with Damian might have had the opportunity."

Lacey frowned. "Evan could never kill Damian. He looked

up to him as a father. And Angie? No, she loved Damian. I can't see Whit having a motive—he earned all of his money from Damian and his business. That leaves Tanya. And me, I guess. But I could never kill anyone." Lacey shivered.

She had skipped the caterers altogether, but Bill saw no reason to complicate her analysis.

"You said you could never kill someone, but I gather you believe Tanya had the fortitude to do so."

"Oh, yes," Lacey said, nodding fiercely. "Tanya is strong. She could do anything."

For the first time, Bill surmised that Lacey Akin was not particularly intelligent, but his instinct told him to be wary of that impression. Some people were clever enough to manipulate others by portraying themselves as slow-witted, and it took a clever person to get away with murder. He reminded himself to be careful around Lacey Akin.

"Why would Tanya do such a thing?" he asked.

Lacey tilted her head, as if she were considering this question for the first time. "Maybe for money. I don't know for sure, but I suspect Damian intended to leave Tanya a lot of money in his will."

"I see. So by killing Damian, Tanya would come into her inheritance now."

Lacey nodded.

"But wouldn't you have the same motive? Did Damian intend to leave you an inheritance?"

"Yes," she said without hesitation, "but love is more important than money."

Love. Did she mean her love for her stepfather? Or love for Evan Hale?

"Tell me about your relationship with Evan Hale."

Lacey sat straight and pulled her shoulders back. "Evan

and I are in a serious relationship." She took a deep breath. "We love each other. We will marry someday."

"I'm happy for you." But Bill felt certain Lacey and Evan regarded their relationship in vastly different ways. He wouldn't mention this concern to Lacey, but he might say something to Evan the next time they met.

Lacey beamed. "Yes, we might marry soon, now that—" Her eyes opened wide.

"Now that what? Now that Damian is dead?"

"No." Lacey wrung her hands. "Well, perhaps that is what I meant, although the words sound horrible. Evan and I had not publicly declared our relationship, but Damian sensed something was going on. He told me he wasn't a fan of the idea."

Bill's estimation of Damian Susskind kicked up a notch. The tycoon knew a player when he saw one, and he didn't much like the idea of Evan breaking Lacey's heart.

"I see," said Bill, then he tacked in a new direction. "I understand that some of the party had whiskey on the back deck after lunch. Did you partake?"

Lacey took a while to respond. Her silence lingered, as if she was still considering their last few sentences. "No, I don't like whiskey, so I had coffee."

"Did you see who poured the whiskey?"

Her eyebrows furrowed, and she hesitated again. "Do you think someone poisoned the whiskey?"

"Not necessarily. I know almost nothing at this point. I'm stumbling around in the dark."

Lacey pressed her lips together as if to recollect the scene. "Damian brought the whiskey out from his study. He showed the label to the others. I didn't see who poured the whiskey, but I assume it was Damian."

Bill asked Lacey if she had noticed anything else of

interest that day, but she had not. They wrapped up the conversation, and Bill left to drive down the mountain. He had never tried fly fishing, but he suspected that Tanya Stafford—a top executive of an outdoor sports company—had spent some time on the water.

THIRTY-EIGHT

Not far from Crozet, Mitch Gentry drove down Hillsboro Lane and parked his squad car in the driveway of an old house. A wave of nostalgia swept over him, as it always did when he visited his ancestral home. The house was white with a dark roof, green shutters, and a portico. Mitch owned the place. He had inherited it from his grandmother, although it came with a whopper of a mortgage. The rental income his tenant paid barely covered the monthly payments. In truth, the house was a break-even enterprise, as it was always in need of one repair or another. Mitch spent two or three days every month working on the place. Thanks to online DIY videos, he now knew a bit about plumbing, fixing sash windows, electrical work, and painting. It seemed like there was always more caulking and painting to do.

But it was worth it. Mitch knew that in his bones. One day, he would play cornhole in this front yard with his kids. They would climb that maple tree. Lulu would sit on the front porch and laugh. They would plant a garden in the backyard big enough to supply all their vegetables. He might even build a chicken coop. The kids could sell the eggs. Of course, it would take a lot of work, and money, to refurbish the house. But he didn't worry about that. He had a savings account designated for the purpose into which he had already stuffed twenty thousand dollars.

Mitch strolled up to the front porch and rang the bell. Holly answered the door with an infant on her hip. Her husband, Ray, worked at the nearby lumber mill. Holly asked if Mitch had gotten the rent check. Yes. She said the bathtub faucet was leaking again. Mitch told her he'd come soon and that she could deduct half of the water bill from the next month's rent. Was there anything else? Well, the wind whistled through the window in their bedroom. Not a big deal now, but come winter, it would let in the cold air. Don't worry. He would fix it before then.

Back in the squad car, Mitch thought, *Caulking and painting. Always more caulking and painting.*

But it was worth it. He knew that in his bones.

Ten minutes later, Mitch pulled into the parking lot of Crozet Pizza.

Richie Lawrence—Lulu's cousin—met Mitch at the front door. Richie was a police officer too. He worked for the Charlottesville police department and spent much of his time on narcotics investigations. Mitch would be forever in debt to Ritchie because at a party long ago, he had introduced Mitch to Lulu.

When they entered the restaurant, the patrons at two nearby tables stopped talking and stared.

"How y'all doing?" said Ritchie.

"Fine," said a man.

"Great," said a woman. "And you?"

Ritchie slapped his stomach with both hands. "Fantastic. It's pizza time."

They agreed to split the large Special pizza, which came with pepperoni, onion, mushroom, green pepper, and sausage.

Mitch's eyes lingered on the menu. "Hey, let's get some of these brussels sprouts for an appetizer."

Ritchie scowled. "Brussels sprouts? In a pizza joint? My cousin has ruined you. She's getting you into the health food thing, isn't she?"

"No, I've always liked brussels sprouts."

"Uh-huh."

Mitch had reached out to Richie because he liked him and wanted to catch up, but also to pick his brain about the MDMA scene in the area.

"MDMA?" Richie's head swayed from side to side. "We don't worry much about that. We have bigger problems with the opioid scene. Prescription drugs are still an issue. Worse than that is the heroin and the fentanyl. I swear that fentanyl is the devil's creation."

Mitch was glad he had taken the job at Wintergreen. If he'd stayed in Richmond, he might be dealing with the same issues as Ritchie.

Ritchie glanced at the nearby tables and leaned closer. "Now that I've worked in narcotics awhile and seen how things play out, I realize we need to attack this problem with a different strategy."

"How so?"

"Most of the overdoses we see stem from a lack of information. Addicts take the wrong dose because they don't know what they have. Illegal manufacturers ignore quality control."

"What do you want to do? Have pharmacists dispense heroin and fentanyl?"

Ritchie lifted his eyebrows. "It might be worth a try. I bet we'd have fewer deaths that way."

Yeah, Mitch was glad he had moved to Wintergreen. He brought Ritchie up to speed on the murder investigation and why he was interested in MDMA.

Ritchie shrugged. “Charlottesville is a college town. Pretty good party scene too. We’ve got MDMA. But the same is true of other nearby cities. Richmond. Harrisonburg. Anyone with money can find MDMA. But the quality? Well, that’s a different question.”

Ritchie’s response was in line with Mitch’s expectations. If Damian Susskind wanted MDMA, he could put his hands on it. And he wouldn’t have to troll poor neighborhoods in his car because he would know someone who knew someone. Mitch suspected the same was true for any of Damian’s guests.

But that wasn’t the only reason Mitch had reached out to Ritchie. The food came, and they chitchatted while they ate. They both had schedules to keep and would have to leave soon.

Mitch sucked in his breath. “Hey, I want to ask you a question.”

Ritchie may have detected a change in Mitch’s tone, because his eyes grew serious. “What’s up?”

“Has Lulu ever said anything to you about me?”

“Yeah, she says you’re the greatest.”

Mitch’s heart pounded in his chest. “But you and I, we both know that’s not true. I’m not the greatest. I’m an average person and an average cop. So what I’m asking is if she’s ever expressed disappointment in me.”

“What? Heck, no.”

“I’m not as smart as her. She’s much smarter than me. And she’s stronger too. Not physically. I’m referring to willpower. You know? If she’s having second thoughts, you should tell me. It's not too late. But after we get married, it'd be a huge hassle for her to dump me then."

Ritchie shook his head. "Dude, where's this coming from?"

"I worry about it."

"Well, stop worrying. Lulu loves you." Ritchie leaned across the table to touch Mitch's shoulder.

Mitch took a deep breath.

"Maybe you're not as smart," said Ritchie, "but who is? Not me. Hell, few people are as smart as Lulu, but that's not the point. Intelligence is only one factor. You're a strong person, Mitch. Not just physical strength, either."

"I hope you're right."

"I *am* right. We all do the best we can. That's what matters. That's how the world works. You do the best you can, right?"

Mitch nodded. "Yeah. Thanks, Ritchie."

After lunch, Mitch waved as Ritchie drove off and then leaned against the trunk to think. Ritchie was a good friend. He wouldn't lie to Mitch.

The sun was high overhead. It was warmer in the valley, and the mountains were beautiful to the west. A mockingbird landed in the grass nearby, pecked at the ground, and flew away.

Mitch got in his squad car and texted Krista to see if she'd made any progress on the background checks.

THIRTY-NINE

Sitting in her cubicle, Krista bit into a tuna fish sandwich, sipped a can of Diet Dr. Pepper, and turned toward the monitor. She had worked a dispatcher shift that morning, and it was nonstop action. First, there was a bear sighting. Then a large branch fell on a house down on Shamokin Springs Trail. On and on it went until her shift ended.

Now, she'd have some time to work on the assignment Alex and Undersheriff Arnie Shields had given her the previous day—background checks on Justin Quintrell and Maddie Katz. She'd focus on Justin first, although he seemed a pleasant young man and was Cindy's son, so Krista could hardly imagine him as a criminal, certainly not a murderer. She began by validating Justin's social security number. Yes, he was an actual person. Then she quickly checked Nelson County records—nothing, which made sense given he had only resided there a short while. His address said Virginia Beach, but if he had been in serious trouble anywhere in the state, it would appear in Virginia's criminal history records system. Again, nothing. As far as Virginia knew, Justin Quintrell had never been arrested or convicted of a felony crime.

And he was handsome to boot, although if Krista had a magic wand, she would cut his hair, remove the tattoo from his forearm, and age him ten years so he'd at least be relevant for her personally.

On to Maddie Katz—Madeline V. Katz, to be more precise. What did the V stand for? Vera. Valentina. Victoria. Or it could be a last name. Vaughn. Vance. Vogeley.

Maddie's social security number checked out, and the Nelson County search turned up a traffic violation from six years earlier. No big deal. Krista had one of those herself. Krista then entered Maddie into the Virginia records system, and several results came back from the search. She paused to read the details and frowned. At the age of twenty, Maddie was swept up in a raid the Harrisonburg police conducted on a private dance party. The raid produced multiple charges for the party organizers—serving alcohol to underage patrons and numerous other offenses. Maddie had been unresponsive at the scene and was taken to a local hospital. Later, she'd been charged with possession of marijuana, but the prosecuting attorney had dropped those charges. Small wonder. With the legalization of marijuana on the horizon, prosecutors could no longer be bothered with pot. Nevertheless, Krista took a note to call Harrisonburg to learn what she could about that party.

The next record for Maddie in Virginia's criminal history system made Krista's heart skip a beat. She moved closer to the screen. Maddie was arrested the previous year for trespassing at a corporate office building in Charlottesville. Krista read the name of the company and did a double-take. Fair Game.

Krista spent the next hour on the phone tracking down the right people with the Charlottesville police department. Only then did she notice the text message from Mitch.

FORTY

Bill took a left off Route 151 onto Monocan Drive, drove through the golf course and past the clubhouse, and turned left to wind his way along twisting streets to Stoney Creek Park. It was a small park with a few picnic tables set among tall oaks and maples. No one else was there. A sign indicated that fishing required a state license and a Wintergreen permit.

A crushed stone path wound down to the creek, where water gurgled around rocks and fallen branches. Bright sunlight filtered through the trees and made the water sparkle. Bill scanned the shoreline upstream and downstream but saw no one. Perhaps it was not the right time of day for fly fishing. Was there an optimal time? Did fish bite on a sunny afternoon?

Bill followed the trail, which led left and downstream. The course hugged the left bank, and after a few turns, he spied Tanya Stafford standing in the moving water. He stepped closer to the bank for a better view. She wore waders, jeans, and a long-sleeved denim shirt. Her brown hair was pulled up and tucked under a dark cap. A light breeze rustled leaves in the treetops. Tanya finished reeling in her line and began to make a new cast. She rocked the rod forward and backward, seeking the perfect spot for her bait. Her movements were relaxed and graceful, and Bill guessed Tanya had done this many times. Finally satisfied, she landed the fly softly on the creek's surface, waited a moment, and then turned the reel to remove slack in the line. After deciding her cast would not land a fish, she reeled in the line and repeated the process to aim for a different spot. Bill watched her cast several times. Tanya stood so comfortably that she was an extension of nature itself, and he was loath to interrupt her flow.

Soon, Tanya moved farther downstream and began casting toward a shaded curve in the bank. The water swirled quietly there, and its darker hue hinted at depth. Suddenly, something disturbed the bait, and Tanya jerked the rod. Bill held his breath and stepped closer to the bank. Tanya lifted the reel higher and adjusted her stance. A shiny fish ten inches long jumped above the water and struggled to be free. Tanya stepped toward the fish and reeled the line in with smooth, even turns. She produced a net Bill had not noticed earlier and scooped the fish from the water. The fish flopped in the net, and Tanya brought her hand underneath the net to keep it still. After inspecting her catch, Tanya carefully disengaged the hook and released the fish into the stream. With a flap of its tail, the fish disappeared.

"Bravo," said Bill, clapping. "Excellent." Tanya's head jerked his way, and Bill waved wildly.

She adjusted her gear and waded across the stream to where he stood.

"You made it," she said with a smile. "The office said you might come."

"I watched you fishing. You were magnificent."

Tanya climbed the bank and shook his hand. In the waders, she stood a few inches taller than Bill. She had a confident grip and shiny blue eyes. They sat on a nearby tree trunk where she had stashed her gear.

Bill asked if she fished often. Not nearly enough. How had she come into it? Did her father teach her? No, Fair Game employees were provided free access to a pool of sports equipment and encouraged to use them. Tanya soon found she enjoyed nature and eventually learned to fish, hunt, and camp.

As they spoke, Bill formed a positive impression of Tanya Stafford. She was a talented and independent woman who spoke her mind, and he would have gladly spent more time discussing leisure activities, but she was also a busy woman, and he had a job to do. Bill shared that the police had asked for his assistance, and he had a few questions.

Tanya shrugged. "Sure. But I'm surprised. Shields told me they no longer suspect me of pushing Damian."

"That's true."

"Case closed, right? Damian had a heart attack and fell off a cliff. It's a bummer, definitely, but what's to investigate?"

Bill then shared that Susskind may have been poisoned with a substance capable of inducing a heart attack.

"Poisoned," said Tanya in a surprised voice. But then her executive instincts kicked in, and she processed the information quietly. As head of operations for a large retail company, she often received unexpected news. Her managers could handle routine activities, but when something ran badly off the rails, they reported it to Tanya.

Bill told Tanya about the alcohol and the MDMA.

"MDMA?" she said, surprised once again.

"Yes, are you aware of Damian ever taking MDMA?"

"No," she said emphatically. "Never. That wasn't his style."

"What about the alcohol?"

"That makes sense." Tanya closed her eyes and massaged her temple as if that gentle motion might improve her memory. "We had a little party on the back deck after lunch. Damian had a new scotch he wanted us to try. I can't remember the name—started with a B. I think he also had wine with lunch."

"Do you remember who poured the whiskey?"

Tanya gazed at the sky and spent another moment with her memories. "Damian poured the whiskey. When he came out of his study, he carried four rocks glasses in one hand and the bottle in the other. I remember because he had to be careful with the glasses when he got to the table."

"Who tried the whiskey?"

"All of the men and me. Angie and Lacey didn't. They don't like whiskey. Personally, I love it, but as usual, Damian poured too much in each glass. I don't believe anyone finished theirs, except perhaps Damian." Tanya turned her head to the side. "So, your theory is that someone poisoned the whiskey. It's possible, I suppose. But the more interesting question is who. Who would have wanted to kill Damian?"

Tanya pondered her question, and Bill let her. Sometimes the best move in an interview was to stop asking questions.

"Lacey certainly had a reason," said Tanya.

Bill leaned in. "Why do you say that?"

"Because she and Evan are spending a lot of time together. At night. If you follow me."

"I do."

"It's not supposed to be public information, but I picked up on the vibe and pressed Evan for details. He fessed up in two seconds but then begged me to keep it a secret. Apparently, Damian was not keen on those two hooking up. If you wanted to remain an heir, you had to stay on Damian's good side. No romantic relationship means much to Evan. There's always another girl at the dance for him. But Lacey is smitten with Evan. She cares a lot. Knocking Damian out of the way would put her one move closer to locking down her dream guy." Tanya put the words *dream guy* in air quotes as if she would have never considered such a goal worthy of pursuit. She pulled off her cap to play with the rim, then said, "Just spitballing here, but if Lacey did poison Damian, that would give her an excellent reason to accuse me of pushing Damian off the cliff. Shields believes Lacey experienced an optical illusion. Maybe. Maybe not."

One of Tanya's characteristics that Bill liked was her coldly analytical approach to gnarly issues. He imagined her debating the opening of a new store with her colleagues. Did the local market demographics fit their target? How close was the planned location to highways they used to replenish inventory? What did the numbers say?

Still, he wanted to get her off the subject of Lacey Akin, so he said, "Describe Damian's relationship with Angie Finch. I understand they were engaged."

Tanya wrinkled her nose. "I didn't consider Angie, but I guess she had a reason too. When Damian broke off the engagement, Angie took it hard. Not that they ended the relationship." Tanya nodded fiercely. "Oh, yes, they were still sleeping together. I don't understand getting bent out of shape over an aborted marriage. What's the big deal? But I guess a woman like Angie Finch dreams of getting a ring on her finger. And then, of course, there's the money."

Bill recalled Angie's red-tinged eyes the previous day. Could that have been an act? How long did it take a regretful killer to shift emotional gears from rage to grief?

"You mentioned money," he said. "I suppose you may have stood to inherit a lot of money."

Tanya lifted a hand of indifference. "Who knows? Damian was all over the place about his inheritance. One year, he loved me. The next year, he hated me. This year, he started chattering about giving most of his fortune to charity. As for me personally, sure, if he left me ten or twenty million, I'd be grateful, but it wouldn't change my life much. I already make plenty to meet my needs. And I plan to work for the rest of my life no matter how much money I have. I *need* work to keep me sane. Work is my life."

It was a soft pitch that Bill couldn't resist.

"On the subject of work," he said, "I gather that Damian was considering hiring an outsider to run the company. How did you feel about that?"

For the first time, anger crossed Tanya's face, and Bill felt sorry for anyone on her team who made a costly mistake.

"You *know* how it made me feel. It pissed me off. I've broken my back for Damian's company. Over the past year, he's been a flake." Tanya pointed at herself. "*I've* kept the thing together. *Me.* I'm the one who made sure everything was moving along as it should. And then he had the nerve to tell me he was bringing in someone else." She held her hands up as if ready to choke a neck. "I could have strangled him. I would have enjoyed it."

Bill kept his face still. He'd had a lot of practice with not showing his emotions. But his heart was racing forward like it did whenever he sensed a confession lingered nearby.

Tanya took a deep breath. "But then I realized he wasn't himself. Damian's mind wasn't as sharp as it used to be. Also, killing him would likely result in me going to prison, and I wouldn't enjoy prison work. So I decided if he hired someone else, I'd search for another job."

Bill thanked Tanya for her time and returned to his car. She was a self-sufficient woman who didn't need another living soul to make her way in the world, and he respected her for that. He didn't want Tanya to be guilty, and her reasons for not killing Damian made sense. But at the same time, Bill believed she possessed a stronger will than any of the other suspects.

At Monocan Drive and 151, a Nelson County squad car roared past from right to left with its lights flashing. Bill wondered what was up. Then he turned right, and his cell phone buzzed. It was a text from Alex Sharp asking him to stop by the office.

FORTY-ONE

Bill found Alex Sharp in the conference room wearing a severe expression. Krista and Mitch sat with him and appeared somber as well. Goodness. Who else died?

"What's up?" Bill said.

Alex said, "Nelson County has picked up Maddie Katz for questioning."

Bill's eyes darted from Alex to Mitch to Krista. Krista nodded back.

"When I met her yesterday, she seemed nice," said Alex. "But it appears we've found our killer."

Bill sat across the table from Alex. His mouth felt dry, and his knee began to bounce.

Alex looked at Krista. "Run Bill through what you found."

Krista consulted her notes. "Maddie attended college in Harrisonburg for a year. She did well in her first semester but then hooked up with the wrong kind of guy and got heavily involved in the party scene. The police raided one party and charged Maddie's boyfriend with narcotics possession.

MDMA was involved. Maddie wound up in the hospital and earned a pot possession charge that was later dropped."

"Okay" was all Bill could say.

Maddie had told him college did not agree with her. That was one way of putting it. But a pot charge didn't prove Maddie had killed Susskind. No, they must have more. Sure enough, Krista was still consulting her notes.

"The boyfriend wound up in prison, and Maddie moved from Harrisonburg to Charlottesville three years ago. She worked at a grocery store for a year, then at several different bars, then got a job as a clerk at the Fair Game store on 29."

Oh, boy, thought Bill, *here comes the bombshell.*

"Maddie didn't last long at Fair Game. Management warned her several times for missing shifts and told her they'd let her go if it happened again. Well, she missed another shift, but apparently, this time she had a legitimate excuse—something about having to help a neighbor in a crisis. This incident created a huge debate within the company that the bureaucracy eventually kicked to the top. Guess who made the final call? Damian Susskind. Thumbs down."

Bill rubbed a hand over his eyes. "All right. What did she do then?"

"According to the vice president of human resources, word somehow got back to Maddie that Damian had fired her. Then, out of the blue, Maddie showed up at the corporate office, high on something, and demanded to see Damian Susskind. Security stopped her and called the police, but not before Maddie threatened to kill Damian."

"Jeez," said Bill. "What a nightmare."

"Maddie's parents hired a lawyer, and the judge gave Maddie a light sentence. Community service. Plus, she had to move back home and get some counseling. That was this past March. Nothing of note since then."

Two days earlier, when the catering crew drove from Cindy's condo to Damian Susskind's house, Bill had noticed that Maddie never played with her phone. She had dropped all of her social media apps. Why? Had she been too busy planning a murder to bother with Instagram? Had Maddie somehow learned that Cindy catered to Susskind and then applied for the assistant job when it came up? Had she slipped MDMA and digitalis into Damian's coffee to exact her revenge? It seemed so implausible.

"How long has Maddie worked for Cindy?" said Mitch.

The question pulled Bill back to the present. "About three months."

"And how long has Cindy had Susskind as a customer?" said Mitch.

"I'm not sure. Maybe six months now."

"That sounds like it then," said Alex.

Quite possibly. Maddie certainly had the opportunity to poison Damian. But motive? Murder was drastic retribution for getting fired from a low-paying job. Then again, he'd seen folks murdered for less. Murder over an insult was not uncommon, but that was typically a spur-of-the-moment thing. Whoever murdered Damian had planned their actions well in advance. Could Maddie have done it? Possibly. In any case, she faced tough questions from Arnie Shields and the sheriff.

What should Bill do? If Maddie was guilty and broke in the face of Arnie Shields's glare, the case would be washed, dried, and folded by the end of the day. But if she was innocent—maybe a long shot but possible—then Bill still had a job to do. Until they heard the news from Nelson County, Bill might as well continue down the path he was on. After his earlier conversations with Evan, Lacey, and Tanya, it was time to give Whit Whitlock an update. Based on what he'd learned from the others, Bill was intensely curious about the contents of Susskind's will.

After the conference room meeting, Bill grabbed a cup of coffee and rolled back around to Alex's office, where the interim chief sat behind his desk typing on a keyboard.

"Got another minute?" said Bill.

"Sure."

"Did state forensics test that bottle of Braemore?"

Alex nodded. "I forgot to mention it. They found the bottle and tested it but detected no trace of digitalis or MDMA. The sheriff wants to keep the house sealed for another day or two, but they have allowed the guests to retrieve their personal belongings."

"It's a shame about the test," said Bill. "I thought that might be it."

Alex regarded Bill like he was the slow kid in class. "I believe Maddie poisoned Damian's coffee, but there's no way to prove that now."

"Yeah, you're probably right. Hey, I want to ask a favor. Reach out to Arnie Shields and ask him if I can visit with Maddie Katz. Maddie and I hit it off well, and she might tell me something she wouldn't tell them."

Alex shrugged. "What if she's already confessed?"

"I'd still like to see her."

"Okay. I'll ask Arnie."

"In the meantime, I'm going to reach out to Whit Whitlock."

Deep furrows formed on Alex's forehead. "What for? If the case is solved, there's no need to rile people up any longer."

At his core, Alex was still a real estate broker who prioritized relationship management, and Damian Susskind's friends and heirs were all potential future clients.

"No case is solved until the hard evidence is in hand," said Bill. "We don't have that yet. Until we do, we should keep plugging away."

"All right, but go easy."

Bill lifted his hands. "Kid gloves, always."

On the way out of the office, Bill stopped by Krista's desk and found her staring at her monitor. Her red hair was pulled out of the way to reveal her long, beautiful neck. Krista was quite a sight in her police uniform, and once again, Bill found it surprising that she was unattached. If you searched for idiot on Wikipedia, you might find a photo of her ex-husband.

"Nice work today," he said. "Great summary, too."

Krista turned and smiled shyly at Bill. "Thanks."

"Did you find anything on Justin?"

"No, totally clean. What should I do next?"

"Hmm." Bill folded his arms. "Good question. Maybe you should do background checks on everyone else, although it seems like we know a lot about them already."

"That won't take long. When that's done, I'll do a deep dive on Susskind himself to see what turns up. I might find a useful tidbit."

Bill doubted Krista would learn much more from her internet searches, but he wanted to keep her engaged and excited, so he nodded and said, "Let's do it. Contact me if you find something interesting."

"You bet."

"How are things at home?"

Krista shook her head. "It's a never-ending circus, Bill. A never-ending circus. Last night, Trevor told me he now officially has a girlfriend."

"Don't say that. Trevor's what, twelve years old?"

"That's right. And he's a little too much like his daddy." Krista shook a finger. "But if he tries any tricks with this girl, he'll have to answer to me."

Bill laughed. "He sounds like a handful. Better keep your eyes sharp."

"I always do."

Out in his car, Bill sent a text to Whit Whitlock to set up an appointment in Charlottesville the next day. To his surprise, Whit had continued to stay at the Mountain Inn and was available to chat in fifteen minutes.

FORTY-TWO

"It's still hot in Charlottesville," said Whit Whitlock, "and it's so nice in Wintergreen, I decided to work here another day."

Whit had suggested they take a short walk on the Highland Leisure Trail, and they now strolled on a paved walkway not far from the Mountain Inn. Whit had been on his computer all day and wanted to breathe fresh air. On the left, the Timbers condo buildings offered their owners a stunning view. Up ahead, chairlift cables bellied to a support tower on the right. They strode past the chairlift station and through a condo parking lot to the trail.

"I'll go back tomorrow to check on MaryEllen," said Whit, "but she's fine. She likes having a few days by herself. It makes her feel more independent."

Bill and Whit both possessed information they were reluctant to share. Bill wanted to know the details of Susskind's will. And as Damian's executor, Whit wanted Bill to keep him apprised of the investigation's progress. Having been married to an attorney, Bill doubted Whit would share anything without getting something in return. With that in mind, Bill gave Whit an overview of the investigators' findings thus far. The forensics results. MDMA. Digitalis. As had the others, Whit expressed great surprise at the prospect that someone had poisoned Damian. Whit had believed all along that Damian fell by accident; whether the accident occurred as a result of a heart attack seemed of little consequence. Even after the forensics report, Whit held the same view. Forensics teams made mistakes. It happened all the time. But then Bill shared the news of Maddie Katz's background and reported that the sheriff had taken her in.

"From the catering crew?" said Whit, incredulous. He stopped on the trail to stare wide-eyed at Bill. "The young woman?"

"Yes."

"That's mind-boggling. So the theory is that Ms. Katz knew they were catering for Damian, and she purposefully laced his food or beverage with MDMA and digitalis."

"Uh-huh. That's the current thinking."

Whit shook his head. "I guess stranger things have happened, but that's one of the more spectacular stories I've ever heard."

"Of course, it could be a coincidence that Maddie was on the catering crew. We don't have hard evidence that she poisoned Damian."

"I thought policemen didn't believe in coincidences."

Bill scratched his neck with a fingernail. Whit made an excellent point. As a rule, Bill regarded coincidences with a great deal of skepticism. Nevertheless, they did occur once in a while.

Tall hardwood trees surrounded the men, and a huge boulder lay on the trail to the left. A woodpecker knocked on a tree high in the air.

Whit pushed his lips out and turned his head to stare in

the direction of the woodpecker. “Then again, if this young woman is guilty, it frees me to execute Damian’s will without delay. That would be helpful.”

“That brings up a subject I wanted to ask you about,” Bill said. He shared that Evan claimed Damian had shifted most of Evan’s share of the inheritance to charity. Tanya had reported that Damian mentioned giving money to charity but said his mind changed from day to day.

Whit frowned. “Of course, I wasn’t in the conversation with you and Evan, but what you’ve told me is inaccurate. Damian intended to shift much of Evan’s share to charity and put the rest in a trust with conditions attached. Damian shared his intention with Evan months ago. The trust was put in place; however, the charitable gift concept was never implemented. Damian flirted with many charities but didn’t make a final decision until a few weeks ago, and the changes were never made to his will. Evan knows all of this because I told him as much.”

“Does that mean Evan will inherit a great deal of money?” asked Bill.

“Yes, provided he meets the conditions of the trust.”

“What about the others? Tanya and Lacey and Angie.”

“They each will receive an inheritance. Angie will inherit far less than the other two but still a tidy sum.”

“And the charity?”

Whit shrugged. “I’m afraid the charity is out of luck. With Damian’s history of continually changing his mind, anything that is not signed already could not be considered valid.”

When Bill paused to consider what Whit had told him, the attorney turned to proceed quickly up the path. For a man who appeared out of shape, Whit moved fast, and Bill had to hustle to catch up.

After a few hundred yards, they reached a wooden overlook platform on the right. The mountain slope dropped away, and they had a clear view down into the valley. The condo ridge was to their left, and Bill ran his eye across the line of condo buildings until he found his and Cindy's. Whit stood with his elbows on the railing.

Bill said, "I understand from some of the others that Damian drank whiskey on the back deck that day after lunch."

Whit considered Bill's statement and then nodded. "Yes, a new scotch that had him excited. Several of us tried it."

"Do you remember who poured the scotch and who drank it?"

After reflection, Whit said, "Evan and I tried the scotch with Damian. And I seem to recall that Damian offered it to Tanya also. I believe Damian poured the whiskey. Yes, I'm almost sure of it."

"What was the brand?"

Whit rubbed his chin. "I'd never heard of it. Brae-something. Braecliff. No, that's not right. Braemore. That's it. Braemore. Why are you interested in the scotch?" But then Whit nodded and answered his own question. "I get it. You think someone may have poisoned the whiskey. But I don't see how."

Neither did Bill, which left the coffee and the tea. He frowned. Maddie had seemed a nice young woman, but her future appeared bleak. At that moment, Cindy texted Bill asking him to stop by her condo. He replied that he'd be there soon, and then he and Whit returned to the Mountain Inn.

FORTY-THREE

When Bill knocked on Cindy's door, she answered almost immediately and stepped into the stairwell landing to be with him. She glanced up and down the stairs to ensure no one else was nearby.

"Kim Wiley told me they arrested Maddie. Is that true?"

Goodness. News traveled faster in Nelson County than it did on the internet.

"I don't know if they've arrested her yet," he said, "but the sheriff brought her in for questioning."

Cindy's eyes seared into him. "And I have to hear it from Kim Wiley? You didn't think to let me know?"

"I . . . I was going to tell you, but things came up." Bill looked at his shoes. "Sorry, I should have texted you."

"Yeah, you should have. When you're dating a cop, people assume you know what's going on. Kim called me to get more information, and I didn't know diddly."

Bill lifted his hands in frustration. Some days, he just couldn't win.

Cindy sighed and said, "Justin's upset. Come in and tell us what you know."

It might have been the first time Bill had seen Justin sitting down without a phone in his hand. Instead, he slouched in the corner of the sofa and stared at the coffee table. The sliding doors onto the balcony were open to the fresh air. Outside, the sunlight against the mountains had softened with the lateness of the afternoon.

Bill told them what the police had learned about Maddie's past. When he revealed the threat Maddie had made at Fair Game's corporate office, Cindy's face grew strained.

"She wanted to kill Damian Susskind?" said Cindy.

Bill shrugged. "I wasn't there. This is third-hand knowledge, but it appears that Maddie uses, or did use, recreational drugs."

"I'm shocked," said Cindy. "She's been a reliable worker. And pleasant too."

Justin shook his head. "I invited her to go to the Edge a few nights ago. She said she doesn't drink."

Bill recalled that the four of them had wine in Cindy's condo the night of the murder. But on reflection, he wasn't sure whether Maddie had even touched hers.

"I don't for an instant believe Maddie killed Susskind," said Cindy, getting herself worked up. "So she poured his coffee. That doesn't prove anything."

Bill took a seat in one of the living room chairs, hoping that Cindy would do the same. "The police have to go where the evidence takes them, and the evidence has blazed a trail to Maddie."

"No," said Cindy. "She's not guilty. I know it."

"But how well do we know her?" said Bill.

Cindy was still standing and had now folded her arms across her chest. "Are you trying to say I don't know how to read people? I've hired hundreds of people in my career. But never a murderer."

Bill nodded to show Cindy he understood her feelings. But truthfully, she had only known Maddie a few months. None of them knew Maddie well. Cindy was still going off of her first impression. His first impression of Maddie was also favorable, but experience told him first impressions were often wrong. The only way to know a person was to observe their actions over a long period.

Justin had gone silent. He sat still and nervously kneaded the palm of one hand.

"Justin," said Bill. "Are you okay?"

"I remembered something. When Maddie and I went for a walk the other day, she mentioned Damian. I didn't focus on it at the time, but now I don't know. I had told her I thought Damian's retreat was awesome and that it must feel good for someone to make enough bank to buy a sweet second home. Then Maddie said Damian Susskind was not who he appeared to be. I didn't think anything of it at the time."

"That doesn't prove she's guilty either," said Cindy, her indignation growing. "I agree with what she said. Rich people are never what they appear to be."

"You're right," said Justin. "That doesn't prove a thing." Then Justin turned toward Bill. "I'd like to see her. Is that possible?"

"Probably not today," said Bill. "The sheriff's department will have their hands full. They'll interview her. She might bring in a lawyer. The prosecuting attorney will need to weigh in."

"Yes, but you can see her, right?" said Cindy with cynicism. "You can do that much. Or can you?"

Cindy's implication was clear—what was the point of dating a cop if it only came with a downside? There had to be some advantage to balance the hassle of everyone knowing you were hanging out with an ex-policeman.

"I already put the request in through Alex."

"Yeah? What did Alex say?"

Cindy had sprinted to Maddie's defense. Why? Surely, she could see how the odds were stacking. Maddie had access to recreational drugs. Maddie had a criminal record. And Maddie had verbally threatened the victim.

"Did you check Maddie's references before you hired her?" he asked.

"Of course, I checked her reference. A bar manager in Charlottesville raved about her."

A bar manager. That was quite a reference. And Cindy had used the singular form of the word reference. Then Bill understood. Cindy was rising to defend the oppressed. Of course, the powers that be would rush to lock Maddie up. Surely, it was Maddie, a young and relatively poor woman, who had killed Damian Susskind, not one of the wealthy and older suspects who had dined at his table. Yeah, well, maybe Cindy had a point.

"I'll text Alex to nudge him," said Bill. "See if I can get in to see Maddie tonight."

FORTY-FOUR

Once at home, Krista baked a store-brand pizza and made a salad of leafy greens and tomatoes from the garden. Over dinner, she listened to the boys' reports of the day's activities, and then she helped them wash the dishes so they could get to their homework sooner. After her conversation with Bill about doing a deep dive on Damian Susskind, Krista had been distracted by everyday duties that demanded her time. More than likely, the next day would be the same, but with the boys back in their room and David and Goliath settled in for an early evening snooze, she could spend an uninterrupted hour on the internet.

A search on Damian Susskind and Fair Game returned bio information and pages and pages of articles and social media references to the company. She flipped through screens. Her eyes flitted down the monitor, stopping on each entry for only a second or two. She became progressively more efficient at discarding routine entries. Store openings. Sales announcements. Tie-ins with local sporting events.

On the seventh screen, an article from the *News Leader,* the local paper for Staunton, caught Krista's eye. Damian

Susskind had made a hundred-thousand-dollar donation to the Museum of Early American Leisure. The museum was a modest institution housed in a former residence on Beverly Street. Krista had never personally visited the museum or even heard of it. Although considered newsworthy, the donation was a modest amount from Damian Susskind's perspective, and after giving the article a brief scan, Krista returned to her search results. But then she paused. The search had returned nothing else of note thus far, and Krista was already fifteen minutes into the hour she had allocated. So, she returned to the article and clicked on the museum link.

The Museum of Early American Leisure was dedicated to preserving artifacts and paintings of leisure activities pursued by residents of the Appalachian Mountains region before 1850. The article had included an image of an oil painting depicting indigenous Americans and settlers playing lacrosse. Krista scanned the museum's website and found a tab for news. The museum had announced Damian's donation several months earlier and included quotes from the president and Damian. The president, a woman named Jane Yarborough, thanked Damian for his support and welcomed him onto the museum's board of trustees. Damian expressed his enthusiasm and verbally committed time and additional money to support the museum's aggressive plans for future growth.

Krista sat back in her chair. The announcement made it sound like the hundred-thousand-dollar donation was only a hint of things to come. This might be a bigger deal than Krista first imagined. She clicked on the *About Us* tab, which led her to a listing of the board of trustees, where she found a photo and a brief bio of Damian Susskind. Krista blinked several times at the name of a fellow trustee, because she knew the woman, at least by reputation. Frieda Chang was an author of steamy romance novels—several of which Krista had read with delight—and also happened to be a resident of the Cliffs, a Wintergreen complex on the ridge next to where Bill O'Shea lived.

Krista swallowed, thrilled at the prospect that the lead might give her a chance to meet Frieda Chang in person. She called Bill.

He picked up on the second ring.

"Hey, Krista."

There was a great deal of background noise on the call.

"Are you driving?" she said.

"Yeah. I'm headed down to the sheriff's office in Lovingston. Going to see Maddie Katz. What's up?"

"I found something."

Krista walked him through the results of her search.

"That's interesting," he said.

Krista disliked it when Bill said something was interesting. It shared almost nothing of what he thought, only that he didn't consider what she'd told him boring. But she didn't probe him for more. Maybe someday she would, but she didn't feel she had the standing to do that yet.

"What should I do?" she asked.

"Try to contact this Frieda Chang. See if she's open to meeting with me in the morning."

"You want me to come along?"

After she'd said the words, Krista realized her tone was borderline desperate.

Bill hesitated, as if considering her question from different angles, then said, "Yes. It's your lead. You should come."

FORTY-FIVE

By the time Bill made his way to Lovingston and found the parking lot of the sheriff's office, the sun had fully set. His headlights shone on the back of an RV painted in the department's colors. A tagline across the bottom read *Unwillingly Donated by a Nelson County Drug Dealer*. Bill chuckled. How resourceful.

Inside, Bill thanked Arnie Shields for letting him come.

With brown hair and a thick mustache, Arnie sat on the edge of a desk and shook his head. He seemed tired.

"Maddie's a sad-looking girl, Bill. In a mountain of trouble, and she knows it."

"Did she confess?"

"Not yet. Can't say that I blame her. We don't exactly have a smoking gun."

"Is she using?"

Arnie shrugged. "Not that I can tell. She's not a meth addict. That much I know for sure—we've seen too many of those here in the county. Her mother came by a while ago and said Maddie's been good for six months now, swears her girl would never do something like this. But it's a heck of a coincidence—Maddie threatens Susskind like that, winds up working at his house half a year later, and then he gets poisoned."

Arnie told Bill to wait in a small interview room and had a deputy bring Maddie in. Dressed in jeans and an old sweater, Maddie's hair needed a touch-up, and her eyes were scared. She wore no makeup but otherwise seemed fine. Bill wondered how her appearance would change after she spent the night in jail.

On the drive over from Wintergreen, Bill had planned for this moment. What could he say that Arnie and the others had not already tried? If Maddie wouldn't confess to them, he'd have no better luck unless he came up with a different approach.

"You put Cindy in a heck of a jam," he said. "When word gets around that her staff poisons the food, she'll have a hard time finding new clients."

"I didn't poison anybody."

"Don't play innocent," he said menacingly. "You knew who Damian Susskind was. You knew darn well because you had threatened to kill him. And you didn't say a word to Cindy."

Maddie squirmed in her chair. "I feel bad about that."

He leaned forward and pointed a finger. "You *should* feel bad. You should feel awful. Now, tell me what happened. Tell me everything."

If he could get her talking and she was guilty, she would slip up somewhere along the way.

Maddie gnawed on a fingernail.

He resisted the temptation to make a remark.

"That other time?" she said. "At the corporate office? The cops arrested me then too. I knew I had to change." Maddie slumped her shoulders. "Jamie, my ex-boyfriend, went to prison. I visited him once, and he told me not to come back. He told me I should run away from that life as fast as possible. But I didn't listen, not until I got arrested in Charlottesville. Sitting in that jail cell, Jamie's advice came back to me, and I made a decision."

"Made what decision?"

"No more partying. No more drugs. I moved back home and cut my old ties from Harrisonburg and Charlottesville. I dropped all my social media."

Bill nodded. That much made sense.

Maddie's fingers rapidly tapped the table. "I got the job with Cindy and thought, *Okay, this is good.* I liked the work, and it was honest. Living at home was okay too. But when I realized Cindy catered for Damian Susskind, I was horrified."

"But you didn't say anything."

The guilt was written all over Maddie's face. "I knew she'd fire me if I did."

Not a bad assumption. At the least, Cindy would have taken Maddie off the Susskind gig, and she might have fired Maddie outright. Bill would have. Why take the risk? On the other hand, if no one gave Maddie a second chance, how could she ever move forward?

"Then I met Justin." Maddie pressed a fist against her left eye. "He went to college and all, but he's still a good guy. And he's going into the Coast Guard. And I thought, maybe, something might happen between Justin and me." Maddie heaved a sigh and threw her hands to the sides. "And then all this happened."

"Are you telling me you didn't get mad when you saw Damian Susskind?"

Maddie sat tall in the chair. "Yes, I was mad. He was a jerk. Another rich guy who stomped on poor people."

"It's a nice story, Maddie, but I'm not buying. You still have a stash of MDMA somewhere from your party days."

Her eyes widened. "I don't. I swear."

"You made a concoction of ground-up MDMA and dried foxglove and then put it in his tea."

Maddie pulled her arms off the table and slumped. Her eyes cut to the door. "They don't believe me, and you don't believe me. My folks can't afford another lawyer, so I'll take my chances with whoever Nelson County gives me. But stop trying to make me confess. Just leave me alone."

"You're telling me you don't have any MDMA."

"Zip. Told you. I left that world."

"But you would know how to get it."

Maddie shrugged. "That stuff's not hard to get."

Bill knew Maddie might be lying to him. He had met excellent liars in his career, and he had long ago lost faith in his ability to judge a person's words by their voice or body language. But pressing Maddie for a confession was doing him no good, so he decided to take a different approach by assuming, for the moment, that she was innocent.

He said, "Have you ever heard of an older man like Damian Susskind using MDMA?"

She shook her head. "No. Not a guy like that. Country club guys get crushed on booze."

"So how did he get it in his system?"

"No clue."

"Why don't you consider my question for a second before answering?" Impatience had crept into Bill's voice. "If you didn't poison Susskind, someone else did."

"Wait, are you saying you believe me?"

"No. Not yet. But if you are innocent, you'd be smart to spend your time trying to figure out who poisoned Susskind and how they did it."

Maddie tilted her head.

"Did you see anything unusual at lunch?" he said. "Maybe one of the others around the table lingered over Damian's coffee long enough to put something in it."

She shook her head. "I don't remember anything like that."

"Give it some more time. Try to recreate every moment from when you first entered Damian's house right through lunch. The best way to help yourself now is to give me something I can use."

Maddie got right to it. She bit her lip, stared at the tabletop, and barely nodded when Bill left the room.

In the lobby, Arnie asked Bill if he'd learned anything new.

"No, she's sticking to the woe-is-me-I'm-innocent line. But I'm not sure she's guilty, either."

"Are you still interviewing Susskind's guests?"

"Yep." Bill shared what he'd learned about the whiskey tasting session and his thoughts on possible motives.

"An eighty-million-dollar inheritance?" said Arnie.

"Uh-huh. Ballpark estimate."

Arnie scratched his cheek. "I have to admit that makes for a lot of motive to go around."

FORTY-SIX

The next morning at ten o'clock, Bill walked up from his condo to the Cliffs, where he met Krista standing by her orange Subaru Forrester. They approached the condo building entrance, and a white poodle yapped from an open window. As they drew nearer, the poodle's warnings became ferocious.

"That must be Curly," said Krista.

"Curly? You know this beast?"

Krista smiled shyly. "I told you Ms. Chang is a romance novelist."

"The spicy kind, right?"

"Uh-huh. Anyway, I've listened to a few of Ms. Chang's stories, and I follow her on Instagram. She's always posting photos of her and Curly in Wintergreen settings."

"Okay."

Bill had read two romance novels in his life, both on the recommendation of his ex-wife Wanda—who ran through them like she ran through tissues—but he had not acquired a taste for them.

After Bill knocked on Ms. Chang's door, Curly's yapping approached from inside and grew louder still.

Krista raised her eyebrows.

Then, one of the tallest women Bill had ever met answered the door. She had to be six feet five or six, but he didn't have time to assess more than her height, as the poodle scampered into the hallway and ran two quick circles around Krista and Bill.

The tall woman laughed. "Don't mind Curly. He has a loud bark but has never bitten anyone."

Curly quieted as soon as Bill and Krista crouched and held non-threatening hands out for him to sniff. Curly decided he preferred Bill's hand and began licking Bill's fingers. Bill scratched around Curly's ears, and the dog ran inside.

Bill stood, and the woman said, "Hello, I'm Frieda."

In dark pants and a turquoise shirt, Frieda Chang towered over Bill. She had a beautiful round face with dark eyes and wore red lip gloss. Her hair was blond and curly. Frieda invited them inside and offered cups of coffee, which they both accepted.

Bill examined her condo. The layout was similar to his, but her furnishings indicated that Ms. Chang knew a lot about style and had the financial wherewithal to match her tastes.

They took seats in the living room, and after introductions, Frieda said Krista's name was familiar. Krista said she had worked dispatch one day when Frieda called about a matter requiring police attention.

"Now I remember," said Frieda, "and I promised you a signed book that I never delivered."

Frieda hopped up and jogged to one of the back bedrooms. She returned with two copies of the same paperback novel—*Sherie's Demise*—and signed one for Krista.

Frieda Chang moved with an athletic grace that made Bill wonder if she had ever played sports, perhaps volleyball or basketball. But he refrained from asking. She likely got that question from strangers all the time.

"Would you like one?" asked Frieda, holding the second book in his direction.

"Um."

"You won't offend me if you say no. I realize the romance genre is not for everyone. Maybe you have a friend."

"Yes, please. Make it out to Cindy." Bill spelled Cindy's name.

He examined the cover briefly. A scantily clad young woman—Sherie, presumably—was held in the arms of a young man with three days of beard growth and a freakishly sculpted bare chest.

"How can I help you?" said Frieda.

Curly nudged Bill's leg, and he leaned forward to scratch the poodle's ears again. "Krista, perhaps you can paint the landscape for Frieda."

"Yeah, okay."

Krista's voice quivered slightly at first but gained confidence as she got further into her briefing. At the end of her summary, Krista asked Frieda if her portrayal was consistent with the facts.

"Yes," said Frieda. "I'm on the museum's board, and so was Damian."

Krista glanced at Bill as if to ask, *Should I continue?* Bill nodded yes.

"Reading between the lines of the article," said Krista, "I gather Damian Susskind had intended to give a larger donation to the charity. Is that correct?"

Frieda nodded. "He promised a huge donation. Forty million dollars' worth of stock in his company—Fair Game."

Bill sat straighter in his chair.

"Forty million," said Krista, a bit starstruck, but she recovered quickly. "What more can you tell us about this donation?"

Frieda paused a moment to collect her thoughts. "It's important to keep in mind that a donation of such magnitude would transform the charity. We could afford a new and much larger facility, hundreds of additional artifacts, and a paid staff. It was exciting for the board, but at the same time stressful, because Damian attached one condition to his generous donation. He insisted that we replace the current director."

"Jane Yarborough," said Krista.

"That's right," said Frieda. "You've done your homework. Jane is a nice person and perfectly capable of managing a museum with an annual budget of a few hundred thousand dollars. But she has no formal training in museum curation and lacks the management and leadership skills demanded by Damian's much larger vision. So, after some soul-searching, the trustees unanimously agreed that we would dismiss Jane once the donation came through."

In her navy uniform, Krista sat perfectly still with her eyes glued to Frieda Chang. The story of Damian's donation and its impact on Jane Yarborough's world had captured Krista's attention like one of Ms. Chang's romance novels. Krista breathlessly awaited the next chapter, and frankly, so did Bill.

"Unfortunately," said Frieda, "the task of broaching the matter with Jane fell to me. I'm afraid I sort of chickened out on the conversation with Jane. Instead of firing her outright, I told her it was merely a concept under consideration." Frieda paused to sigh. "Jane was upset, and of course, she guessed right away that a donation of that magnitude could only come from Damian."

"What's her status now?" asked Bill.

Frieda shrugged. "She's still the museum's director. I last spoke with Damian two weeks ago when he said the paperwork required for the donation would be completed within a week or less. Now, I don't know where it stands, which is problematic concerning Jane's status. After hearing of Damian's death, I planned to give it a few days and then try to sort the details by tracking down the executor of Damian's estate."

Based on what Whit Whitlock had told Bill in their last meeting, Frieda was in for quite a shock because the donation had never gone through. It wasn't Bill's place to deliver news on behalf of Damian's estate, but he did share with Frieda that Whit was the executor.

Neither Bill nor Krista had more questions for Frieda, but they stayed to finish their coffee. Bill shared that he lived in the Vistas condos next door, and Frieda said he must visit the next time she had neighbors over for wine.

Frieda nodded at the novel in Bill's hand. "You can bring Cindy too."

"Thank you. We'd like that."

At the door, Bill stooped to pat Curly's head. The day was off to a good start—he had made two new friends.

Outside in the parking lot, Krista asked, "So, should we consider this Jane Yarborough a suspect?"

"Why would we do that?"

"I know it seems a remote possibility, but she has a motive. By killing Damian, she could prevent the donation from going through and save her job."

"But she wasn't even at the house. We can't figure out

how anyone else poisoned Damian, let alone someone who wasn't there."

Krista pressed her lips tightly together and nodded.

Jeez. Bill had shut her down, which he knew was a mistake. He had no monopoly on bright ideas and needed all the help he could get. Two heads were better and so forth.

He said, "On the other hand, you make a good point regarding motive. Jane Yarborough may know something about the donation that we don't. It certainly won't do any harm for you to interview her in person. You should contact her."

Krista's demeanor brightened visibly. "Okay. Sure. Should I ask her to come to the station?"

"No. People naturally grow nervous when summoned by the police. They tighten up. You want her as relaxed as possible. Try to get her to share everything with you that she would share with a friend."

"Do you want to come?"

He shook his head. "You ride solo on this one. I've got more stuff to do here and may drive into Charlottesville again."

FORTY-SEVEN

Earlier that morning when Bill peered over his balcony railing, Mr. Chips was nowhere to be found. Perhaps the groundhog had slept in. After the interview with Frieda Chang, Bill strolled down to his condo building to get his car. Once he passed Cindy's building, he glanced right toward the ridge's edge and spied Mr. Chips nibbling on greens near his burrow entrance.

Bill waved. "Wait there, Mr. Chips. Be right back."

Inside his condo, Bill picked up a bright red beefsteak tomato and then hustled outside again. Having set the goal of getting a little closer to Mr. Chips every day, Bill now hoped to cross the ten-foot line. He held the tomato high and jiggled it to capture the groundhog's attention. Mr. Chips stood straight and dropped the greens.

Bill then repeated the routine he had established. Slow steps toward the target. No sudden moves. Everything was going according to plan. Twenty feet. Fifteen feet. Ten feet. Bill's heartbeat accelerated.

But suddenly, Mr. Chips stood straight and turned his head as if to listen for something. Bill frowned.

"Take it easy, Mr. Chips. I have a nice fat fruit here, but you only get it when you let me come a few feet closer."

It was as if Bill had said nothing at all. Mr. Chips turned his head farther to the side and lifted his nose to sniff. What in the heck? Mr. Chips pulled his head back, and then his whole body jerked. In the next instant, the groundhog rushed to his burrow entrance and disappeared.

"Dang it," said Bill. He stomped toward the entrance and leaned over to snarl. "What is your problem? You were happy to wait yesterday. Don't think I'll drop this tomato for you to eat at your leisure. These things aren't free, you know. This is a two-way street."

But then Bill heard a noise coming from beyond the drop-off of the hill. The grasses on the slope rustled. He sensed movement and got the unmistakable impression that another life-form approached. Then, a dark furry form rose above the slope not ten feet away. His heart pounded, and his eyes bulged.

Holy Peter, Paul, and Mary! It's a bear!

Bill dropped the tomato and fell on his butt in the grass.

But the bear kept coming. The mammal moved leisurely, one huge paw in front of the other. The black omnivore would reach Bill in a few instants.

Bill crab-walked backward, his eyes glued to the bear. The bear sniffed Mr. Chips's burrow entrance, pawed at it once, and noticed the tomato. Bill kept scrambling, his arms and legs a blur. The bear sat on its haunch, grabbed the tomato with both hands, and lifted it for a close inspection. Bill managed to stand and continued to increase his margin of safety. After sniffing the fruit, the bear decided it made for a suitable snack, and the tomato disappeared down the bear's gullet in the next instant.

Wait a minute. Bill knew that bear. The same varmint had

stolen his coffee and danish a few months earlier. Bill didn't harbor any ill will, although he was glad the bear had settled for Mr. Chips's tomato. On that other occasion, Bill's neighbor, Mrs. Spooner, had laughed at Bill and delighted at the bear's presence. She even had a name for the bear. What was it?

Ms. Betsy.

Bill waved. "H-hey, Ms. Betsy."

In answer to his greeting, Ms. Betsy rose and ambled toward him.

"You can stay there if you want to," said Bill.

Nothing doing. Ms. Betsy had places to go, and Bill stood in her path. He hustled to the sidewalk and then up the steps toward his building. Fortunately, Ms. Betsy paid him no mind. She sniffed his car door but apparently detected nothing of interest. After examining two other vehicles in the lot, she made her way into the woods and was soon gone from view.

Inside his condo, Bill poured a glass of water and sat at his dining table to wait for his heart to settle. Good lord. He lived in a wilderness area. What had ever possessed him to leave the safe confines of a civilized city? But in the next moment, he knew the answer. No matter how hard humans tried to create artificial structures of beauty, the results paled compared to what lay a few strides from his door. City dwellers scurried about in a frantic search for their next thrill. Better to take a walk in the woods.

Which reminded Bill that he had an appointment to do just that. He glanced at his phone. Better hurry or he'd be late for his meeting with Angie Finch.

FORTY-EIGHT

Bill drove across Fawn Ridge Drive, turned right on Laurel Springs Drive, and pulled onto the right shoulder at the spot where the Old Appalachian Trail crossed the road. Angie Finch stood next to a parked sedan.

She had texted Bill the previous night. Would he take her to the spot where Damian died? Of course.

Angie wore jeans and a windbreaker. The day was chilly, and the sky filled with heavy clouds that blocked the sun.

They exchanged greetings, his calibrated to match her state of grief, hers dull and short.

"Are you still at the Mountain Inn?" he asked.

She nodded. "Whit says I can stay at Damian's retreat until it's sold, but the sheriff still has the house sealed." She gestured to the road's shoulder. "Is that where they parked?"

"Yes. They came in Evan Hale's Land Rover."

Angie turned toward the trailhead. "Okay. Let's go."

Bill led the way through the forest. The clouds and treetops allowed so little light through that it seemed as if dusk was close at hand. Having worn only a sweater over a T-shirt, Bill had underdressed for the weather.

The trail wove around the mountain's contours. Although not athletic, Angie had no trouble keeping up. Every time Bill turned to check, she was scarcely a stride behind him, and he concluded that she must walk or jog for exercise. He picked up the pace.

They reached the halfway point without saying a word, and Bill decided that now might be the best time to ask a few questions. Who knew what state she'd be in after visiting the overlook? He started by asking whether Angie remembered the young caterer named Maddie. She did.

"Did you ever meet Maddie before she worked with Cindy?" he said.

"No."

"Did Damian ever mention her?"

"No, why do you ask?"

Bill explained that the sheriff had taken Maddie into custody and gave the reasons why.

"Good heavens," Angie said angrily. "She poisoned his coffee?"

Bill turned toward her and held up a cautionary hand. "We don't know that she's guilty yet. The prosecuting attorney has not filed charges."

"But you're certain that *someone* poisoned Damian."

"Yes, it appears so."

A dangerous rage filled Angie's eyes. It seemed that dark notions crossed her mind, but she didn't share them with Bill. He shivered.

When Damian broke off their engagement, how had she reacted? Had she cast those fiery eyes on him? Was her grief a ruse? No, she couldn't fake that. Or could she?

He turned to continue the hike and soon switched topics.

"I understand some of the group had a scotch on the back deck after lunch," he said. "Did you join them?"

"No, I don't like scotch. But it wasn't unusual for Damian to share whiskey with his guests. He kept meticulous records from each tasting session. I typed up his notes on every bottle. Wait, I see where you're going now. Someone may have poisoned the whiskey."

"Did you see who poured the whiskey?" Bill asked.

He had to wait for Angie to formulate an answer.

"Damian poured the whiskey," she said. "He tried to carry the bottle and four glasses out from his study, and I ran over to help him."

Bill asked if Angie recalled the brand, but she didn't.

"The others told me the scotch was labeled Braemore."

"I don't recognize that brand," she said. "And I remember all the brands because of my work on the tasting files. Damian must have found that scotch recently."

For the remaining distance to the overlook, Bill pondered Angie's statements. By her admission, she had handled the glasses on the back deck. Had she slipped something into Damian's scotch?

The trail inclined upward, and the forest brightened. The overlook was ahead and to the right. Hairs stood on the back of Bill's neck. How would Angie react when she reached the place of Damian's death? He slowed his pace and glanced at her. Angie fixed her eyes on the opening through the trees. Bill passed the last tree and climbed to where the dirt path turned to stone. The edge was twenty feet farther out, but they could see the vista from where they stood. The valley lay far below them. In the next instant, Angie strode past Bill toward the edge, and he raised a hand as if to stop her.

Bill's hands were clammy, and he could scarcely catch his breath. He took another step closer and then another. His throat grew tight. Angie stood at the precipice, fearless, or perhaps uncaring of the danger. Bill drew nearer, and the overlook fell away into space. The wind blew across the mountain's face, and the treetops moved in unison. Bill imagined Damian falling to his death.

Angie stepped even closer, and Bill suddenly realized why she had wanted to visit the overlook.

"It takes my breath away," she said, and she lifted her arms toward the mountain range in the distance.

Bill took a hesitant step toward her. And then another. His hands started shaking.

"It's a beautiful place to die."

"Angie, you're far too close. Please come away."

She spread her arms wide.

Oh, no. Don't. Don't jump.

Angie stood on tiptoes. Now. She would do it now. She would bend her knees and leap into the open air.

Bill stepped forward, grabbed Angie's elbow, and pulled her away from the edge.

She curled into him, and he wrapped his arms around Angie to quell her shaking. She was in that state for only a few moments, then she pulled away and plodded toward the forest. Bill caught up with her at the first tree. Her fingers idly touched the bark.

"I wasn't going to jump," she said. "I would never do that."

Such a wave of relief had overcome Bill that he would agree with whatever she said. "Of course you wouldn't. But I was afraid you might fall." As a precaution, he remained standing between her and the overlook.

She gazed toward the Shenandoah Valley. Her face had grown pale, and her lips trembled. "I never imagined he would die like that. Falling off the edge of a cliff. It's an unfitting way for a sportsman to leave the world."

"I don't know that it makes any difference in the end," said Bill. "But he didn't suffer. I guess there's that."

Angie frowned. "Such a violent ending. I had hoped his heart would allow him to go in his sleep."

Bill recalled that Damian had grown tired over lunch. Had Angie guessed he would take a nap? Had she laced his whiskey with digitalis? Enraged at him one moment and in love with him the next, she had wished for him a peaceful ending, but an ending nonetheless.

Angie may have guessed where Bill's mind would go, as her eyes grew hard and she said, "I didn't poison Damian. I loved him. One of those other jerks did it."

Easy words to say, but killers rarely confessed, and Bill hadn't expected to get such an admission from Angie.

They spoke little on the return hike to Laurel Springs Drive, and Bill spent the time considering what else Angie could tell him. Angie and Damian had been lovers. Despite breaking off the engagement, Damian might have shared details with her that he'd kept from the others.

Standing next to Angie's sedan, Bill said, "Is there anything else you can tell me that might be of use?"

Angie pursed her lips. "Like what?"

"Did you know the terms of Damian's will?"

"I don't know all the details, but I know the basic numbers. Damian enjoyed sharing those. They were to change a lot this year because of the museum donation."

Bill nodded to indicate a keen interest in the numbers, and Angie went through them. Before the museum donation came up, Evan, Tanya, and Lacey were each set to receive twenty million, and Angie would get five. But the museum grant would result in deep cuts in those numbers; Evan's and Tanya's shares would each fall to five million, and Lacey's share would fall to ten million. But Angie would stay at her original level.

A smile came to Angie's lips when she explained that Damian had not used any of her share to fund the donation.

"What about Whit Whitlock?" asked Bill.

"Whit's share was two million. His didn't change either."

Bill rubbed his chin. The charitable donation, which had not gone through, would have drastically reduced the three primary recipients' inheritance. Assuming one of those three had the emotional and psychological profile required to commit murder—admittedly a long bridge to cross—they had powerful motivation to do it now.

"I remembered something else," said Angie. "Whit came to the retreat the night before Damian died. He often came to discuss business in person. They were in Damian's study for an hour or more. At one point, I was in the kitchen and heard them arguing."

"Arguing how? Like shouting?"

"No, not shouting, but Damian raised his voice."

"Do you know what they were arguing about?"

She shook her head. "It might not mean a thing. Damian often got overly excited when he discussed business."

Angie thanked Bill for taking her to the overlook and left. Bill watched her car pull away and thought, *If Damian often got overly excited when discussing business, why did Angie bring it up?*

Then his phone rang. It was Alex Sharp.

"I got a call from Arnie Shields. Maddie Katz has asked for you to visit again."

FORTY-NINE

The Staunton Museum of Early American Leisure was located in an old but well-restored house in the Beverly Historic District not far from the Woodrow Wilson Presidential Library. The flower beds on both sides of the raised porch were bursting with brilliantly blooming white and red roses. A narrow driveway on the left led Krista to a small parking lot that contained only one other vehicle, a Hyundai SUV with a dent in the left rear panel.

At the top of the porch, Krista opened a screen door and entered the foyer. A staircase ahead led to the second level. She guessed that the large rooms to her left and right were once the living room and dining room, respectively. A hall in the middle led to the back of the house. The rooms were adorned with paintings and display cases. As far as Krista could tell, she was the only person in the museum.

"Hello?" Krista called weakly. Her stomach ached—this was her first interview for an investigation, and she knew she would mess it up.

Upstairs, the wood floor creaked as someone shifted their weight. Footsteps approached the stairwell, and then a woman in slacks and a white top came down. She was slender, a few inches taller than Krista, and appeared to be in her mid-forties. Her blond hair was parted neatly in the middle. Jane Yarborough offered Krista a strong handshake and a confident smile. She had blue eyes and walked with her shoulders back and her chin held high.

"Thank you for taking the time to meet with me," said Krista.

Jane gestured to the empty rooms on either side. "As you can see, we're not busy this morning." Then Jane Yarborough critically examined Krista from shoulders to shoes. "It's too bad you have to wear that uniform."

Krista's face grew warm. "Well, it comes with the job."

"Yes, but it doesn't have to be such a boxy thing. You have a cute figure. Imagine if those pants were form-fitting. Jeans would be even better, with knee-high boots. And that navy shirt is depressing. Imagine a nice light color like fuchsia or mango. With the shirt tucked and a badge, you'd appear official, but you could walk with pride. And you'd turn a few heads as well."

Krista laughed nervously. "I'll mention it to the chief, but he's not big on fashion."

Jane laughed loudly. "I'm not surprised. Would you like a quick tour?"

Sensing that Jane wanted to show off the museum, Krista agreed. They spent ten minutes on the first and second floors, and to her surprise, Krista found herself engaged by the various displays. She would have imagined that early Americans—both indigenous and settlers—had spent most of their time scrounging a livelihood from the land. On the contrary, Jane claimed, leisure time was plentiful, and the people invented new forms of competition and entertainment. Games that involved balls and sticks and running and throwing.

Plays. Singing. Painting. And sculptures. The list went on and on.

At the end of the second-floor circuit, Jane offered Krista coffee.

"Yes, thank you." Bill O'Shea was always drinking something at the police station. Coffee. Diet Coke. Water. Perhaps taking long sips provided him with pauses in conversations that he used to formulate questions and consider answers.

"I envy you for working in Wintergreen," said Jane, after taking a chair at a small table in what appeared to be a break room upstairs. "It's beautiful when the leaves first begin to change."

"Do you get to Wintergreen often?"

"Not really. I have a friend from school who lives there. Diana Morgan. Do you know her?"

"No." Krista jotted Diana's name in her notebook.

"Diana invites me up now and again. In fact, I was there a few days ago."

Now that Jane had taken their conversation to Wintergreen, it seemed a good time to start the interview, so Krista said, "As I mentioned on the phone, we're investigating Damian Susskind's death. Did you know him well?"

"Such awful news, to die in a fall like that. I can't imagine." Jane sat relaxed at the table and maintained solid eye contact with Krista. Despite the genuine nature of Jane's words, her tone displayed no affection for the dead. She might have been discussing a change in Staunton's downtown traffic flows. "I knew Damian professionally, of course, given his position on the board of trustees. But I didn't know him well. We were never social friends." With her last sentence, a hint of anger entered Jane's voice.

"I gather from others than Susskind intended to make a

large donation to the museum," Krista said. "A game-changing donation."

Jane's body grew tense. "Yes."

"I understand that the intended donation had a condition attached. Damian wanted you to step down. Is that correct?"

"I never discussed the matter with Damian, but one of the other directors told me as much." Jane straightened her shoulders. "I was upset, of course, but after a bit of soul-searching, I realized that's how the world works."

"How so?"

"We have a tiny museum in a small college town that's lucky enough to be interstate-accessible." Jane gestured toward a painting of people wearing simple clothes dancing in a field. "Damian wanted to build a shiny new museum. Fulfilling his vision required someone who could negotiate with the city and buy land and procure hundreds of new artifacts. I bought into his vision and believed I was the perfect person to carry it out. Obviously, Damian disagreed. But as we both know, the people with money get to make the decisions."

Going by her words alone, Jane had accepted that the donation would result in her termination. But Jane's general disposition struck Krista as inconsistent with someone who would soon have to search for a new source of income. On the contrary, she appeared confident about her future. Bill had told Krista it was his understanding the donation would not go through. Therefore, Jane's job was safe. Did she know that already?

"So, what happens now?" Krista asked.

Jane shrugged. "I don't know. I called Frieda Chang, the director who talked to me earlier, but she didn't have a final answer for me. So I'm in limbo."

Krista expressed empathy with Jane's situation and then

asked if Jane could think of anything else that might be relevant to the investigation. Jane couldn't, and the conversation meandered into small talk. The two women had something in common—they were both divorced, although Jane did not have kids. They both expressed light-hearted dismay at the prospect of dating in the digital age. Jane asked if Krista was seeing anyone special. No. Krista asked the question in return and got a similar answer—Jane had shared dinner with one man a few times, but it was going nowhere.

After leaving the museum, Krista sat in her car in the parking lot and decided she was unlikely to become Jane's friend. For starters, they had dissimilar backgrounds. Jane had graduated from Mary Baldwin College in Staunton and married a local businessman who she still bragged about even though they'd been divorced for ten years. Krista had attended one year of community college but then got pregnant and dropped out.

Krista reviewed the notes she'd taken, reflected on the conversation, and added a few more notes. From what she could tell, Jane Yarborough and the Staunton Museum of Early American Leisure were a dead end. At the same time, Krista wondered if she had asked all the right questions. It was probably a case of rookie nerves, but she couldn't help feeling she had missed something.

FIFTY

Back in Lovingston, Bill once again found Arnie Shields in the lobby of the sheriff's office.

"Where's the sheriff?" said Bill.

Arnie tilted his head vaguely toward an area of the ceiling behind him. "Up in the courthouse working on a new deal. We're trying to raise money for a drug rehab program. They have one in Charlottesville, but that's a long way for these folks to drive."

"Yeah. Good luck with that. What's Maddie's deal?"

"Who knows? She won't talk to me. But we've had a development on our end. A deputy remembered seeing Maddie's mother selling dried flowers at the farmers market in Nellysford."

"Dried flowers? So, what, you believe Maddie learned to extract digitalis from foxglove by watching her mother make dried flowers?"

Arnie lifted an eyebrow. "Perhaps. Maddie's folks have a big back garden. Lots of different flowers. We should have a search warrant this afternoon. If Maddie made poison, we'll find traces of her work."

Bill wondered how the deputy knew Maddie's mother and how Arnie knew the Katzes had a big back garden. Then he realized Nelson County had one high school. It was an everybody-knows-everybody situation.

"How about you?" said Arnie. "Learn anything new in Wintergreen?"

Bill walked Arnie through his latest interviews. No big revelations, but his views concerning motive were gradually coming together.

Arnie smiled. "Sounds good, but if we find a digitalis lab in the Katz home, we'll have this case wrapped up."

"Yeah. Let me know if you do."

"Sure thing. And you let me know what Maddie has to say."

"You bet."

~

Maddie Katz had bags under her eyes that weren't there the previous day; otherwise, she looked good for someone who'd spent the night in a jail cell.

"You okay?" he said.

"Yes. Breakfast was good. They have a little kitchen in the back, and a deputy made scrambled eggs."

"Make sure you post a five-star review."

Maddie chuckled and said, "I didn't get much sleep, though. Not their fault. I thought about the morning at Susskind's house like you asked me to. I went through every moment from when we loaded Cindy's van until the police sealed the building." Maddie shook her head. "I wound up with nothing. If someone poisoned Damian, I didn't see it."

Bill was a bit annoyed but tried not to show it. Why the

heck did Maddie drag his butt to Lovingston if she didn't have anything new?

Maddie leaned toward him. "But I remembered something else."

Okay, he thought, *this had better be good.*

"I don't recall his name, the younger guy in the group that day."

"Evan Hale."

"Yeah, him. When I first met Hale that morning, he seemed familiar, but I couldn't place him. I chalked it up to one of those things where someone looks like someone else you know. But with all that time last night, I remembered where I'd seen him."

Bill sat straight. The hairs on his scalp tingled.

Maddie nodded, confident. "I saw Hale at a dance party in Charlottesville."

"When was this?"

"About a year ago. It was a pop-up party in a warehouse on Avon Street. Hundreds of people showed up. A lot of heavy partying. We were all high."

Maddie faded away from the interview room. A smile came to her lips, as if she remembered that her former life was quite a thrill. But then she blinked and came back.

"Anyway, there was a ton of Molly at this party. People said a man in the corner was giving it to girls for free. One of the guys in our group asked me to check it out, so I did. In the corner, there was a long bar stocked with nothing but cans of sparkling water. Five bucks a can. The only alcohol at the party was what people brought themselves. Anyway, three chick bartenders were back there selling sparkling water."

Bill had never been to a warehouse dance party. He imagined it as being dark and noisy and crowded.

Maddie said, "These two other dudes were standing off to

one side. One of them fit right in—he was young, had a beard, and wore a long-sleeved T-shirt with horizontal stripes. The other dude was older and dressed in a white collared shirt." Maddie paused to point her index finger at Bill. "That guy was Evan Hale."

Huh. Evan Hale at a dance party. Not a complete shock.

"What happened then?" Bill said.

"I asked the first guy about the Molly, and he gave me a happy pill just like that. I asked him how much, and he said, 'No charge, dude. We're spreading the love. Have a good time.'"

"And Evan?"

"Didn't say a word. He checked me out from eyelashes to toenails and then smiled and nodded."

"Sounds strange," said Bill. "What did you make of it?"

"I have no idea. If I had to guess, I'd say it was their party. They paid for the warehouse and the music for fun. The Molly was rocket fuel."

Bill gnawed on a knuckle. Evan Hale had sworn to Bill he had no idea how Damian would have put his hands on MDMA. Apparently, that was a lie. But the forensics team hadn't found MDMA in Damian's house, which led Bill and the others to conclude that whoever poisoned Damian had also pumped him up with MDMA. If that wasn't true, if Damian had taken the MDMA himself, it turned things around from the killer's perspective. At the time, Bill had expected Damian to take a nap after lunch. If Damian had died in his sleep, would anyone have pushed for an autopsy? Doubtful. But Bill didn't share those thoughts with Maddie.

"That's interesting," he said.

Maddie smiled for the first time in a while.

Bill asked if she had anything else. She didn't. He suggested she try to relax and promised he'd be back soon.

Outside in the lobby, Arnie Shields had left to handle something else. Bill walked to his car and sat inside for ten minutes. Then he called Mitch Gentry and kicked the MDMA subject around a bit. Next, he texted Evan Hale to see if he could meet for lunch. Evan was working at the office, but he would meet Bill at the original Burgers Galore on Charlottesville's downtown mall.

FIFTY-ONE

After the call with Bill, Mitch picked up the key to Damian's Susskind's retreat at the office and then drove up to Devils Knob Loop. Wintergreen patrol officers had taken turns checking on the house for the past three days. Mitch had done quick walk-throughs a half dozen times on his rounds.

"It's worth a shot, Mitch," Bill had said. "The forensics team searched the house, but they might have missed something. Damian Susskind wouldn't keep recreational drugs in the open. He would have hidden them."

But it was a huge retreat. Three stories. Six bedrooms. Four balconies. Five and a half baths. A large living space and kitchen on the first floor. And a game room in the basement. There were hundreds of good hiding places for small items. Mitch walked upstairs to the bathroom of the master suite, pulled on gloves, and checked the underside of each drawer. He inspected the hollow towel bars. He pulled a picture off the wall and turned it around to check the backside.

This search was crazy. Mitch could spend a week in the

house and still not check every conceivable hiding place. He had to narrow down the scope of his search. Would Susskind hide his stash of recreational drugs in the master bath? Maybe. It depended on where he typically took the drug. Yeah. That's progress. Bill had said Susskind was most likely taking MDMA on the sly. Angie Finch suspected he had taken something, and Evan Hale might be in on the secret, but Damian wasn't throwing wild Molly parties. Mitch figured he could reasonably eliminate the common areas and the guest bedroom suites from his search. That left the master suite and Damian's study. Between those two, Mitch would bet on the study, so he tromped downstairs.

Upon entering Damian's study, Mitch's eyes gravitated toward the whiskey collection on the back shelves. He did a quick estimate, between a hundred and hundred and twenty bottles. Scotch. Bourbon. Rye. Irish. When Mitch did drink, not often, he generally consumed beer. He pulled a few bottles from the shelf and turned them around in his hand. Artful labels and clever names. Clear amber liquids.

Mitch sat in the leather desk chair and tried to think like a rich sixty-five-year-old with a faulty heart.

I used to be a young man, but now I'm old. I want to feel young again.

Where would a man who wanted to amp his night with a half a hit of Ecstasy hide his stash? Mitch glanced toward the bathroom. No, Damian wouldn't hide it there. He would pour himself a slug of whiskey and then reach for the pills. Mitch opened each drawer and inspected them closely. No luck. He got up and looked at the monitor stand. Nothing. Next, he checked the edges of the desk. Then he examined the items on top of the desk: an electric pencil sharpener, several books in a stack, an antique windup clock, and matching pen and paperclip holders. Mitch pulled the tray out from the pencil sharpener and spilled some shavings on the desk. He picked up the antique clock, inspected it, and decided it was made of one solid piece of wood with a clock insert. What about a hidden cutout in one of the books? His heart rate increased. That could be it. But when he flipped the pages, his hopes fell. He sat back in the chair, stumped.

He was ready to move to the bathroom when his eyes fell on the wooden pen and paperclip holders. The paperclip holder was short and the pen holder tall. Mitch frowned at the pen holder. It was eight inches tall, but nearly half of each pen stuck out from the top. Mitch dumped the pens onto the desk and turned the holder upside down. The bottom was felt-covered. He ran his finger around the holder's edges and then gave the base a slight push, which caused a spring to pop open the cover of a hidden compartment. Mitch turned the holder right side up, and a little plastic bag of pink pills fell out.

FIFTY-TWO

Bill parked in a garage building in Charlottesville, crossed Water Street to enter the downtown pedestrian mall, and met Evan Hale at the entrance to Burgers Galore.

"Are you ready for the best burger of your life?" Hale asked.

Bill's stomach had grumbled about food on the drive from Wintergreen, and his taste buds watered when Hale said burger.

Inside, Evan gave him a quick tour of the dining room. Seventies rock played softly from hidden speakers. Back-to-back booths lined the right wall, and a long bar with stools occupied the left side of the room. The middle section was filled with square tables for four. It was a few minutes past noon, and the lunch crowd occupied three-quarters of the seats. The young hostess recognized Evan and smiled. She called Evan by his first name and escorted them to a booth. After handing them menus, the hostess cast another smile at Evan and returned to her station.

"I was surprised to hear from you," said Evan. "We spoke only yesterday."

"When people lie to me, I like to follow up in person as soon as possible."

On the drive from Wintergreen, Bill had decided to put Evan Hale on his heels. Now Evan chewed the corner of his lip.

Bill said, "You told me you'd be surprised to hear of Damian taking MDMA, but it was you who gave him the drug in the first place."

Evan frowned, playing innocent. Bill doubted Evan could keep it up for long.

A waiter stopped by to see if they were ready. Bill ordered the mushroom burger with swiss cheese, fries, and a Diet Coke. Evan chose a salad with grilled salmon.

When the waiter had departed, Bill leaned closer and said, "Your restaurant is called Burgers Galore. How can you order fish?"

Evan's face had lost its color.

"I advise you to admit that you gave Damian MDMA," said Bill. "Lie to me again, and you'll have the police poking into your affairs. It would become awkward given your strained financial situation."

Evan swallowed hard.

Bill grew tired of waiting and threw out a hand of impatience. "Well? Say something."

"Okay. After rehab, Damian complained that he wasn't his old self. He grew tired easily. Did I have something that would pick him up? Make his evenings more fun?" Evan grimaced at the recollection. "I gave him some pills and warned him to cut them into thirds or quarters. Damian reported back to me that it was a miracle drug. He'd never felt better."

"Did you give him MDMA the day he died?"

"No, definitely not. But when Damian miraculously

recovered after lunch, I knew he'd taken a pill. I would have told you earlier, but MDMA is illegal. If my bank found out, they wouldn't extend my loan."

Bill's distaste for Evan Hale increased by the hour. But had he killed Damian Susskind?

"Your lies put you in a bad light," said Bill. "Maybe you poured the whiskey. Perhaps you lined Damian's glass with poison."

Evan shook his head violently. "No. No."

"Why should I believe you now? You lied to me about your inheritance as well. You said Damian was cutting your share drastically to make room for a charitable donation."

"He *did* tell me that. He picked a charity in Staunton. Pioneer sports paintings and so forth."

"Yes, but you also knew that the will did not yet reflect the donation. As soon as Damian signed a new will, your inheritance would fall by three-quarters." Bill's eyes scanned the restaurant. "That extra fifteen million would make a huge difference for your business. You could pay off your loans."

"You can't believe that I would kill Damian for money." Evan wrung his hands. "The old man meant a lot to me. He made me what I am."

Bill held up a hand to keep Evan from blathering on. "Plus, with Damian out of the way, you could carry on with Lacey openly. You could even marry her."

Evan's eyes grew hard and angry. Bill didn't care.

"When I add it up," Bill said, "you have more motives than a stray dog has fleas."

Evan stood and said, "I have to get back to work."

"What about your salad?"

"You eat it. Tell the waiter to put lunch on my tab." Before leaving, Evan leaned forward and whispered harshly, "You don't know nearly as much as you think."

"Please, enlighten me."

The young man snorted and said, "Figure it out yourself." Then he marched from the restaurant.

Bill enjoyed the mushroom burger immensely. He admired Evan Hale's ability to create a compelling combination of great food, a relaxed ambiance, and excellent service. But then Bill recalled Hale's parting words. "You don't know nearly as much as you think." He nibbled on a last French fry, but it didn't taste as good as the others.

FIFTY-THREE

After his meal, Bill called Tanya Stafford at Fair Game's corporate office to ask whether he could stop by for a brief visit. He reached Tanya's assistant, who put Bill on hold and then came back to say Tanya was on her lunch break and free for thirty minutes. Could Bill get there in time? Yes, he was in the area.

The day had grown warm but was comfortable in the shade. Bill dodged through shoppers and diners toward the mall's western edge, where he came to a shiny new office building. He rode the elevator to the third floor, and a receptionist gave him directions to a corner of the building. Once there, an assistant escorted him into Tanya's spacious office.

She sat behind a large modern desk, eating a sandwich wrap and studying a monitor. When Bill entered the room, she looked up, finished chewing, swallowed, and said, "That was quick." She appeared to be in an excellent mood.

The view through the window behind Tanya was stunning. Rolling hills, hardwood trees, and high meadows in the distance.

"I was at Burgers Galore having lunch with Evan."

Tanya wiped her hand on a napkin and walked around her desk to shake Bill's hand. "I wish I'd known. I could have joined you."

"You would have been disappointed. Evan didn't appreciate my questions. I'm afraid he believes I suspect him of murder."

Tanya gestured that they should sit at a small round table with four chairs. "Evan should relax. You're just doing your job. Anyway, I heard Nelson County arrested one of the caterers."

"They have, but they haven't charged her yet. Frankly, I'm not sure Maddie's guilty."

"And so, you have questions for me as well." Tanya settled into her chair. She appeared relaxed and confident in a short-sleeved red top and gold hoop earrings.

"You seem cheerful today," said Bill.

"Do I?" Tanya glanced back at the monitor on her desk. "I received a good report from a new store that I had concerns about." She pursed her lips. "Perhaps I shouldn't celebrate given that Damian's only been gone a few days."

Three days to be precise. No matter how high a person's stature, when they were gone, the clock kept ticking, and the world moved on. Who would notice if Bill died? His kids would mourn him for a long time. And maybe his ex-wife Wanda as well. Cindy would shed a few tears. Others would notice his absence for a short while. But the heart of the world wouldn't miss a beat. Damian Susskind had been a big deal during his lifetime, but now he was a small island in a fast-rising stream. Soon the waters would rush over him, and in a few short years, those whose life he had once filled would think of him no more than once or twice a month.

Tanya nodded solemnly. "Damian was a great man in his day. And a fine mentor to me, that's for sure. Not that I wouldn't have been successful anyway. People with drive make their way sooner or later." Tanya grimaced slightly. "And the harsh truth is Damian lost his edge the last few years. His mind wasn't as sharp. When I first met him, he could recite yesterday's sales numbers from memory. He would do a store walkthrough with a general manager and spontaneously give her twenty ideas for how to improve sales. At the time, I was amazed. I could never possibly be that good." Then Tanya shrugged. "But now, I *am* that good. I have been for years. And Damian? In the last few monthly review meetings, he had trouble remembering the GMs' names. It was sad, to be honest. Truly sad."

Had Damian realized that his grasp of the business was weakening? He had started the company at a young age and built it into a regional retail empire. He had reigned supreme, but the peak had come and gone. In his mid-sixties, his body and mind had failed him. If he had lived, how long would he have kept his place on the team before the game of life pushed him to the side? If not for the poison, how would the end have come? Sitting in a luxurious retirement home relating his glory days in a shaky voice? Was that Bill's destiny, minus the luxury? Was Damian better off this way?

"I imagine you have questions for me, right?" said Tanya.

"Yes, I wanted you to clarify a point you made earlier concerning Damian's plans for his inheritance. You said he changed his mind often. But others have told me he clearly described the recent change he wanted to make."

Tanya adjusted her weight in the chair. "I'm sorry if my words mischaracterized the situation. Damian changed his mind often over the years, but you're right. He was clear about wanting to give a lot to that charity in Staunton."

"Did you also know that implementing the change would take some time?"

"Whit mentioned it would take a while. Something to do with Damian's donation coming in the form of company stock."

"How much would the change impact you personally?"

Bill already knew what Angie had told him, that Tanya's share would fall from twenty million to five million, but he wanted to hear what Tanya said.

"Candidly," she said, "it's a big number. Of course, the stock value varies from day to day, but my share would have decreased by fourteen or fifteen million."

"That *is* a big number."

"Yes, but as I mentioned in our last conversation, I don't work for the money. Even so, the donation is a prime example of how Damian was losing his grip. He planned to give away forty million dollars. A lot of money that could do a lot of good. There are billions of people in the world who need help with food or water or medicine. They have no power in their homes. Damian could have helped some of those people. But what did he want to do? Preserve paintings of pioneers playing games. I'll tell you straight up; I'm glad it didn't go through."

"Who told you the donation didn't go through?"

Tanya pulled her head back, perhaps concerned that she'd said something out of turn. "Whit called me this morning."

"Why? Why would Whit give you that update today? Any special reason?"

Bill had to give her credit. Under pressure, Tanya kept her cool. Her eyes were steady. "I sent him a text asking about it."

Who could blame her? Fifteen million dollars was a lot of

money, even for a woman who claimed she wasn't motivated by the accumulation of financial wealth.

"You realize that this gives you a powerful motive for killing Damian," he said.

Tanya inhaled deeply, and her eyes smoldered. "When we first met, Bill, I liked you. You seemed like a hardworking regular guy. But I like you less with each meeting."

He shrugged. "I *still* like you. You're a hardworking, successful business executive, and I admire you for that. But my job isn't to make friends. My job is to find a killer. And I have to ask you straight up—did you kill Damian?"

"No. Despite my earlier words regarding Damian's precarious mental state, I still cared for him. He helped me a lot, and I will miss him."

Tanya's lip trembled, and Bill realized that she did care for her old mentor. But a murderer could retain a warm feeling for their victim in a back corner of their otherwise cold heart. After a moment, Tanya's steely resolve returned.

"Now, if you don't mind," she said, "my lunch break is over, and I have a company to run."

"Of course," said Bill. "Thank you for your time."

~

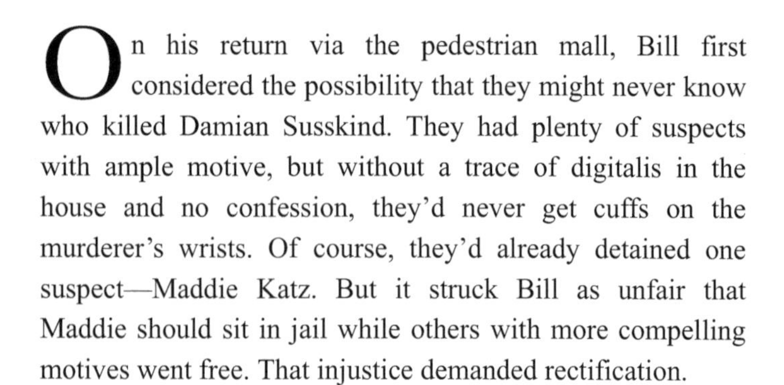

On his return via the pedestrian mall, Bill first considered the possibility that they might never know who killed Damian Susskind. They had plenty of suspects with ample motive, but without a trace of digitalis in the house and no confession, they'd never get cuffs on the murderer's wrists. Of course, they'd already detained one suspect—Maddie Katz. But it struck Bill as unfair that Maddie should sit in jail while others with more compelling motives went free. That injustice demanded rectification.

Back in the garage, he pressed the starter button for his Mazda, and another assignment for Krista popped into his mind. It was a long-odds approach to the problem, but he was running short of ideas.

FIFTY-FOUR

For the entire time that Arnie and Bill kicked around the topic, the sheriff hardly said a word. He sat back in his swivel chair with his hands on his belly and stared at Bill through eyes like slits. Bill had never met the sheriff. Though a man of few words, the sheriff seemed a nice enough boss. No yelling in Bill's presence. On the other hand, Undersheriff Arnie Shields was none too happy.

Arnie, sitting in one of the two chairs across the desk from the sheriff, thrust out a hand and said, "Bill, she threatened to kill the victim in the presence of others."

"True," said Bill, "but she was under the influence. Maddie's straightened up since then. She's worked for Cindy for three months now and never put a foot wrong. Always clocks in on time."

"And she poured the coffee," said Arnie.

"One of the other guys might have poisoned the whiskey."

"There's another connection," said Arnie. "Forensics found MDMA in the victim's blood, and we know Maddie has often used MDMA."

"Yeah. I need to catch you up on a couple of things."

Bill related the new facts that led him to conclude Damian had taken MDMA himself. First, Maddie had reported seeing Evan Hale and his buddy handing MDMA out at a party.

"She what?" said Arnie. "Why didn't you tell me that?"

The sheriff frowned.

"I should have," said Bill. "But when I came out, you weren't in the lobby. Then I got distracted, so I'm telling you now."

Bill added that Mitch had found Damian's stash of MDMA in the study and that Evan Hale had subsequently admitted to supplying MDMA to Damian.

Arnie's face grew flushed, and his eyebrows scrunched together. "Evan Hale, that low-count fancy, I'll put Charlottesville on to him."

Then the sheriff said, in a bass voice so low he could have sung for the Statler Brothers, "Let's move on from the MDMA, Arnie. No one cares about that. Do we have enough to keep Maddie Katz locked up or not?"

"I don't know," said Arnie, clearly upset by the MDMA twist.

"How did you make out with the search of her house?" asked Bill.

"Nothing doing," said Arnie. "If she made digitalis from foxglove, we found no trace of it in the house."

"What's your view?" the sheriff asked Bill.

Bill shook his head. "We don't have anything more on her than we do on these other guys. And frankly, they each have a lot more money on the line than Maddie would make in a lifetime clerking for Fair Game."

The sheriff nodded. "Yeah. I think we should let her go. Arnie, let's get the commonwealth's attorney on the line."

The sheriff shifted his eyes to Bill. "Give us the office for a while, okay?"

Bill stood to leave and said, "I'll stick around to give her a ride if it swings that way."

"It could take an hour or more," warned the sheriff.

"No problem."

~

When the sheriff's deputy gave Maddie Katz her keys and other stuff, she thanked him by name.

Once they got outside to the parking lot, Bill said, "Do you know that deputy?"

Maddie nodded. "Cliff and my older sister knew each other in school."

"Are you okay?"

Maddie seemed okay, though her clothes were wrinkled and her hair needed tending. A heavy cloud cover had turned the sky gray, and Maddie looked up and smiled. "I'm fine now. It feels good to be free."

Maddie told Bill she lived fifteen minutes away. He drove through the little town of Lovingston and turned south on US Route 29. They passed the county library, a Baptist church, a casual Italian restaurant, and a motel. After a section of forest, they passed Nelson County High School on the right. Bales of hay dotted the field on the left.

"Why did they let me go?" Maddie asked.

"They believed you were a murderer. Now they're not sure."

"Do you think I'm a murderer?"

"No. You caught some bad luck, that's all. But you should know that deputies searched your home, so your parents might be upset."

Maddie stared ahead at the four-lane highway with her hands laying inert in her lap. "My parents have a lot of reasons to be upset with me."

"It's not your fault that someone killed Damian Susskind."

Maddie mulled that thought and said, "I guess Cindy will fire me for not telling her the truth. Won't she?"

"You'll have to ask her."

"And the thing with Justin," she said, her voice sinking, "that was never going to work anyway, with him being in New Jersey or wherever."

Bad luck had given Maddie the right to feel sorry for herself, so Bill let her flounder in silence. They turned right on a two-lane road that passed by mown fields and farm-houses and a winery. He gave her another minute but then couldn't resist pushing back. Self-pity never offered anyone a helping hand.

"What do you want?" he asked. "What do you want out of life?"

Maddie frowned and turned her head in his direction.

"Take your time," he said. "Think it over. It's a relevant question for anyone."

They crossed a small bridge, and the road curved to follow a creek. Rust-colored cattle grazed on a hillside. They passed a small white house with a dark pitched roof and well-tended flower beds. A young woman in jeans and a T-shirt checked a mailbox on the roadside. It was a beautiful place to live.

"I want a future," said Maddie. "All I want is a future I can look forward to."

Bill nodded. "That's reasonable. Here's the good news. You already have a future."

"You know what I mean."

"I'm serious. You're twenty-four years old. I'm sixty. You've got a lot of future ahead of you. If Cindy doesn't want you back, find another job. If long-distance love is not for you, search for another guy. If you don't like living in the country, move back to the city. Keep working and learning, and I guarantee your future will be bright. But you must keep one harsh truth in mind."

"What's that?"

"There's no shortcut path to long-term happiness."

For the rest of the drive to Maddie's home, Bill chastised himself for trying to play the sage. Young adults hated that crap, and for good reason. There was nothing worse than an old fart rattling on about bright futures and stuff when no one knew what disasters lay around the corner. Hell. The dinosaurs thought they had a good thing going right until the moment the asteroid struck.

Nevertheless, when Bill dropped Maddie off, she thanked him for the ride.

On the drive back up the mountain to Wintergreen, Bill's mind returned to the investigation. Whoever poisoned Damian had a lot to gain by his demise, and they had executed their plan with great care. Maddie wasn't guilty. No, it had to be one of the people sitting around that table. If he kept chipping away at the problem, sooner or later, new information was bound to break loose.

FIFTY-FIVE

By the time Bill reached the top of the mountain, he felt the effects of a late-afternoon energy sag, so he stopped by Café Devine. Kim Wiley took his order for a half-caf latte from behind the cash register. Her nephew Nathan stood back in the kitchen working on something. While Kim fixed Bill's coffee, he perused the nearby rack of wine specials. A Bordeaux with a clever label was priced at $19.99. Hmm. Maybe he should get two.

Kim waved him over, and he paid for the wine and coffee. No one else was in the store.

"Have you seen Cindy today?" asked Kim. Her voice hinted at mystery.

"No. I've been gone. Why? What's up?"

Kim glanced over her shoulder toward the kitchen. "Nathan, watch the store, will ya? Bill and I are going to catch a gab."

"Yes, ma'am."

Kim led Bill to a two-top table at the side of the store. Bill's chest tightened.

Leaning forward in her chair, Kim said in a low voice.

"Cindy stopped by for some milk earlier, and I tried to engage her in a little chitchat. She was having nothing of it. Hardly gave me two words."

Bill did his best to keep a straight face. It was unlike Cindy to forgo such an opportunity. At least once a week, she returned from a visit to Kim's store bursting with mountain news. Then again, it had been a tough few days, and he pointed that out to Kim.

Kim frowned as she considered Bill's observation. "I suppose it has been tough, but Cindy didn't appear sad to me. She seemed angry. Very short with her words."

"Angry?"

"Yes. Did you do something to get her worked up?"

Bill put his hands on his chest. "Me? No. I don't believe so."

Then again, Bill found women to be a never-ending source of puzzlement. He had been married to his ex-wife, Wanda, for twenty-seven years and never wholly figured her out. And though his relationship with Cindy was in its early stages, he had learned he should avoid missteps and miscommunications whenever possible.

"You might want to check with her," said Kim.

"Thanks. I'll do that."

"How's the investigation going?"

"We're making slow progress. I'm not sure whether we're moving forward at all. Have you heard anything of interest lately?"

At that moment, the bell that hung from the front doorknob jingled. Two women strolled inside and paused at the cold beverage display.

Kim glanced their way and lowered her voice again. "Maybe so. Do you remember I said Lacey Akin was spending a lot of time at Evan Hale's condo?"

"Sure."

"They've decided to take things to the next step."

"What next step?"

Kim pointed at her ring finger.

"No," said Bill.

Kim nodded hugely. "You know Barbara Capaldi, right?"

"Yes." Bill had met the woman briefly during the Lou Thorpe investigation.

"Barbara knows Lacey from the tennis center. They're good friends, I gather. Anyway, Barbara had lunch with Lacey yesterday and got the scoop. Lacey was bubbling over like a shaken bottle of champagne. She told Barbara in strict confidence that she and Evan Hale will get engaged soon now that Damian Susskind has died."

"That's interesting."

"I'll say. Damian was hard set against the marriage, which I can understand given Evan's reputation. But, of course, you can't control people's lives from the grave."

How convenient for Lacey, and Evan Hale, that Damian should die at this moment. It freed them to pursue their marital bliss without delay. And, given that Damian's charitable donation had not gone through, they had a heap of money to ensure their happily ever after. Was that what Evan had referred to when he claimed that Bill was uninformed?

In his car, Bill called Cindy to see if she cared for a glass of Bordeaux.

"No, thanks."

Kim was right. Cindy's voice carried an undertone of irritation.

"Is everything okay?" he asked.

"It's fine. I'll see you tomorrow."

Then Cindy hung up. An abrupt end to a short conversation. What in the world had he done now? For a moment, he considered stopping by her condo to find out, but he resisted the temptation. She'd feel better in the morning.

He went home and popped his head around the corner to check on Mr. Chips, but the sun had nearly set, and the groundhog had already hit the sack.

After a quick dinner and some television, Bill did the same. It was a long and restless night. He might have grown bored staring at the dark, but Bill had a tricky puzzle to occupy his mind.

FIFTY-SIX

By six o'clock the next morning, Bill was dressed, fed, and driving down the mountain on his way to Charlottesville. He had three targets on his list and figured his best chance at seeing everyone was to hit them early. After taking the Fifth Street exit, Bill turned left and pulled into a convenience store for a cup of coffee. Back in his car, he sent texts to Lacey Akin, Evan Hale, and Whit Whitlock. Lacey answered him first. She had a meeting at nine o'clock but could meet him at a coffeehouse on the pedestrian mall at eight. Bill got there early.

Having already eaten breakfast and had his share of coffee, Bill opted for a bottle of water. Lacey ordered oatmeal and a fancy tea drink. She wore a cute skirt with a white top and sensible shoes. They sat outside at a round metal table with metal chairs, and Bill shooed away a pigeon that plucked at crumbs on the ground. Bill thanked her for meeting on short notice and then dropped his bombshell. The mountain gossip wire was abuzz with the news of her and Evan's pending engagement.

"Who told you that?" she said, not pleased.

"I'm sure you told more than one person, and you can assume they all told someone else. But I can't understand why you two would move so quickly after Damian's death."

Bill let the implication hang in the air—the two events were linked. She knew it. Evan knew it. And Bill knew it.

Lacey had managed to consume three spoonsful of her oatmeal, but now she pushed the bowl to the side.

"I've spoken out of turn," she said. "We're not engaged yet, but we're as close as you can get without actually saying the words. We were holding off because of Damian's expressed misgivings. Of course, I wanted Damian's blessing, but he became agitated whenever I broached the subject. He even threatened to cut us out of his will, although I don't believe he ever would have done that."

"I assume you two are madly in love."

"Of course."

Bill pointed at her. "Be careful about that part. Love can mean different things to different people. For example, some say love is worth more than money."

"It *is* worth more. My love for Evan means everything to me. More than the air I breathe."

"If that's so, why didn't you tell Damian to get stuffed?"

"I would have, but—" Lacey cut herself off, and her eyes caught fire. For the first time since he'd met her, Lacey's good-girl persona vanished. Gone were the timid step-daughter and the self-sacrificing social worker. Apparently, Lacey could push back when it came to certain aspects of her personal life. "It's none of your business anyway."

Bill raised his hands in surrender. "You're right. I'm nobody, just a retired cop on loan to the Wintergreen police department. I don't even have a uniform." Then he leaned forward. "But you don't have much of a choice. You can talk to me, or you can talk to the Nelson County sheriff."

Lacey folded her arms and breathed loudly through her nose.

Bill unhurriedly opened his water bottle. Then he nodded toward her oatmeal. "I'm ruining your breakfast. Please, finish before it gets cold."

"All right," Lacey said, "I wanted to defy Damian and marry anyway. Who was he to bar my happiness? My birth father told me as much. He said Damian was trying to control me with his money, and as long as I allowed him to do that, I could never be my own person."

That was good advice, Bill thought, *but difficult to follow with twenty million dollars dangling in front of your nose.*

Lacey's hands gripped the table's edge. "Here's the thing. Evan needed the money for his business. Unfortunately, he's expanded too quickly, and the banks are giving him a hard time."

Wait. What?

"How could your inheritance solve Evan's financial problem if Damian was still alive? Are you saying that Evan poisoned Damian?"

Lacey shook her head emphatically. "No. That's not what I meant at all. Evan believed he could convince Damian to guarantee his loans, but not if we were engaged."

"Oh."

With each revelation, Bill liked Evan Hale even less. The word despicable came to mind. Bill would see Evan again that very day if he had to turn over every rock in Albemarle County.

"What did you know of Damian's intention to donate money to the Staunton museum?"

Lacey sighed wearily, as if the subject of money only served to push her happiness further away.

"I don't know. I guess it was Damian's money to do with

as he pleased. It's not much of a museum today, but Damian had a grand vision for its future. It was to become his passion project when he left the business."

"Did Damian tell you how the donation would affect your inheritance?"

"Yes. He said my share would fall from twenty to ten million. But how much money does a person need? I was fine with it."

Bill pointed at Lacey's oatmeal again, and this time, she followed his suggestion. He tried to imagine her poisoning Damian. How would she do it? She'd bring him a bottle of scotch she knew he couldn't resist and then line one of the glasses in his study with a digitalis potion. Perhaps she had poured Damian a sample and then smiled coyly as he drank the poison. She had solved her problems and moved her love within reach.

Really? Love was a strange beast, indeed, but did it have the power to transform this innocent girl into such a monster? Surely not. A chill ran down Bill's spine, and his mind was filled with doubt.

FIFTY-SEVEN

Bill found Evan Hale's Charlottesville home address by searching the public directory on his phone. Evan lived only a few blocks north of the downtown mall. He had not returned Bill's earlier text, but it was only eight thirty, so Bill decided to test his luck with a stroll.

He headed north on Second Street, cut diagonally northeast through the Market Street Park, and made two more turns before walking north several blocks into a quiet neighborhood. According to the address, Evan Hale lived in a remodeled, painted-brick townhouse. The two-story building was gray with black shutters and beautified with carefully landscaped flower beds. The flagstone walkway led to a front porch that ran the width of the house. On the porch, white rocking chairs invited guests to relax and enjoy the view.

After admiring the home, Bill approached the porch. When he reached the steps, the door opened, and Evan Hale came out dressed in running gear.

Evan blinked several times.

"Words escape me," he said. "You're a recurring nightmare."

"You never returned my text."

"What text?" Evan fumbled with a tight pocket to extract his phone. "You texted me at seven? Don't you sleep?"

"I would expect a hard-charging executive like you to wake up at five, pound the Peloton for an hour, and be at the office long before now."

Evan shook his head. "That's an old paradigm. You're showing your age. The workday never stops or starts—it's twenty-four seven."

"Sounds brutal. Nevertheless, can you spare me a few minutes?"

"All joking aside, I need to get this run in now. Care to join me?"

Bill wore khakis and the wrong kind of shoes. "Why don't we start with a brisk walk?"

Evan took advantage of Bill's reference to the word brisk. They rapidly retraced Bill's steps south and then turned left on High Street. Redbrick buildings lined the road, and they passed the offices of a law firm and a Thai restaurant. Evan leaned forward and swung his arms. Bill wrestled with where to start.

"I met with Lacey this morning."

Evan glared at Bill but didn't break stride.

"Word on the mountain is you two will become engaged soon. Any truth in that?"

Evan only grunted. They reached a red stoplight, and a car approached from the left. Evan ran across the road not twenty feet in front of the vehicle. Bill waited. The driver leaned on her horn. Once the car had passed, Bill crossed over. He increased his stride, but it still took most of the next block for him to catch Evan. The early morning sun shone brightly, and Bill regretted that he had left his sunglasses in the car. His shirt began to cling to his skin, and he pulled it from the side.

"Should I take that stunt back there as your way of avoiding the question?" said Bill.

"Lacey and I won't be getting married anytime soon."

"That's not what she said."

The next stoplight turned yellow, and Evan jogged into the intersection before the light turned red. Bill hustled to keep up.

Bill sensed that Evan was struggling with what to say, and he wished Evan would hurry his words or slow his feet. They crossed Park Street, walked two more blocks, and then turned left on Eighth Street. Up ahead on the right was an old cemetery.

"Sometimes Lacey hears what she wants to hear," said Evan. "We've said many words to each other, but I have never actually proposed."

"I see," said Bill. "So this is a misunderstanding."

The tortured look returned to Evan's face, but Bill didn't feel like giving him any more time.

"Let's face it," said Bill. "You're a jerk."

Evan pulled up short to glare at Bill, and Bill expected him to offer an objection, but then the younger man's shoulders sagged. They had reached the cemetery, and Evan trudged toward it through overgrown grass. Grave markers from earlier centuries lay in straight lines across a gentle downward slope. Evan leaned against the stone wall that bordered the cemetery.

"Damian didn't want you to marry Lacey," said Bill. "If you did, he would disinherit you, so you poisoned him. The upside was too great to pass up. You knew the charitable donation had not gone through, so your share was still twenty million. With that money, you could pay off your bank debt.

Plus, you and Lacey could get married. Although frankly, I'm not sure about that last part."

Evan made a fist and whacked it against the stone wall. "You're right. Damian didn't want me to marry Lacey. He told me I wasn't fit to marry her. But you missed a key point —Damian was smart. He put my inheritance into a trust that pays out at five percent a year. That in and of itself is not a problem. Five percent of twenty million is a lot of money to spend in a year. Even if the charitable donation had gone through, five percent would have been a nice big chunk. But the trust comes with a condition. If I ever marry Lacey Akin, I won't get another cent."

Bill nodded. Yes, Damian Susskind *was* smart.

"Lacey said you would ask Damian to guarantee your loan."

Evan snorted bitterly. "He laughed off that request. Damian said a tussle with the banks was a great character builder. He said all I had to do was stand firm, and they would restructure the terms. He was right. They made an offer yesterday."

The young man smacked his fist against the stone wall again.

Bill winced.

"Yeah," said Evan. "Damian saw right through me. You called me a jerk. Damian called me a cad. Whatever I might be, one thing's for sure—I won't be marrying Lacey." Evan's eyes tightened. "And to tell you the truth, it's a relief. I know who I am. If I married Lacey, I'd make her life miserable soon enough. She doesn't deserve that. She doesn't deserve to marry a louse like me."

FIFTY-EIGHT

Bill didn't have to travel far to reach Whit Whitlock's office. It was a few blocks west on High Street. But Whit couldn't meet until ten o'clock, so after Evan Hale ran north on Eighth Street, Bill returned to the pedestrian mall for some window shopping. He browsed a bookstore and purchased a book that promised to relate four billion years of evolution on Earth. Sitting on a bench in the sunshine, Bill read a few pages and then received a text from Cindy.

Do you want to have lunch at my place at 12:30?

Even if the meeting with Whit lasted an hour, he could make it back to Wintergreen in plenty of time.

You bet. See you then.

He took Cindy's invitation as a good sign. Perhaps he had only caught her at a bad time the previous day.

Bill checked in with Krista to see how she was doing on her assignment to locate liquor stores within a hundred miles that carried Braemore. It was a slog, but she was making progress. Had she seen Mitch? He was out doing rounds. Krista suggested they have a meet-up with Alex that afternoon. Good idea. Could she organize it? Sure.

After the call, Bill sat with his eyes closed for five minutes and considered the material he needed to cover with Whit. They had last met two days earlier, and Bill had learned a lot since then.

Whit's office was in one of the old brick buildings Bill and Evan had passed earlier. The small lobby had hardwood floors and white walls decorated with landscape paintings of the Blue Ridge Mountains. A receptionist showed Bill to a conference room, and Whit joined him a minute later.

Whit asked Bill for the latest, and Bill said he had spoken with Tanya, Lacey, and Evan in the last twenty-four hours.

"I bet Tanya was happy," said Whit.

Bill reflected on that conversation. "Yes, she was. Something about new store results."

Whit smirked.

"Did I miss something?" said Bill.

"The board of directors had an early call yesterday morning and elected Tanya as the new CEO for Fair Game. I gather from your expression that she didn't tell you. Perhaps she wanted to keep it confidential until the press release."

"Oh, that must be it."

Or, thought Bill, *she might have wished to avoid underscoring her motive for killing Damian Susskind.*

Bill said, "I thought they planned to hire an outside CEO with more experience."

Whit shook his head. "They decided against that path, and frankly, I agree with them. With the loss of Damian, continuity at the top is important. It's not the right time to bring in a new face."

Maybe that was the best course, but it was a change from Damian's intention and convenient for Tanya.

"By the way," said Bill, "I gather from Tanya and Evan

that you have already told them the museum donation will not go through."

Whit answered without hesitation. "Yes, that's true. I couldn't see a reason not to tell them; although, I will not pursue execution of the will until the investigation is complete."

"And what if we can't solve the case? What if the investigation is shelved indefinitely?"

Whit's eyes grew concerned. "Is that possible?"

"Yes. I'd say there's a high probability at this point."

Whit held his hands clasped on the conference room table. He twiddled his thumbs. "I don't know what would happen in that scenario. I'll need to do some research. It would delay the inheritance settlement, perhaps for years."

Whit's eyes wandered to a window that overlooked a side street, and Bill guessed he was wrestling with this new complication. Whit was a conscientious attorney. After handling Damian's personal affairs for decades, he had one last job to do, maybe the most important one of all. Having been the source of Whit's new worries, Bill didn't want to ask the next question, but he had no choice.

He cleared his throat to catch Whit's attention. "I gather you argued with Damian the night before he died."

Whit frowned. "No, I don't think so."

"This would have happened in his study at the retreat."

Whit continued searching his memory, and then his eyebrows lifted. "Oh, Angie must have told you that. It wasn't a knock-down-drag-out fight or anything, but she's right, we did have a minor disagreement, and perhaps Damian raised his voice for a sentence or two."

"What did you argue about?"

Whit chuckled and then shook his head. "The same as always. Deadlines. Damian was impatient to donate shares to the Staunton Museum. Whenever Damian came up with a bright idea, he believed it should happen at the snap of a finger. But these things take time. The delay was driven by tax consequences. I told him if he didn't care about getting the full value of the tax deduction, we could transfer shares the next day, but of course, he *did* want the full value of the deduction. So I had to communicate with the charity's back office to ensure their nonprofit 501(c)(3) status was in order. It does no good to figure this stuff out after the fact. If I had screwed that up, we would have had a *real* argument."

"I get it. I've had my share of demanding bosses."

Whit folded his arms on his chest, and a small smile came to his lips. "Yeah, he was demanding, but he was also brilliant. I doubt I'll ever have a better client."

Bill rubbed his chin. What else could he ask Whit? Oh, right.

"I'm sure you can understand that I'm trying to figure a motive. Correct me if I'm wrong, but Damian's demise means Tanya and Evan and Lacey will each come into large sums of money."

Whit nodded. "Yes, definitely."

"And what about you, Whit? Are you in the will? Do you have the same motive?"

At first, Whit continued to nod, but then he tilted his head to one side. "Theoretically, yes, I have the same motive. I was in the will, but my share was a day at Virginia Beach compared to their Mediterranean cruise. I told Damian he should leave me out altogether because I'd made more than enough in fees over the years."

"I'm going to switch gears on you now," said Bill. "Let's go back to the whiskey you each had on the back porch. You said earlier that Damian poured the whiskey. Did anyone else touch the glasses?"

Whit tapped a finger against his lips. "Damian brought the bottle himself, and he poured the scotch. I don't remember who brought the glasses. Was it Angie? No, Damian brought the glasses too, but he had trouble managing things at the table with both of his hands full, so Angie came over to help out."

Bill thanked Whit for his time and made his way back across the pedestrian mall to the parking garage. He hardly noticed the drive through Charlottesville to I-64 West. It had to be the whiskey. Maddie or Justin could have poisoned Damian; they had access to the coffee and tea. But Bill had already crossed their names off his list. Justin had no connection to Damian, and Maddie, well, Bill believed her statement. Which left him with the whiskey.

FIFTY-NINE

"Yes," said Cindy into her cell phone. "I'm aware of that. You don't have to keep telling me the same thing."

For the umpteenth time, her ex-husband had pointed out that Justin's enlistment in the Coast Guard was an eight-year commitment with active-duty service of two to four years.

"It's a lifetime decision with no turning back," said Kevin.

"Sheesh."

Kevin was drawn to hyperbole like a drunk to a drink.

When Kevin's name had appeared on her phone, Justin was sitting next to her studying his laptop. Cindy had rushed onto her balcony to take the call. Kevin had called Cindy twice a day as part of his pressure campaign to get Justin to change his mind.

"Have you called Justin yet?" Cindy asked. "It's his decision." She had made this point with Kevin several times.

"Yes, I have. Justin says he's made up his mind, but I can tell your boyfriend has brainwashed him."

"I never said he was my boyfriend."

"Uh-huh."

The door to her condo rang. Bill, undoubtedly.

"I have to go," she said.

"Make a move, Cindy. We're running out of time. Justin will listen to you."

Back inside the condo, Justin was thanking Bill profusely for all he had done to get Maddie out of jail, but as far as Cindy could tell, Bill had simply done his job. Although why he continued to work on the case was another mystery. Didn't Nelson County have detectives?

Bill and Justin went back and forth a few times, with Bill being modest and Justin ladling out more praise.

Then Bill turned to her. "Maddie is afraid you might fire her."

"Why would I do that?"

Justin's head turned at the sharpness of her tone. Bill blinked twice and then shrugged. "I guess she's worried you might be angry that she failed to mention she once threatened to kill your client."

"Don't overdramatize the situation," said Cindy. "She made a mistake way back when. Who of us hasn't? Let's not punish her unduly because she's young and a woman."

Justin and Bill exchanged glances as if they believed she had come unhinged. Whatever. To heck with them.

She stepped into the kitchen to prepare lunch. Justin said he wanted to get in a run before eating and went down the hallway to change.

"Is everything okay?" said Bill. "You seem a little anxious."

Cindy sighed. What was the matter with her? Snapping at Bill like that when he had done nothing to deserve it. "I'm sorry. I'm on edge with Justin leaving soon." She glanced toward the hall. "I'll tell you more after he's gone for his run."

She pulled lunch supplies from the refrigerator: egg salad for sandwiches that she had prepared earlier, raspberry hibiscus tea, lettuce, and red grapes. Bill washed the lettuce and grapes, and she toasted ciabatta rolls in the oven. Justin left to run, and they sat down to a lunch of sandwiches, grapes, and ruffled potato chips.

"I'd just like to say," said Bill, after his first bite, "that this is the best egg salad sandwich I've ever eaten."

Cindy wiped her mouth with a napkin. "Thank you. The secret is to add chopped celery—not too much—dill weed, and a pinch of ground white pepper."

Bill nodded as if it all made sense, but Cindy knew he'd never remember the ingredients she had shared.

"You were saying that you're anxious about Justin leaving," he said.

"I don't know if it's the right move, him joining the Coast Guard."

Bill pulled on his ear. "Okay. It's a big step for sure. Some kids don't do their homework and join up before they're ready, which can be a problem. But Justin has lined up the pros and cons, and he's excited. I'm sure he'll be fine."

That was easy for Bill to say. Justin wasn't his kid.

"How do you know he'll be fine?" she said. "You don't know if he'll be fine. No one knows. He might be miserable. This might be the worst possible decision he could make."

Bill put his sandwich down and wiped his hands on a napkin. "Did I miss something? You were okay with this earlier. You saw this move as Justin taking a step toward stability. What happened?"

Cindy's head ached, and her stomach churned. "I spoke with Kevin. That's what happened."

"Your ex?"

"Yes. Kevin. Justin's father."

"Okay."

"Kevin can be a jerk at times, but I still consider him one of the smartest people I've ever known."

Although Cindy had not meant to imply that, in comparison, Bill was *not* one of the smartest people she'd ever known, that *was* what she believed. Kevin was smarter than Bill by a wide margin. Not that Bill was dumb, not at all. When it came to street smarts, he had plenty, and he also possessed an uncanny ability to read other people's thoughts. But that was different than the intelligence required to make strategic moves like deciding between the Coast Guard and graduate school.

Nevertheless, Bill may have taken some offense at her statement because he then said, "What does smart Kevin say about Justin joining the Coast Guard?"

"He believes it's a bad idea. A terrible idea."

"What does Kevin have against the Coast Guard?"

"It's not that the Coast Guard is bad, but graduate school or law school would be better. Kevin says no one important ever served in the Coast Guard."

Bill scowled. "That's silly. The Columbia chief of police is a Coast Guard vet. He's a great leader and an excellent cop."

Cindy raised her hands in frustration. "You've underscored Kevin's point. Coast Guard vets become policemen and firemen and facility maintenance managers. They don't become CEOs and professors and politicians. They don't run the world."

That stopped Bill like a visiting team's last-second victory squelched cheers for the home team. He didn't appear angry. Just pensive. Mighty pensive. She had gone too far.

"I didn't mean that," she said. "I got caught up in the argument."

"I'm sorry. I have completely lost my appetite, so I will go."

"Don't leave, Bill. Not like this."

"Listen. Justin's not my son. He is your son and Kevin's son." Bill put his hands together as if he might pray. "But still, you have to know this is Justin's decision. He's twenty-seven. He's not a child."

Without another word, Bill got up to leave. Cindy tried to stop him to no avail.

When Cindy touched his arm at the door, Bill said, "Let's call it a day."

He walked out, and she heard his footsteps on the stairs. What did he mean by that? Let's call it a day. The argument? Lunch? Or their relationship?

What had she done?

SIXTY

Bill got in the Mazda and took it for a spin. He drove down Blue Ridge Drive, did the Shamokin Springs Drive loop, and jagged right over to Laurel Springs Drive. He went all the way to the summit and then came back down Devils Knob Loop to Wintergreen Drive.

His mind didn't register the gorgeous scenery. He was mad at himself for making a fuss at lunch. Cindy was wound up over Justin leaving, and he should be able to understand that. His mother had cried the day he left to join the army. Kevin was probably the smartest guy in his class. Lord knows Bill wasn't. But where did that leave Cindy and Bill? Was he smart enough for her? Wanda had never criticized Bill for not having a college degree. They had argued about everything else at one time or another, but not that.

Bill found himself at the stop sign next to the Mountain Inn. Where the heck was he going anyway? He turned right, looped back up past the Market, and then drove down to the kids' summer camp area. He parked haphazardly in the empty lot and grabbed a windbreaker from the back seat. A cold front was rolling in, and dark clouds advanced from the east. Bill strolled onto the wooden deck that overlooked the zip line and snow tubing park. No one else was around. The zip line was shut down for the summer, and the tubing hill had months to wait for artificial snow. The sign above a closed snack bar bragged of hot chocolate for sale. Bill moseyed past lonely tables and empty chairs to the deck's edge, where he gripped the railing. Fog crept across the valley floor, and a stiff breeze blew against his face.

How did the murderer get digitalis into Damian's bloodstream? He had been sure the forensics team would find digitalis in the bottle of Braemore. But they didn't, and that meant Bill had failed to think like the murderer. He must go back to the beginning. If the murderer had put digitalis in the bottle itself, they would have run the risk of poisoning the whole crew. So, the murderer had brought two bottles of Braemore, with and without poison. Once the deadly pour had been made and handed to Damian, the murderer poured the rest of that bottle down the half bathroom sink. But forensics had not found an empty whiskey bottle.

The fog continued its advance up the mountain.

Bill was stuck. His mind kept tumbling through the logistics of poison delivery. The MDMA had thrown them for a loop, a false clue that had changed Damian's behavior that day. The murderer had expected Damian to lie down for a nap and never rise again. And then the team had wasted all that time on Maddie when the will obviously drove the motive. It was infuriating. It all had to do with the timing somehow.

His mind returned to Cindy again. Her ex-husband, Kevin, still had the power to wind her up, which didn't shock Bill. He knew from his experience that after you lived with a person for many years, they never completely left you, even though you sometimes wished they would. But still, his relationship with his ex-wife, Wanda, was different than that of Cindy and Kevin's. He and Wanda never argued anymore, and whenever her name appeared on his phone screen, his heart rate jumped.

What would Wanda say about the spat he'd had with Cindy? Wanda might give him a better perspective. After all, she also had grown children and an ex-husband. But Bill had yet to mention to Wanda that he was seeing someone new. Was he ready to broach that subject, and if so, should he share with his ex-wife the details of an argument he'd had with his new girlfriend? No. Surely, that was a bad idea.

But having been a corporate lawyer for many years, Wanda might assist him with the case by helping him think through certain aspects of Damian's will. He called Wanda but got voicemail. Below him, the fog climbed the mountainside, advancing as if it were a living, breathing entity intent on conquering Wintergreen. Slightly unsettled, Bill stepped back from the railing and sat at one of the abandoned tables. Then Wanda called.

Her cheerful voice restored his spirits. She and an old girlfriend—whom Bill had met many times—had plans to meet for dinner that night. After some chitchat, Bill gave Wanda a broad outline of the investigation and the specific question that had prompted him to call. Then Wanda, in her usual thorough manner, proceeded to ask him clarifying questions. Their ensuing conversation absorbed Bill so thoroughly that he lost awareness of his surroundings. He closed his eyes to focus on the points Wanda made, but he was distracted by the friendly tone of her voice. Wait. What did she say? Are you sure? Wanda elaborated to ensure he understood. When he did, she said she had to run, and they ended the call.

Bill felt moisture on his face, opened his eyes, and saw only white. Eerie mist drifted over him, and he couldn't see the railing six feet away. Startled, Bill stood and turned to find himself completely immersed in the fog. He couldn't see the parking lot. The quiet was immense—not a single bird or leaf made a sound. The unstoppable fog rolled past him and marched toward its destination with victory assured.

A running engine approached through the fog, and Bill's spine tingled. Tires rolled over gravel down the hill and into the parking lot. The engine idled a moment, and then the tires turned into a parking space. Bill's heart raced ahead. The engine turned off, and the car door opened. Bill took a step and brushed against a chair. Shoes strolled across the gravel to the wooden deck. Bill struggled to quiet his breathing. What if it was the murderer? He had pushed the suspects hard with his questions, and the guilty party may have decided Bill was too close. The slightest sound would give away Bill's location. He stepped softly around the table. He needed a weapon. Could he bash the murderer with a chair? No, better to slip away. The footsteps crossed the deck toward him but then stopped. On tiptoes, Bill moved toward the snack bar. His heart was in his throat.

"Bill?"

Bill heaved a quiet sigh, not entirely sure.

"Where are you, Bill?" said Mitch.

Relief washed over Bill. He laughed nervously and said, "I'm here."

Mitch emerged from the fog in his uniform. "Jeez. I can't see a thing in this fog."

"Yeah, it's bad."

"I called your phone, but you didn't answer."

"Sorry. I was on another call."

“I got on the radio to ask if anyone had seen you. Officer Hill said you’d come this way. Alex wants me to work the case full-time now. What’s the next step?”

“Back to Charlottesville,” said Bill. “We need to go shopping for whiskey.”

SIXTY-ONE

They caught a break with the Braemore. As things turned out, the scotch had only been available in Virginia for a month. Krista, in her usual efficient way, found a friendly administrator at the state-run Alcoholic Beverage Control Authority. The administrator told Krista that only three stores within a hundred miles had ordered the whiskey so far, all of which were located in Charlottesville. One ABC store had not managed a single sale. The second store had sold three bottles in a single transaction, paid for with a credit card by a man named Sutherland who lived in Gordonsville. The ABC store at the Barracks Road Shopping Center had sold two bottles of Braemore in a cash transaction two weeks earlier. Which is why Bill and Mitch now sat in the squad car parked outside the same store.

"You start the conversation," said Bill. "The uniform will get things going."

Mitch and Bill stepped through the front door, and a chime sounded. A few customers were in the aisles shopping. At the counter on the right, a tall skinny clerk with a ponytail helped a woman with her transaction. When the door chime sounded, they both looked at Mitch. The clerk pulled his head back. The woman smiled.

"How y'all doing?" said Mitch.

"Can I help you, officer?" said the clerk.

"Which way to the scotch?"

The clerk pointed, and Bill and Mitch walked to that aisle to peruse the display. The Braemore was located with other single malt specialty brands on the next to the top shelf. Bill pulled down a bottle, examined the label, and handed it to Mitch, who carried it back to the counter. The clerk now stood at the counter by himself.

"Do you have a manager on duty today?" said Mitch.

"Doug's in the back office. He's the assistant manager."

"I'd like to speak with him, please."

The clerk picked up a landline phone at his side, spoke briefly with Doug, and in a few moments, an obese man with a thin mustache exited a door next to the wall of cold beverage displays. Doug glanced around the store. Every customer was staring in their direction, and Doug suggested they go into the back office. Mitch took the bottle with him.

"Is there a problem?" said Doug, after they were all seated in a cramped office. A monitor dominated his desktop.

"Not with the store," said Mitch. He added that they were trying to identify a customer who had purchased two bottles of Braemore recently.

Doug turned toward the monitor, typed on his keyboard, and waited for the screen to change. He gave Mitch a tight smile. "The computer's slow today."

"We've got time."

A screen came up, and Doug typed in some more words, then waited again. With the next screen, he frowned. "That was a cash transaction. It's going to be difficult to identify the customer."

"What about video?" said Mitch. "Can we get the footage for that day?"

Doug shook his head. "We have an old security system. We don't keep that much history."

"Who made the sale?" said Bill. "It's a distinctive brand. Maybe the clerk would remember the customer."

The assistant manager raised his eyebrows skeptically. "We transact hundreds of sales every day."

"It doesn't hurt to check," said Mitch.

"You're right," said Doug. "No harm in that." He turned back to his screen and got an answer in a few seconds this time. "We're in luck. Percy made the sale. He's the clerk you met out front. Shall we go see him?"

Doug and Mitch stood, but Bill remained seated.

"Maybe you could spell Percy at the register and send him back here," said Bill. "We'll only keep him a few minutes."

Doug nodded eagerly. "Sure. I'll send him right back."

Percy entered the office in less than a minute and sat in Doug's chair. Mitch handed him the bottle of Braemore and explained what they needed.

The clerk turned the bottle in his hands. "Two of these in a cash deal?"

"That's right," said Mitch.

Percy closed his eyes and gripped the bottle as if that might refresh his memory. "Yeah, I remember that transaction because I didn't even know we had the whiskey in stock. It had only come in the previous day."

Adrenaline rushed through Bill. He yanked his phone out, hurriedly typed in the password, and then flipped to his photo library. Years ago, he had learned that keeping suspects' photos on his phone made his job easier.

"They bought two bottles of Braemore and one bottle of Glenfiddich," said Percy. "I don't know Braemore, but Glenfiddich is a fine scotch and more reasonably priced."

"Is this the customer?" said Bill.

Percy frowned. "Nope. Not that guy."

Bill sat back, dumbfounded. He had been confident. But facts were facts, and Percy showed no hesitation. Bill swiped to another photo. "Here." He thrust his phone toward the clerk again.

Percy shook his head. "I didn't say the customer was a man."

"A woman bought the Braemore?" said Bill. "Are you sure?"

Percy cast a dubious glance toward Mitch and said, "Yes, I'm sure."

Bill was even more surprised and, frankly, disappointed. He searched his photo library again.

Holding out his phone, he said, "How about her?"

The clerk shook his head.

Bill showed Percy yet another photo and got the same response.

Frowning, Bill turned toward Mitch.

"I know it doesn't seem likely," said Mitch, "but maybe it's the assistant."

"Nope. Let me think."

Bill dialed back through the conversations he'd had with various suspects. He must have forgotten something. Then he remembered the location of the liquor store.

"Hang on," he said. He pulled up his phone browser and searched the internet. It took a full minute to find what he sought. When he did, a sinking feeling entered his chest, but he held out his phone anyway.

"Yep," said Percy. "That's her."

~

Outside in Mitch's cruiser, Bill explained what had happened. Mitch asked a few questions, and they discussed the next steps. Then Bill went back into the store and bought a bottle of Glenfiddich.

SIXTY-TWO

Mitch did not know Charlottesville well and used the cruiser's nav screen for directions. From the shopping center, he drove southeast on Barracks Road across Emmett Street and up into a hilly residential area.

Bill called Krista at the office. He needed her to make a run to Damian Susskind's house and then out to the state forensics lab in Roanoke. Tell them it was a rush. On the way back, she should drop by Staunton again.

Barracks Road became Preston Avenue, which Mitch followed to McIntire Road. Once through the stoplight, he turned left into an area north of downtown. It was a beautiful neighborhood with brick homes and lush gardens. Shiny vehicles sat parked in the driveways: BMWs, Mercedes, and Teslas. Wow. The detached guest home on that property was bigger than Mitch's rental house.

"How much would these homes go for?" he asked.

Bill studied the next house, a two-story mansion with a brick driveway and a fountain. A manicured boxwood hedge lined the street.

"I don't know. Several million dollars, I'd guess."

Mitch whistled. He and Lulu would have to win the lottery to move into this neighborhood. But Mitch didn't share that thought with Bill.

Bill's knee bounced. His eyes searched ahead for the next street sign.

"Take a left here," he said, his voice tense. The next house had a big flower bed that ran the length of the facade. "Hold up a minute. You see that flowerbed?" Bill pointed. "After you drop me off, drive around the neighborhood and scan the gardens."

"Hang on." Mitch fiddled with his phone and showed the screen to Bill. "That's it, right?"

"Yep. The blooms can grow as tall as five feet. Purplish-white bell-shaped flowers."

"Foxglove."

"Uh-huh."

After another block, they pulled up to a house with a dark pitched roof. Two large magnolia trees framed the front porch. An SUV was parked in the driveway on the right.

Bill took a deep breath and blew air out through his lips. "Okay. I'll check the beds in front and peek at the backyard. Then I'll search the nearby blocks. You go farther out."

Two streets along, Mitch pulled the car over to collect his thoughts. He wanted to make sure he had all the pieces sorted correctly. Would he ever be as good at police work as Bill? Perhaps not. Bill had a knack for figuring out the motives of others, bad people and good people. Then again, Bill had more experience than Mitch, three decades' worth. And Bill had worked as a detective in a city. For the first time, it occurred to Mitch that if he wanted to be a good detective, and he did, he might have to leave the Wintergreen police department.

Time to stop daydreaming and get to work. Mitch rolled

slowly down the street to examine the flower beds on both sides. Leafy azalea bushes were long since out of bloom. Roses flourished in the bright sun: red, yellow, white, and pink. He spotted chrysanthemums and marigolds and pansies.

Mitch pulled to a stop at a cute house on a small corner lot, more of a cottage than a house. Surely, this place would go for less than a million dollars. Even so, on a policeman's salary, he could never afford it. But a dentist could. Lulu could.

Back to work. Mitch glanced to the yard on the left. What were those flowers? Bright purple, but no white, and they were the wrong shape. His eyes scanned the nav screen, and he plotted a new route in his mind. This could take hours. He pulled forward, made a right at the next corner, and continued with what he knew could prove to be a fruitless search.

Azalea bushes. Rose bushes. Gardenias. Marigolds. A trellis was overflowing with orange trumpet vines. He picked up the pace, and the flowers began to blur. Another street. Another street. Loop back to the right. At one point, Mitch grew confused. Had he passed this street already? His mind kept returning to his earlier thoughts of real estate and career. Then he realized he'd passed one yard without giving it a glance. He pulled to the curb and closed his eyes.

Lulu had warned him about this—random thoughts bred inattention, and inattention bred mistakes.

Mitch shifted into reverse and returned to the last yard. Wiry bushes laden with bright yellow blooms lined the front of the house. Though they were not foxglove, Mitch reflected on their shimmering color—the bushes glowed. He rolled the cruiser forward and paused at the next yard. The limbs of a bush hung heavy with green leaves and deep blue chrysanthemums. The next house held more treasures. Mitch lost himself in the gardens of the neighborhood. His heart rate settled. Marigolds. Sunflowers. Gladiolas. More roses. More chrysanthemums. All the colors of the rainbow. Burgundy. Mango. Blue. Fuchsia. Burnt orange. Purple. White.

Wait.

Mitch slammed the brakes. He blinked several times.

The large two-story home had shuttered windows and a dark front door. On either side of the house, camellia bushes and holly trees provided lush greenery. Various flowers bloomed brightly in the yard: pansies, begonias, and foxglove.

He parked and hustled to the flower bed. Someone could quickly harvest them at night, even in the daytime, because the foxglove plants were only a few long strides from the street. Mitch's heart fluttered, and he hurried to the porch. The doorbell came with a security camera. Before ringing the bell, Mitch crouched to gauge the camera's field of view. The foxglove plants were not visible, but the camera might capture a person approaching from the street.

A tall thin man with nearly white hair answered the bell, surprised to find a police officer on his doorstep. Mitch explained his quest. The man was an avid gardener and coaxed his foxglove plants to bloom all summer long by cutting the flowers at precisely the right time. He knew that foxglove was poisonous if ingested, but he'd never had any trouble with it.

Mitch asked to view the stored footage from the home-owner's security camera.

"Absolutely," said the man. "I've got it here on my phone."

"This could be from as long as a month ago."

The man frowned. "In that case, you'd better come inside. We can search the history faster on my laptop."

SIXTY-THREE

Several hours later, Bill, Mitch, and Alex Sharp sat in the conference room at the Wintergreen police station. In the center of the table, the only remains of a large everything pizza were the box and a single slice.

Arnie Shields from Nelson County was on the conference phone. Krista had dropped the evidence off in Roanoke and called in from her car. She had muted her phone because of the ambient noise.

"That sounds pretty good," said Arnie.

"We need the test results first," said Bill.

"Won't the security tape be enough?" said Alex.

"Yeah. Should be," said Bill, but he was a constant worrier at this part of the game. The case wasn't closed until they had a guilty verdict in hand. "But maybe we could tie the knots a bit tighter."

"What did you have in mind?" said Arnie.

Bill rubbed his hands together. "Arnie, I propose that you tell the key players Nelson County is releasing Susskind's house because you've solved the case. If I'm right, the killer would like nothing better than to have five minutes alone in that house."

"What are we going to do?" said Alex. "Hide inside the house? That seems a bit cloak and dagger."

"Yeah," said Bill. "It would be better if we had cameras. Can you handle that, Arnie?"

Arnie took his time responding. "Yeah. We could, but it would take a while. My best guy for that is out sick. I'd have to see if we can call him in."

The ambient noise from Krista's car intruded on the call. "I can handle the cameras," she said. "We have wifi access, right?"

Arnie confirmed that they had the wifi network password, and Krista said she'd work on the cameras as soon as she returned from her meeting in Staunton.

"We could be at it all night," said Bill.

"No problem," said Krista. "I'll get my mom to watch the boys."

"Thanks, Krista," said Alex. "That's fantastic."

The five of them spent the next twenty minutes discussing logistics. Then they got to work.

SIXTY-FOUR

Mitch spent most of the night tucked into a camp chair behind a bush near the wooden stairway of Damian Susskind's back deck. He wore a heavy jacket, gloves, and a cap to keep out the chill. Bill had warned him to take special care because it was difficult to gauge a suspect's level of desperation. Bill's message was clear—Mitch should keep his eyes open for a gun.

After returning from her fruitless meeting in Staunton, Krista had rigged security cameras inside Susskind's retreat. She now sat with John Hill in an out-of-town neighbor's dark garage. Her location was close enough to the wifi signal from Susskind's house for her to monitor the cameras. Bill and Arnie Shields hid in the bushes near the front door. Alex and another patrolman sat in Alex's truck in a driveway farther down Devils Knob Loop. Arnie had confirmed earlier that the target had a key. Mitch didn't expect anyone to come his way, but Bill had said someone should wait at the back entrance to be safe, and Mitch had volunteered.

He checked his phone for the time—5:20 a.m. They were all tired. They had traded good-natured radio banter to keep each other alert for the first few hours. Arnie had said they would call it off at eight. Still no word from the forensics lab. What if it came back negative? Would a killer go free? Mitch opened another Slim Jim and munched it down, his third of the night. He took a few sips of water and then stood to stretch. He turned his shoulders left and right and bent over to touch his toes. Down the mountain somewhere, a car engine struggled to climb the hill.

In the dark forest to his right, the mountainside dropped off several hundred feet to the White Oak townhomes area. No chance the suspect would come from that direction. An experienced hiker like Mitch would find it a struggle, even in the daytime. Something rustled leaves in the darkness, perhaps a field mouse. Mitch wiped a hand across his face.

"Vehicle approaching," said Alex over the radio. "A large sedan."

Mitch stretched his arms above his head and then behind his back. Every twenty minutes or so, a random car passed by and got them excited. Then, inevitably, the driver rolled past Susskind's house.

"Hey! Look sharp," said Alex. "It's a Mercedes."

Mitch turned the volume down on his radio.

"Headlights turning into the driveway," said Bill. "We're going offline."

Mitch switched his radio off. A dim light shined around the house's edge and into the forest. Mitch's heart rate increased. He stepped closer to the stairs. The vehicle's engine hummed softly in the night. Mitch expected it to stop, but it kept running, as if the driver couldn't decide whether to stay or go. Then the engine turned off. Mitch strained his ears and heard footsteps on gravel. The headlight continued shining twenty seconds longer and then switched off. A sudden wind blew in the treetops, but no sound came from inside the house. Mitch made fists and relaxed them. By leaning to the right, he could see a back window. It was dark.

He counted sixty seconds. Two minutes. Three. Then he stopped counting. What the heck was going on?

Suddenly, a door rattled on the patio and swung open. Light shined onto the deck and through cracks between the boards. Mitch crept silently onto the stairs. Heavy footsteps sounded on the decking above him. Mitch put his hand on his holstered gun and took two more steps. He considered unclasping the gun but feared that would make a sound. The footsteps approached Mitch's side of the deck. Liquid poured over the side and onto dead leaves on the ground. What? Oh, they were pouring out the whiskey.

Then more footsteps sounded from the front side of the deck, and a light flashed across the decking.

"Okay, now," Arnie Shields warned loudly. "That's enough."

Mitch took another step.

The suspect uttered a sharp cry, and the bottle made a thud when it landed on the ground. Lots of noises came from the decking. Feet hurried from the far side, and the suspect approached the stairs. Mitch looked to the top of the stairs, and a flashlight's glare blinded him.

"Hey," he shouted. "Stop!"

Mitch took another step, and then the flashlight hurtled toward him. Something hard crashed into Mitch's face and chest, and he tumbled backward and fell. Mitch's back slammed into the ground, and his head snapped. A heavy weight landed on top of Mitch, and he lost consciousness.

In what seemed a moment later, someone grabbed Mitch by the shoulders.

"Mitch. Mitch."

Mitch blinked his eyes open. A loud ringing noise faded into nothing.

"What's going on?" he said.

"Are you okay?" said Bill.

Mitch scrambled to his feet and shook his head. "Yeah. I'm fine."

Bill turned toward the forest. A crashing sound came from the woods below them, and a light flashed in the trees. "He's trying to get away."

Mitch pushed Bill toward the stairs. "Drive down to White Oak. I'll go after him."

With his flashlight on the ground, Mitch trudged down the steep hillside. The irregular slope was chock-full of rocks and saplings and demanded fierce concentration. A level stretch of ten feet was followed by a steep drop-off that forced Mitch to his knees. The suspect crashed loudly fifty feet farther down the hill. He was gaining ground on Mitch. Never mind. They'd both be lucky to avoid breaking an ankle or a leg. Mitch stepped into a hole filled with dead leaves and gasped at the sudden plunge. His lungs heaved. He pulled his foot out of the hole and tested his ankle. Everything worked fine.

Mitch moved left to get around a boulder. The suspect had gone right, but the ground was leveler this way. Mitch angled across the hill. He aimed his flashlight twenty feet ahead and got into a rhythm. He cut a switchback down the hill. Fifty feet left. Fifty feet right. A loud crash sounded in the woods, and the suspect yelped. Mitch was gaining ground and hurried through another switchback. Fifty feet left. Fifty feet right. He climbed over a fallen tree and paused to catch his breath. The suspect was behind him now and a hundred feet to the right. A trail ran through the woods here somewhere. The downslope grew steep again, and Mitch took a risk by leaping out and down the hill. His boots slid in the dead leaves. He leaped and slid again. One more time. If only his luck would hold out.

What's this? A level spot on the hillside.

Mitch aimed his light across the hill and spotted a yellow trail marker. Up the incline on the right, the suspect moved more slowly, hurt, or perhaps just winded. Mitch kept his light down and trotted along the trail. When he reached the spot directly below the suspect, Mitch switched off his light and hid behind a tree.

His heart pounded. The suspect thrashed in the woods behind him. Mitch closed his eyes and took deep breaths. The suspect stumbled and swore. Mitch opened his eyes and turned. The suspect stepped onto the path, and Mitch ran toward him like a linebacker blitzing a quarterback. Mitch smashed into the suspect's chest to knock him down and then flipped him onto his stomach. The suspect squirmed, but Mitch had him pinned to the ground with his knee. Both men heaved. It was a good while before Mitch could speak clearly.

Then he said, "I'm sorry, Mr. Whitlock. I have to cuff you now."

SIXTY-FIVE

Bill, Arnie, and Alex sat in the Wintergreen Police station conference room with Whit Whitlock. Arnie had called for a squad car and two deputies but said he didn't mind if Bill asked a few questions while they waited. Arnie made Whitlock affirm his rights and then gave Bill a nod.

Mitch had brought in a tray and four cups of water. Whit sat at one end of the long table with his hands around a cup. He hadn't said a word.

There was only one thing Bill needed from Whit. Everything else had fallen into place. But he should warm Whit up first. Where to start?

"By the way," Bill said, "that whiskey you poured over the side was Glenfiddich. We sent the other stuff for forensics testing. You were mighty clever, though, up to a point."

Whit stared blankly at the wall. He seemed sleepy.

"You knew Damian couldn't resist trying a new scotch, so you brought a bottle of Braemore to the retreat. Before coming, you emptied the Glenfiddich bottle and refilled it with Braemore from the second bottle laced with digitalis. When Damian wasn't looking, you poured him a healthy slug of the poisoned Braemore from the Glenfiddich bottle, then put the Glenfiddich bottle back on the shelf. Damian liked the whiskey so much he wanted to serve it to the others. Of course, by then, you had placed the untainted bottle of Braemore on the desk in front of Damian. My guess is you thought Damian would simply take a nap and have a heart attack in his sleep. Is that right?"

Whit sniffed but didn't say anything.

"I'll bet you planned to pour the laced whiskey out that day, but Angie thwarted you by working in Damian's study all afternoon. Then Nelson County, god love them, closed the house, so you couldn't get rid of the bottle. Not until tonight, of course."

Nothing from Whit yet. The silent treatment. Whit sipped his water. Maybe an attack would shake him up.

"It was inconsiderate to have your sister MaryEllen buy the scotch. Let me guess. You asked her to do you a favor since she worked close by at a Barracks Road clothing store."

No reaction. Strange. Whit had always seemed warm and friendly. Was that an act? Had he hidden his true character all along? Maybe he was in shock. Perhaps he couldn't believe his well-made plans could go so badly wrong. The MDMA had been an enormous setback. No one would have suspected foul play if Damian hadn't gone on the hike. No autopsy. Death by cardiac arrest. Happened all the time.

"It took me a long while to figure you for a suspect," said Bill. "You're down for two million in the will. A fair sum, but not enough to risk prison after you've already made a pile from Damian over the years. The donation's delay tickled my curiosity. While the delay benefited each of the chief suspects financially—Evan, Tanya, and Lacey—you were the only one who could influence the timing. I consulted a corporate lawyer who checked out Fair Game's stock and the Staunton museum while we were on the phone. She couldn't see how it could possibly take longer than a week or two. A determined lawyer could get it done faster. You *were* determined but not in that direction."

Whit gazed at Bill with a blank expression, as if Bill were discussing the weather in Patagonia.

"But why did you delay the donation?" said Bill. "I couldn't sort that out. When Krista—our communications officer—suggested we investigate the charity, I considered it a waste of time. But Krista went down there and chatted with your friend, Jane Yarborough. Or is she your lover?"

Without so much as a blink, Whit lowered his eyes to the paper cup he held in his hands.

"Krista didn't like Jane on her first visit," said Bill, "and she liked Jane even less after last night's chat."

Whit's body shrank into itself. His shoulders hunched, and he lowered his head. Was he even listening? No matter. Bill was on a roll and couldn't stop.

"Jane claims she knew nothing about it," said Bill, "but Krista believes she's lying, and so do I. The first time you and I had a conversation was at the Edge on the night of Damian's death. Do you remember? You said you were dating someone new. I only missed Jane by a couple of minutes that night. I saw her on the patio behind the inn, but I didn't know who she was at the time. Last night, I recognized her face on the museum's website."

Bill leaned forward. This might be the best chance they'd get. They had no evidence attaching Jane Yarborough to the crime, and she and Whit were both too smart to leave a digital record of their plot.

"Tell me," said Bill. "Jane devised the whole scheme, didn't she? By preventing the donation, you would save Jane's job. In turn, she would show her appreciation in many ways. You'd get two million more from the will on top of what you already have, making you a nice catch for Jane. I bet you expected to marry her after a suitable cooling-off period."

Nothing from Whit. Absolutely nothing.

"Jane told Krista the two of you had gone to dinner a few times, but it was nothing serious. According to Jane, she had already decided to break things off. Jane was shocked, positively shocked, to hear we believed you were involved somehow in Damian's death. Do you really want to go to prison by yourself?"

By then, Bill knew all was lost. He could hear the frustration in his voice. Whit had little to gain by implicating Jane Yarborough at this point. The county would charge him for willful premeditated murder with malice aforethought. The prosecuting attorney might throw Whit a bone if he cooperated, but the attorney would have to make an offer before Whit said a word. On the other hand, perhaps Whit's shielding of Jane was a sign of true love. And it was remotely possible that Jane was innocent. Not likely, but possible.

Perhaps Whit had other reasons for his silence, motivations buried so deep no one else would ever understand them.

Bill had gone through a period years ago when he felt compelled to read works of Shakespeare. He had read all of the plays and the sonnets. Whit's silence reminded him of a character from one of the tragedies. Bill couldn't recall the name of the work. The character he had in mind had orchestrated a great man's downfall by process of sinister manipulation. Once found out, the villain never said another word.

SIXTY-SIX

Early one evening, Rachel Dunn pulled her BMW into the Mountain Inn parking lot and turned off the car. She checked her outfit. White jeans and sandals with no heels. Bright top. Denim jacket. Manicure and pedicure. Perfect highlights. And Gucci sunglasses. She felt good about the day. Lugging her equipment to five different appointments was hard work but good exercise. Her business was growing. One regular customer had referred her to a woman who lived down in Stoney Creek. That had led to three more regulars, and Rachel was now considering dedicating Tuesdays and Thursdays to the valley to save herself commute time. She might also trade the BMW in for an SUV. Wrangling her massage table into the BMW was a pain, and she could put signage on an SUV.

Yes, business was good, but that was enough planning for one night. Rachel was treating herself to dinner at the Edge for no reason other than it being a Wednesday. Some people pitied a forty-something woman dining alone, but they had it wrong. Why sit at home alone eating dinner in front of the

TV? You wouldn't make any new friends that way, and Rachel Dunn was always in the market for a new friend. Besides, the hostesses, servers, and bartenders all knew her at the Edge, and she enjoyed their company. Fred at the front was a fellow Washington Commanders fan. Anja always had juicy mountain gossip. And Raleigh at the bar told good jokes and made a mean martini.

Rachel hiked up the stairs to the Mountain Inn and crossed through the lobby to the back patio area. While the air had been still in the parking lot, an early fall breeze blew up the ski slope and rustled leaves on either side of the brick walkway. Yellow and orange had crept into the treetops. Fall would arrive soon.

Up ahead, a man exited the Edge, and Rachel's keen eyes recognized the athletic figure of Evan Hale. Evan appeared dispirited with hunched shoulders and hands in his pockets, which surprised Rachel, because according to her sources, he had recently come into a great deal of money. When Evan noticed her figure at a distance, he straightened his posture and pulled his hands from his pockets. Rachel could read his mind. There's a woman. Look sharp. But then Evan recognized her, and his shoulders slumped again. His eyes focused on the sidewalk and only glanced her way at the last possible moment. She gave him a curt nod and continued walking. Jerk.

Inside the Edge, Rachel stopped to chat with Fred about the Commanders' upcoming game. When Fred asked if she would dine at the bar, Rachel indicated that she would, but at the entrance to the dining room, she paused to scan the tables and booths for familiar faces. Next to the window on the left, a woman sat alone and stared at a nearly full glass of beer. Goodness. It was Lacey Akin, looking as if she had no friends in the world. Rachel did the math and marched straight to Lacey's booth.

"Hey, Lacey," she said in a cheery voice. She extended her hand for Lacey to shake. "I'm Rachel Dunn. We met once when I came to Damian's house for an appointment."

Lacey's eyes showed no recognition, but she shook Rachel's hand anyway.

"I was Damian's masseuse," said Rachel, by way of explanation. "I'm sorry for your loss."

Lacey tilted her head. "Masseuse?"

"That's right. Mind if I join you?" Without waiting for an answer, Rachel slid into the booth seat across from Lacey and smiled. Lacey was on the verge of breaking into tears. Wasted tears, as far as Rachel was concerned. Even so, she leaned forward and lowered her voice. "Do you need a moment? I have a tissue." Rachel opened her purse, rummaged around, and held her hand across the table.

Lacey grabbed the tissue like an overboard sailor lunging for a ring buoy. She pressed the tissue against her eyes and then blew her nose.

"I passed Evan outside," said Rachel.

Lacey's eyes widened, and the blood drained from her face.

"Let me guess," said Rachel. "He broke up with you."

"How could you possibly know that?"

"I carry a crystal ball in my purse too." Then Rachel laughed, trying to bring levity to the moment.

But Lacey's lips dropped into a sad frown.

Rachel said, "I know you feel crappy, and if you want to have a good cry by yourself, I'll leave you alone. But here's the truth—if you sit in this booth and cry, another person will come by and try to make you feel better. You might as well stick with me. Later tonight, when you're home alone, you can do the tears-and-sobs thing up right."

The key to pulling a victim back from the brink of a self-pity abyss was to surprise them. Shoulder rubbing and empathetic boohooing were tantamount to a good solid shove. But if you confused them with words, curiosity forced their minds to try to make sense of what you'd said.

"Are you with me?" Rachel said.

"I don't know."

It was progress. An opening. Time to throw in a few hand gestures.

"I'm not trying to belittle your feelings," said Rachel, "but let's take a step back and assess the situation with a clear eye. Okay? You're in your upper twenties, right?"

Lacey lifted her head and pulled her hair out of her face. She was a pretty thing—sparkling blue eyes.

"I'm twenty-eight," Lacey said.

"Good. The bad news is you've lost a boyfriend, someone you hoped to marry. But is that truly a downside? Believe me —and I have *a lot* of experience with men—Evan Hale was no great catch."

Lacey pursed her lips.

"Now, let's get to the good stuff," said Rachel. "You have a beautiful face and an attractive figure. And unless I'm mistaken, you have inherited an obscene amount of money. I'm forty-eight and have worked hard my whole life. I don't have anywhere near that kind of money. So, on those facts alone, which of us should be sad?"

Lacey pulled on her earlobe. "I don't understand. Are you trying to say you're sad?"

"No, it's a trick question." Rachel threw her hands out for the big reveal. "Neither of us should be sad. We're both lucky to be alive and living in a wonderland called the USA. So let's stop moping, send back that beer, and order the Edge's most expensive bottle of wine."

Lacey clamped her upper teeth onto her lower lip, mulled Rachel's proposal, and said, "That's a great idea."

SIXTY-SEVEN

Krista glanced at the kitchen clock. 9:35 p.m. She should tell the boys to start getting ready for bed. They were in the back room watching a Spiderman movie with the dogs. Maybe another ten minutes.

She was pleased with her performance in the Damian Susskind investigation. Krista had found clues using her internet sleuthing skills, interviewed a suspect twice, and gotten a compliment from Alex Sharp for her self-taught knowledge of surveillance cameras.

The only wrinkle in the story—and Krista considered this a monster wrinkle—was how things ended with Jane Yarborough. "Don't worry about that," Bill O'Shea had said. "These things happen." The important point was that they had caught the murderer. Worst case, Jane was an accomplice. She might have put ideas into Whitlock's head, but he was the one who planned and carried out the act. Without testimony from Whitlock, Jane was presumed innocent. Still, Krista would never drive into Staunton without thinking about her.

Krista turned her attention back to the monitor. She had sat down at the computer ninety minutes earlier to check her personal email for a few minutes. After that, she had planned to relax and listen to the story of Lance and Daphne. But then she had done an online search for Virginia criminal justice schools, and the clock's minute hand had raced like a NASCAR driver around a track.

Krista had asked for a few minutes of Alex's time at work that day. Would he consider allowing her to leave work early twice a week to pursue higher education in criminology? "Heck, yeah," Alex had said. Not only that—he would find money in the budget to cover her tuition.

There were several accredited programs within an hour's driving distance that conducted evening courses. If Krista got her butt in gear, she could apply in time for a January start. But first, she had to talk to the boys. How would they react to her coming home late two nights a week? At fourteen, Ashton would likely enjoy time without her close supervision. At twelve, Trevor might be too young. Maybe she should start with an online program. Sheesh. Big decision. That was enough for one night. It was 9:45 p.m. She really should get the boys moving toward bedtime. Krista glanced at her headset on the coffee table next to the couch. Maybe another ten minutes.

SIXTY-EIGHT

Mitch pushed the lawnmower in ever-decreasing squares on the front lawn. He enjoyed mowing because it required little concentration. With earmuffs on to block the noise, his mind was relatively free to contemplate pending decisions. Mitch had wrestled with a big decision for a week, but he had finally pinned it to the mat.

Across the street, children played kickball in a vacant lot. To avoid car traffic, they had placed the home base closest to the road and the other bases farther into the field. A teenager rolled an easy pitch to a little boy. The boy kicked the ball to the right of the second-base girl, who took her time retrieving the ball to give the kicker every chance to reach first base. Mitch finished the last square of the lawn, circled the shrubs by the street, and stowed the mower in the garage.

Inside the kitchen, he fixed a glass of ice water and leaned against the counter. Sitting at the kitchen table, Lulu frowned mightily at her laptop.

"Whatcha working on?" he said.

She moaned in frustration. "This stuff doesn't work. No way it works."

Mitch pulled on his chin. Lulu rarely got upset and almost never when at her computer; she was a whiz with home technology. He was the one who often needed help, and he had never stumped her with an IT question. He moved to stand behind Lulu and touched her shoulder. She was messing with a spreadsheet.

"What's that?" he said.

Without turning around, Lulu put her hand on his. "I can't go to dental school. I worked the numbers a lot of different ways, but the answer is always the same. We can't afford it."

Mitch leaned closer to the screen. "Show me."

Lulu pointed to a bold number in the lower right corner. "This is the killer—my projection of our outstanding debt when I graduate from dental school. Four hundred and twenty thousand dollars. We can't sign up for that."

As it happened, Lulu's spreadsheet was related to the decision Mitch had contemplated the last few days.

"I don't think those numbers are right," he said.

Startled, Lulu pulled the neighboring chair out for Mitch to sit. "Do you want to check my math? I can't work during school, so we're down to your salary for four years. I input the projected tuition and fees, and I drastically cut our living expenses. But we still have principal and interest payments on my current loans. It just doesn't work."

Mitch drank from his glass to give the conversation a pause and then said, "I disagree. I've figured out a way to pay tuition and fees without borrowing any more money."

Lulu's eyes searched his. She was highly intelligent, and there was only one possible way for Mitch to raise that kind of money. Lulu shook her head. "No."

"Yes. It's the only answer that makes sense."

"You can't sell your ancestral home, Mitch. I can't go along with that. It's not right."

"It's not *my* home. I never lived there. And I already met with an agent."

Lulu continued to shake her head.

Mitch took both of her hands in his. "The real estate market is hot now. Even a broken-down house like that one can fetch a lot of money. I'll take two weeks off and work to get it ready. Then we put it on the market. The agent believes we can clear three hundred thousand after paying off the mortgage."

"But it's your dream home."

Mitch shrugged. "Nah. I've given it a lot of thought. It was more of a notion than a dream. Here's my new plan. We sell the house to pay for school. You work your tail off, graduate, and start making the big bucks. Then we can buy *our* dream home."

Lulu gazed at him fondly and then threw herself into his arms. She kissed him madly.

He enjoyed a few kisses and then reluctantly pushed her away. "I'm all sweaty. Let me take a shower first."

Mitch stood and strode toward the hallway. He heard Lulu behind him and turned around. "Where are you going?"

"I can't wait, Mitch. We're taking that shower together."

SIXTY-NINE

On that same warm afternoon, Bill returned from a walk and came across Justin and Maddie in the parking lot outside Cindy's condo building. They both wore running shoes, shorts, and long-sleeved shirts. Maddie also wore a cap, and Justin had a bandana tied around his neck.

"What's up, guys?" said Bill. He hadn't seen Cindy since their argument over Justin's enlistment. He was dying to know where Justin had landed but was afraid to ask.

"Justin's joining the Coast Guard," said Maddie.

Justin smiled. "I'm headed to Cape May tomorrow."

Bill nodded. "Cool."

Justin said, "Dad wanted me to consider going back to college, but I have zero interest in grad school. I'd rather learn about boats. What's wrong with that?"

Bill perceived that Justin had asked the question rhetorically.

But Maddie said, "Nothing. As long as you stay in touch."

Justin's face grew flushed. "Oh, I want to stay in touch, but you're not on social media, so . . ."

"Send me an email. Better yet, send me a postcard."

"For sure. I'll send a card every week."

Listening to the young adults make plans, Bill felt as useful as training wheels on a teenager's bike. He changed the subject. "Where are you two headed?"

"We're hiking Crabtree Falls," said Maddie. "It's Justin's first time."

"They say it's cursed," said Justin.

"I've heard that," said Bill. He gave them a wave and turned to go. "Make sure you stay on the trail. You'll be fine."

Bill continued past Cindy's building and toward his own. But after Maddie's car had disappeared from view, he turned back and made his way to Cindy's front door.

"Hey, Bill," she said. She seemed pleased to see him. "I was going to call you. Come in. Can I get you a glass of water or something?"

"No. I thought I'd knock and see if you were around. Maybe we should talk."

Bill had never been one to avoid conflict. He liked Cindy a lot and had hoped their relationship would transition to a more formal state. He still did. The form that took was not a matter of conviction for Bill. Marriage seemed a long way off. But exclusivity? Girlfriend/boyfriend? That could happen. Or so he had thought until the tense conversation around Justin's big decision. Now, he wasn't sure. But either way, the important thing was for them to discuss the matter and figure out where they stood. Confusion would only lead to anxiety, and no one needed that.

"Yes," said Cindy. "Let's talk." She strolled into the living room area and sat on the couch. Not for the first time, Bill realized he found Cindy to be quite attractive. He sat next to her.

"I ran into Justin in the parking lot," Bill said. "He told me he's headed to Cape May."

Cindy sighed. "It's fine. That's what he wants to do. And it'll be fine. Like you said earlier, it was his decision to make all along."

"I'm sorry I got in a huff the other day."

She shook her head and leaned toward him. "It's not a big deal." She touched his hand.

Hope swelled within Bill. His fingers tingled. Perhaps they could weather this storm without losing momentum.

"I like you," she said, "and I want us to be friends."

Friends?

"But perhaps we moved forward too quickly," she said. "At this point in our lives, it might take longer for us to get used to a new person. What do you think?"

Bill tried not to show it, but hope escaped from him like air from a punctured tire. Nevertheless, he appreciated her sticking with the truth. And he knew he wasn't Shakespeare. No words of his would magically woo her on the spot.

"It is true," he said. "As we grow older, it becomes more difficult to change direction in a hurry. I'm glad we're friends, Cindy. And I want you to know that no matter what happens, you can always count on me."

The rest of their conversation was pleasant but of little consequence. Naturally, they discussed the investigation for a while. Then the topic changed to the weather. Cindy thought fall was coming on faster than it had in recent years. Neither of them could believe it would soon be October. Another year three-quarters gone.

At the door, Cindy kissed him on the cheek. It was a slight change from earlier partings when their lips had met. But Bill noticed.

SEVENTY

Back in his condo, Bill sat on the couch with slumped shoulders. The list he had prepared for upgrading the condo's interior was more than a page long, but he couldn't get excited about working on any of it. Although generally happiest if actively engaged in doing something, Bill was also old enough to recognize when an unexpected downturn called for sitting still.

Emotions were tricky at this point. Anger was a temptation. But who deserved his anger? Cindy? Surely not. Himself? No, his interactions with Cindy, both in word and deed, were consistent with his values. Nor should he quarrel with the reality. Be sad? Yes. Be angry? No. Facts were facts.

And as he nearly always did after giving a situation due consideration, Bill saw the bright side. He enjoyed being in Cindy's presence a great deal, and she wished to remain friends. Plus, the situation might change in his favor over time. Sure. It almost certainly would.

Bill glanced toward the picture windows and noticed that dusk was approaching fast. He stepped onto the balcony. The sun behind him cast orange and purple hues onto the rounded tops of the Blue Ridge Mountains. Far below him, Lake Monocan was a tiny mirrored surface in Stoney Creek. A broad-winged bird glided across the mountain's side.

Bill's gaze settled on the lawn below him, and he spotted Mr. Chips nibbling greens several feet from his burrow entrance. Bill's heart gathered speed. He grabbed a fat beef-steak tomato from the counter and hustled outside. As Maddie had instructed, Bill held the fruit aloft to attract Mr. Chips's attention. Then Bill slowly approached his furry friend. Twenty feet. Fifteen feet. Ten feet. Bill stooped, assuming what he hoped was a friendly posture, and crept forward. Eight feet. Six feet. Bill crouched.

Mr. Chips's chest fluttered, but his eyes never left Bill. He dropped the greens.

Bill extended his palm upward with the tomato held lightly by his fingertips.

Mr. Chips took a cautious step closer. Another step.

Bill held his breath.

Then Mr. Chips scampered forward, grabbed the tomato from Bill's hand, and hurried back to his burrow entrance. Mr. Chips stood erect and gnawed the tomato furiously—just like in the YouTube video.

Bill said, "There's nothing like a juicy tomato, eh, Mr. Chips?"

The groundhog declined to answer, as he was busily storing calories for the long, cold winter ahead.

THE END

ALSO BY PATRICK KELLY

Thank you for reading *The Overlook Murder.* I hope you enjoyed Bill O'Shea's latest adventure.

Return to the Wintergreen Mystery Series in book three, *Murder in White.*

A female hiker disappears in a snowstorm

As president of the Old Virginia Gun Club, Cassandra Key calls for a trustees' meeting at the beautiful ski resort of Wintergreen, Virginia. Cassandra–a huge fan of outdoor sports–ignores a harsh weather forecast to undertake a solo hike across mountainous terrain. But then she disappears.

Wintergreen Fire & Rescue organizes a search mission, and many volunteers respond–including retired homicide detective Bill O'Shea. Despite herculean efforts, the search effort fails, and the next morning, a ski patroller finds Cassandra buried in snow. She is deceased–shot twice in the chest by a high-powered rifle.

The short-staffed Wintergreen Police Department asks Bill O'Shea to assist them with the investigation. After initial interviews, Bill has suspicions about several gun club trustees, including Cassandra's ex-lover, the ex-lover's fiancé, and an underling scheming for Cassandra's job. But what Bill can't sort out is how anyone shot Cassandra in the middle of a snowstorm from four hundred yards. Will Bill and his friends solve the mystery of a murder in white, or will a Wintergreen killer go free?

If you love beautiful mountain settings, a charming cast, and

intriguing plot twists, you're going to love the Wintergreen Mystery Series!

Clean read: no graphic violence, sex, or strong language.

Murder in White is available in print at Amazon and in eBook format at Amazon, Barnes & Noble, Apple, and other online stores.

Join the Readers Club to make sure you don't miss the next Wintergreen Mystery. As a bonus for signing up, you'll get a free Bill O'Shea novella—*The Curse of Crabtree Falls*.

The Curse of Crabtree Falls

When a friend invites Bill to hike Crabtree Falls, he eagerly accepts, but then he hears the story of the curse. Not given to superstition, Bill is compelled to investigate the mysterious waterfall that has doomed lovers since 1851.

Join my readers club and be the first of your friends to read the next Wintergreen Mystery.

www.patrickkellystories.com/newsletter-signup

ABOUT WINTERGREEN

Several years ago, we bought a condo in Wintergreen, Virginia, to escape the hot Texas summers. Not by coincidence, our condo is in the same location as the one owned by Bill O'Shea. Groundhogs scrounge greens from the lawn beneath our balcony. Sadly, the groundhog named Mr. Chips is a fictional character. Black bear sightings and stories are common.

There are many hiking trails in and around Wintergreen. The overlook in the story is a combined portrayal of three separate overlooks that appear on a winding trail along the northwestern edge of Wintergreen. American Chestnut trees were once the dominant species of hardwood tree in this area but were largely wiped out by chestnut blight in the early twentieth century.

Most of the places and establishments mentioned in the story are real; however, the characters and events are all fictitious. The Wintergreen Police Department does a fine job of protecting the community. The police procedures depicted in the novel are from my imagination and undoubtedly an inaccurate portrayal of how a real police department would go about its business. As a writer, my interest lies primarily with the mystery and the interaction of the characters.

As always, my wife Susie tried to help me write a better book. She is the love of my life.

ACKNOWLEDGMENTS

Thank you to Lori at Great Escapes Book Tours for working tirelessly to support the cozy genre and for hosting a fantastic book tour.

Sleepy Fox Studios designed the book cover. Liz Perry of Per Se Editing edited the manuscript.

Several Wintergreen residents were kind enough to read an early draft and give me feedback, including Emily Ferguson, Valerie Calhoun, Katie Moran, Linda Ehinger, and Debby Missal. Thank you to the many people who work hard to make Wintergreen a wonderful resort community.

Praise for *The Wintergreen Mystery Series*

"The prose was compulsively readable, well-written, and engrossing. The pace was steady and character-driven. There were plenty of suspects and the ending was unexpected with a nice twist." **- PamG, top 100 Goodreads reviewer**

"The Mountain View Murder" is an excellent start to a new mystery series. Protagonist Bill is an instantly likeable main character, and I enjoyed learning more about him as the story progressed." **- Barnes & Noble reviewer**

"This was really an excellent mystery, and I was happy to realize it is the first book in a new series, so (hopefully) many more to come!" **- Barnes & Noble reviewer**

"I found this book intriguing, suspenseful, full of twists and turns. I found the storyline riveting from the first word until the last word." **- Barnes & Noble reviewer**

FIVE STAR AMAZON REVIEWS!!!

"The spectacular descriptions of the Appalachian mountains, and true to life engaging characters make this a book to come back to. I'm ready for the next in the series."

"Wonderful characters are woven into a suspenseful whodunnit that will make you laugh and cry. Welcome to The Wintergreen Mystery Series. It's going to be a fun ride!"

KEEP IN TOUCH

If you enjoyed meeting Bill O'Shea and his friends at Wintergreen, lend me your email address, and I'll keep you posted on their next adventure.

www.patrickkellystories.com/newsletter-signup

Follow me on:

www.goodreads.com/patrickkelly

Instagram: pkellystories

Facebook: patrickkellywriter

Made in the USA
Middletown, DE
03 October 2023